Blade of Lightning

The Stormcrafter Chronicles

J.T. Moy

CENTAURUS
PRESS

Published by Centaurus Press, Auckland, New Zealand.
See www.jtmoy.com for further publications. 19052022

Cover illustration and design by Jeff Brown Graphics.

Blade of Lightning
ISBN 978-0-473-61189-7 (Kindle)
ISBN 978-0-473-61188-0 (Epub)
ISBN 978-0-473-61187-3 (Hardback)
ISBN 978-0-473-61185-9 (Paperback)

*For my parents.
Thanks for having me!*

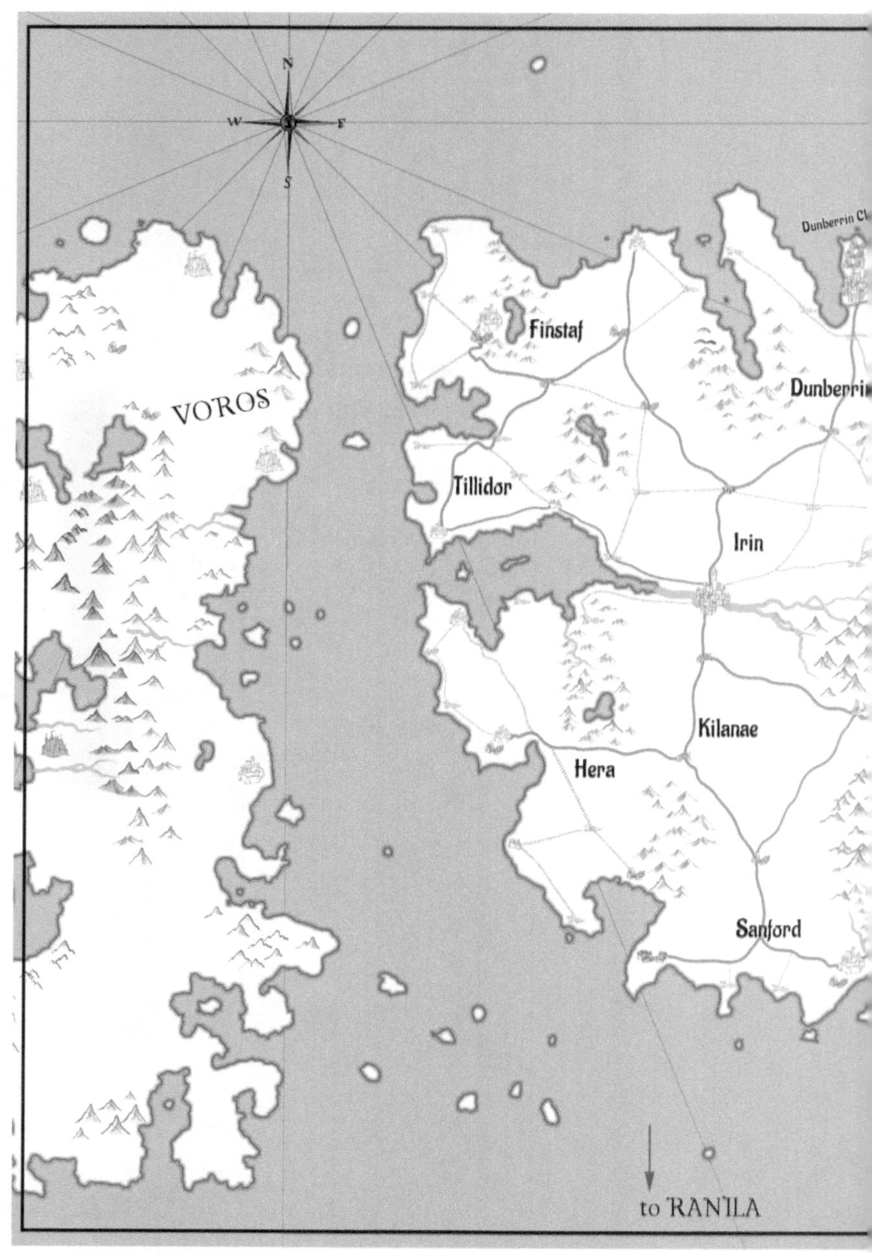

N
W
E
S
VOROS
Finstaf
Dunberrin Cl
Dunberri
Tillidor
Irin
Kilanae
Hera
Sanford
to RANILA

FAUCONY
to PIHAAT
STROCK
Jurn
ELLIPTA
ASCORIA
to ZURA
Cerik
HUSVAN
NERA BOA

Chapter 1

The Edge

Karisa—Castle Sanford, Province of Sanford, Ascoria

Karisa Rauhalik gasped for air and rolled to her side, away from the Vor king. His hands had loosened around her neck just as her life-force had begun to slip away. Each time, death edged a little closer; each time less narrowly escaped.

So cruel, was this king of the Vors. Since raiders captured her, after ambushing her company a few months before, Karisa had been a slave in King Harek's harem. And in that time, he had already murdered two other courtesans.

She had to escape before he killed her, or worse—handed her to her father. She would flee tonight.

"Why do you not beg?" the king asked. "Why do you not struggle? Do you not fear death?"

He could not have been further from the truth. She woke some nights, drenched in fear and sweat from nightmares of dying.

"Are you so terrified that you do not even fight for your own life?"

"I wish only to serve you." Her throat could only manage a whisper. She knew that if she rewarded his cruelty with fear, more would follow. She had seen the other women. Women who trembled under his gaze, who screamed and thrashed under his ministrations, only to splutter and die in his hands. She wouldn't be one of them—she knew what he wanted and refused to give it to him.

"I think you enjoy it. I think I pleasure you very much."

"Yes, your highness," she replied, her voice raspy.

"Liar," he said. "I'll break you one day. I'll hear you wail and cry. Now, get out—I have a massacre to attend."

The guard, who had been standing at the tent entrance all the while, parted the flap for Karisa to leave, but not before clamping an iron collar around her bruised neck.

Clutching a blue silk wrap to her chest, she walked out into the nipping cold, ignoring the snarling hound and its handler stationed outside.

Under a full moon, thousands of armed figures had assembled in an open field on the forest's edge nearby.

Guided by flaming torches, eager but hushed voices boasted and chided one another in the semidark while *torgue* leaders and commanders ranged between the armed warriors, calling out orders.

"They're moving out already?" Karisa asked her harem guard.

"We expect the Ascorian column to march through the pass in the morning," said the man. "The king commands all units to be in place before the sunrise."

"God have mercy."

She trailed the guard back to the tent she shared with the other two women. Karisa was the longest serving. They called her the king's favorite, but it was only because she had outlived the rest.

"Boe," she said the guard's name, once they had reached the warmth of the tent and he had attached her chain to the central pillar. Silina and Gertrid stared wide-eyed at her from under a blanket they shared, fearful and thankful that the king had chosen her that night instead of one of them.

"Boe, you are so kind to me." She looked from his bulbous nose up to his uneven eyes—one always squinty. But even so, he wasn't an ugly man, just plain, a face who might have come to watch her on stage a dozen times but whom she wouldn't remember.

During the walk between tents, she had illumanced her appearance subtly. Over the past weeks, she had noted that Boe eyed her longingly when her hair was back-lit gold and loose around her bare shoulders.

She shook her hair out, and it glistened in the candlelight. Her face illuminated with magic to hide her bruises and highlight her cheek and jaw angles, blue eyes, and plump lips. She passed him a tip of the silk wrap.

"Wrap me." She spun and swayed in front of him, covering herself yard by yard, as his breathing hastened with desire. Of course, he had been watching when Harek touched her. They all did. But unlike the rest, Boe would look away, pinch-faced, when the punishment grew harsh.

When the length of silk was gone, she touched his arm and placed her lips close to his ear. "Tonight . . . it must be tonight we run away."

Boe breathed fast and an artery pulsated on the side of his temple.

"Loosen my collar? My neck hurts terribly." Wincing, she pulled at the restraint. The plain iron device wrapped in leather was the first barrier to her escape.

Mesmerized, he keyed the lock open, then shot a glance over his shoulder.

Karisa tailed a second bolt of silk around her neck and over the collar. "An hour after you are relieved, I will meet you at the latrines. Bring the uniform," she whispered into his ear. The final act of a month of whispers and promises to him had now arrived.

Nodding, he retreated to wait for the rest of his duty outside the tent entrance with his fellow guard.

Seeing the other girls' shocked gazes—a guard would be fed to the *gargantors* for unlocking a girl without permission—she lay between them and pulled them close.

"I'll come back for you when I reach help." She promised she'd find her sister, Vixhana, a captain of an elite warrior unit called the Nightwraiths, and lead Vixhana and her unit back to assassinate the Vor king and retrieve the two women. She was sure her detailed observations of the Vor guards' routines would help them return unobserved. The hounds and dragons, with their sensitive ears and noses, would be their only concern.

"Take us with you," Silina said, eyes pleading. Her once proud and haughty face quivered, a tapestry of purple and blue bruises.

"I won't be long. I promise. Now hush, you must try to sleep." She blew out the candlelight and waited.

An hour after she heard the changing of guards, Karisa unhinged her collar and began an invocation—one with which she had little practice. She knew well the illusions that drew focus and attention to herself; however, the light-annulling invocations that the nightwraith warriors used were more complex—they absorbed light so they wouldn't even cast a shadow. When she had been a child, Vixhana had instructed her in the technique, but because it hid rather than beautified her, she had never used it again.

She drew on her memory of Ella, her little dog. On that evening in the castle, a few days earlier, during the banquet of celebration, she had seen a dog that looked exactly like her Ella cowering in a metal cage. It was a delicate, tiny-boned dog and had been protected by bars from the slavering war hounds that had paced nearby. She had ached to hold the trembling creature and had found herself conflicted when her father finished talking with the king and approached her to say, "You left it behind. Be a good girl and you'll get it back."

Despite the fear for her pet, she basked in that joy of knowing Ella was alive and used the emotion as fuel to nullify any light that touched her.

At the rear of the tent, her shadow hands tugged at the canvas until there was enough of a gap for her to slip through.

Since she had last been outside, the horde of warriors had filtered into the trees, leaving only a scattering of tents and a bare garrison of guards and camp followers.

She would have to escape through the Vor army in the surrounding forest—or around, if she could find an "around." She chewed her lip. *Damn, I should have fled yesterday.*

Boe, poor lovesick Boe, waited by the latrines wrinkling his nose. It was a perilous place to walk in the dark; a misstep meant a bootful or two of excrement. She found him at the furthest trench.

He startled and almost dropped the package he held when Karisa whispered in front of his face. "Don't be frightened. I'm going to take your hand and you will be invisible, like me."

"How—"

"Shush. Into the tree line, so I can put on the clothes."

Several yards into the forest, she dropped the lightvoid invocation and pulled the puffing harem guard into an embrace behind a dense of shrubs. She kissed him lightly on the lips. She owed him that, at least.

"We must keep moving," Karisa said breathlessly, pulling on the oversized Vor warrior outfit and boots he had brought as best she could, then threw away the ridiculous silk wraps.

"Give me your dagger," she said, and then tucked the sheathed weapon into her belt. "Which way do we go? Which way is the pass?"

Hesitantly, she invoked a stick-thin illumancer beam to light their path through the forest. Boe stared at the brightness emitting from her hand and up into her face.

"It's just light magic. I can't turn you into a toad or anything, silly."

"I don't know about this. Maybe we should go back," he said, his voice a higher pitch than normal. "They'll send hounds after us."

"Don't worry"—she cupped his hands with hers —"everyone will be too distracted by the battle to notice us gone. By then, we'll be safe. You're my hero, my rescuer—my brave, strong Boe."

They inched through the forest, neither knowing for certain which way to go, except that glimpses of the moon through the branches told them they were heading away from the camp.

After what seemed like an hour, they froze at the sound of a voice ahead. Karisa dismissed the lightbeam, dropped to a crouch, and channeled a light-nullifying cloak around them both.

"Is it them?" she whispered, fearing they had crept up on the back line of Vors waiting in ambush of the Ascorian army column that was expected to pass down the forest road in the morning. She swore silently, having hoped somehow with luck, prayer, the grace of God, that they would stumble out of the forest into an Ascorian sanctuary—an abbey or monastery perhaps— or at least get a clean run to a village or town.

"This way." Boe pulled her toward a direction perpendicular to the path they had been walking. She gave his hand a grateful squeeze. Her shoulders were aching with tension and her neck was painful to turn from the choking the king had given her.

A few minutes later, she tugged on Boe's hand to pull him to a stop.

The dimmest of lights ahead.

More warriors.

Again, they adjusted their course but only to stumble into more close encounters: the clank of a weapon, muffled speech, looming silhouettes—requiring changes to their path almost every few hundred yards.

"Stop," Karisa said finally. "We're going in circles." They were huddled behind a fallen tree after a voice had challenged them and cued them to scramble away for several minutes. It felt as though they were surrounded. She continued to cloak Boe and herself with lightvoid magic until the mental effort was too much to continue and counted her breaths until the woods went silent.

Boe's insecurity returned. "The king will be furious when he finds you gone."

"Doesn't matter. We'll be safe back with my people."

"Your people are about to be ambushed and slaughtered. We could still go back."

"It's too late . . . we don't even know which way 'back' is." She fumbled in the dark and found his shoulder. "Do you hate me so much that you'd abandon me now?"

Boe's hand clasped hers. "I would die for you, but the king is even worse than death . . . you weren't around when he flayed alive Iain just for groping one of his slaves. He tolerates no insult to his crown."

"Then better to die together than suffer that sadist." Her fingers found his face and stroked his cheek. "Let's rest. I'm tired."

Curled in Boe's arms for warmth, she succumbed to the fatigue from a day of abuse and a night of flight and fell asleep, numb to the surrounding danger.

Sometime later, she startled awake to sounds nearby: a hedgehog nuzzled through leaves a few yards away, and a lark sang a hesitant morning melody in the distance. The forest canopy had brightened with yellows and reds, while white boughs stood like the legs of lithe dancers.

"Wake up." Karisa shook the wonky-eyed guard awake. "We have to be away from here before the fighting starts."

Under the golden hue, they walked and mostly avoided the Vor warriors lying in wait. The two times they stumbled across hidden men and women, a hasty lightvoid invocation cloaked them and they vanished into the trees—careful to make sure they didn't betray their presence with the movements of bushes and branches they brushed past.

"Did you see that? A ghost . . ." a fearful voice trailed away.

The trees and undergrowth thinned until tan hills undulated ahead. Encouragingly, there had been no sign of humans for the past hour, and Boe had spotted some wild berries that were tart and seedy.

"Ugh, they're gross. Sure they're not poisonous?" Her face twisted into a wince.

"Dunno . . . at least we'll die together," he said, copying her words from the previous night, then smiled at her with the blackberry juice dribbling into his beard. At least he was trying; thankfully, the big-nosed guard had grown bolder since their rest, quelling some of Karisa's misgivings about bringing the man along.

The guard squinted at the sky and reasoned that they were heading north because the sun had risen to their right. If he was correct, they had skirted the massed armies and could break out straight to the Reynford River and follow it to the City of Irin. "How far is it? The city?" he asked.

She shrugged. "Four, five days, maybe?"

"And you will vouch for me when we come across soldiers?"

"Of course. As long as they don't kill us on sight. It'll help if we can replace these outfits with some regular clothes. And we should cut that hideous beard off." She mimicked a snip of scissors with her fingers and flashed him a smile to lighten the mood. She then scanned the empty hills before setting a brisk pace away from the edge of the forest.

It was midmorning when they first smelled smoke. Behind them, pillars of smoke rose from the direction of the forest and carried with the breeze. Signs that the ambush had begun.

"Glad I'm not near those damn firemages, they burn everything in sight," Boe said.

The hills soon flattened to a tan, grass-swept expanse. In the distance, a road cut north with a few homesteads nestled along its side, each surrounded by farmlands of brown, dug earth. And on the horizon, a signaling tower stood like a lighthouse overlooking the sea of toiled dirt. Karisa heartened at the sight that promised a return to true freedom.

"We must hurry to one of the buildings and borrow some clothes," she said, pulling tight the oversized trousers and tossing her hair to cover her neck.

It was then that they saw dozens, scores, and then hundreds of figures emptying out of the line of hills that they had just abandoned—running and tripping along the road or through the fields and plains. Some so close that she recognized the pigeon-chested chest plate, steel cap, and brown leathers of Ascorian conscripts. Some bore swords or spears but most were empty-handed. They threw desperate glances over their shoulders.

Enemy horsemen followed and swept through the fleeing troops with axe and sword, cutting swathes through the men and women crisscrossing the open ground, unable to escape the murderous mounted warriors.

"Run, Boe!" Karisa yelled, her gullet rising. She turned from the routing mass and ran.

Pounding feet and frightened cries sounded faintly in the distance. Several Ascorian soldiers hurtled out of the hills toward her and Boe; then, like frightened fish, they veered away and scattered.

A minute later, four or five horsemen crested the hills and shouted excitedly as they chased down the fleeing soldiers. They were Vor skirmishers, whose usual task was to harass the flanks of a battle. But now that their enemy was routing, their bloodlust transformed them into merciless cutthroats.

"Faster!" Boe shouted at her, grabbed her hand, and propelled her along.

The skirmishers could cut them down in an instant. She had to do something. She steadied her mind and forced her fear aside to summon an inkling of joy to channel into her illumancy. Ridiculously, a childhood memory returned to her—she and her mother prancing and laughing through meadows similar to the ones around her. She hung on to it and plunged into a lightvoid.

She and Boe vanished from sight, leaving two small flickering pools of black on the ground, as though the sun were directly above but with no substance to view.

"Keep running . . . we need to get to some cover. I can't keep this cloak up for very long," she said. By now, the horsemen had run down the soldiers and were casting about for more victims; a couple stared in their direction for several seconds. One then shouted a command, turned in the opposite direction, and kicked his horse into a canter toward another group of fleeing Ascorians.

Several minutes later, exhausted from the lightvoid magic but within the cover of some bushes at the base of a hill, Karisa and Boe stopped to catch their breaths as she dropped the invocation and watched her hands and arms reappear.

From their cover, they could see that the routing Ascorians were thinned out over the plains, and the road and farms were littered with bodies. However, at the head of the road coming out of the hills, an organized group of Ascorian soldiers fought a thin-lined retreat against a mass of Vor warriors. A small cloud of red and green spiraled over the battle. Sleek draconic forms swooped down to rake talons across heads and shoulders, then circled around for another attack.

Armored horsemen and footmen on both sides thrust and chopped at each other. Firemages roamed the battle line, with the occasional burst of flame to engulf the occasional soldier or two. Pillars of smoke trailed their paths from the forest out onto the plains.

"Hideous beast," Karisa said, watching as a huge four-legged beast bounded into the fray and tossed bodies aside like sticks, ripping through the brittle flank. "Sickens me to my core."

The monster, a gargantor, was a favorite of the Vor king. Some days before, she had been forced to watch as the animal—almost the size of an elephant—tore apart and devoured a prisoner with its daggerlike claws and serrated maw.

Minutes later, the Ascorian line collapsed under the combined fury of the gargantor and Vor warriors. A few Ascorian horsemen turned their mounts, threw down their banners, and galloped for their lives. Their cowardice was infectious, and others followed in panic.

Distracted by the battle, neither Boe nor Karisa noticed the Vor skirmishers until they were already upon them.

Six blood-splattered riders surrounded them, axes or chipped sword blades held menacingly at their sides, and snarls etched into their faces. A broad-shouldered woman, with blue tattoos around her short neck, cantered forward and tipped her head to examine them. "What have we here?" she asked. Her face then turned to curiosity. "Wait . . . deserters? Deserters from our own ranks?"

Boe stepped in front of Karisa with his hand on the pommel of his sword.

"Tell them I escaped and you're taking me back," Karisa whispered to the outmatched guard.

"She escaped and I—"

"Is that so? What I know is that she's the king's pleasure. I've seen her around." The woman slid from her horse with her blade in hand.

"I caught her. I'm returning her," Boe finished, his voice shaky.

"I don't think so. Holding hands like lovers and hiding like thieves. I know what's going on here," she said with a smirk. "You've been letting your trouser-snake do your thinking."

"I haven't touched her."

"You should start thinking with your head. Now, thinking of brandishing your sword at me . . . that's not good thinking either."

Boe removed his hand from the pommel of his sword.

Opportunities were streaming away. Karisa had to act. All the skirmishers were looking toward her. It had to be now.

She thrust her hands outward and invoked a

blinding lightburst—light flared in the hills like a blast of sun.

Horses neighed and reared, tipping their riders up, and the warriors lifted hands to eyes. Two men fell to the ground, one dangling with his foot caught in a stirrup. The thick-necked woman cried out in alarm, and her hand darted up to cover her eyes.

"Quick, with me." Karisa grabbed Boe's hand and invoked the lightvoid cloak, disappearing into a pool of black. She pulled the guard to the top of the hill, then ran down the other side. They needed to find more cover, but scanning as she ran, she found there was little to help except low bushes and the occasional tree.

"Where did they go?" a male voice shouted from the other side of the hill.

"The whore's a lightmage, you idiot. Get back on your horse," the female warrior's voice could be heard shouting back at him. "Spread out and search for them."

At the bottom of the hill, Boe tripped, and his hand slipped out of hers. His body snapped into sight just as one of the horsemen crested the top. "Here's the man," the skirmisher shouted.

Karisa heard thundering hooves as the riders descended on them. She reached down for Boe's hand, but in her panic and inexperience, she lost focus on the lightvoid completely.

"Here's the woman."

In fear, she turned to the charging horseman and gasped in horror as a battleaxe cleaved through Boe's head. The blade emerged through the guard's face with blood and brain tangled through thick, dark hair. He stood for a second, then his legs crumpled and he collapsed to the ground, blood pumping out of the ruinous gouge in his head.

"Tie her up before she vanishes again," the woman warrior commanded, trotting down the hillside. However, the fight had left Karisa. Exhausted, unable to fuel another lightvoid, she slumped to the ground, defeated. Her dagger was knocked out of her grip and a rope looped around her hands and neck.

Months of hope, thwarted. She growled a curse of frustration. Now more than ever, freedom seemed so distant.

She would try again. But she needed greater help.

She prayed that Vixhana and Jaks would keep their oaths. No one else would come for her.

Chapter 2

Desperate Times

Jaks—The Village of the Jurns, Ascoria

Jaks squinted against the morning sun as he reached the plateau-top of the village of the Jurns. He examined the ancient huts of gray stone surrounding the staircase that led up from the caves below, uncertain which was the infirmary that housed his sister. He had a debt to repay her.

It had only been a day since Grandmaster Mulgrave and Meila had departed on their journey back to the Ascorian capital. A day since Jaks had abandoned electromancy for its part in critically injuring his sister Vixhana. And a day since deciding to self-exile.

Guilt weighed heavily on his mind. He would do whatever he could to keep her alive.

Around him, villagers garbed in skins and furs of wild animals busied themselves at all manner of tasks. Three *kaikushkas* spun flaxes into baskets, and several more of the elderly women tended cooking pots over firepits. A crew of men chipped away at a pile of rocks; a neat stack of rectangular blocks sat next to them, the product of their craft. And at the edge of the village, a band of young men hauled on ropes as voices shouted up from the canyon below. When the carcass of a black bear finally breached the top, the group cheered, then dragged the dead animal over to an awaiting butcher.

A hunched woman, as though reading his mind, raised a crooked finger and pointed at a nearby building with a sloping slate roof.

He nodded thanks and hurried past.

As he opened the door, he saw he was in the right place.

Two figures lay in separate wooden cots. Furthest away, Vixhana faced him. But only her closed eyelids, nose, and mouth were visible; the rest of her face was covered in bandages. A thin, narrow tube trailed into her nose through to her stomach. Tavis lay on the nearer mattress of animal furs, and a bench of healer's tools and shelves of stoppered stone jars lined the far wall.

The windows in the hut were shuttered to the chill, and a cheerful hearth, flued to evacuate the smoke, warmed the building. A woman, with her back to Jaks, wiped the brow of the enfeebled apprentice.

"How are they?" Jaks asked, hoping the tribeswoman understood the Ascorian tongue.

She turned, and he found himself staring at Xanra, the chieftess's daughter.

Intense green eyes gazed at him from beneath

slender eyebrows. Delicate ears peeked out from beneath a braid of auburn hair wrapped around her head like a crown, and soft lips pursed at the sight of him.

"Close the door. You're letting out the heat," she replied in Ascorian. In the warmth, she was dressed only in a light leather tunic and leggings.

As Jaks obeyed, the woman continued. "Your sister is stable. But Mother says only Hodrin knows what will come of the lightning damage and the fall on her head." With her words, guilt stung at Jaks again.

"Will she live?" he asked.

Xanra shrugged. "Perhaps. Perhaps not. She barely moves other than to sigh and twitch." She wrung out the used cloth in a clay bowl filled with water. "Your friend, though, has a better chance. At times, he murmurs and his eyes flutter as though ready to wake."

"He is not my friend. To be honest, we've traded a lot of ill feeling between us. I don't know whether to be sad or happy about his condition. I came to see Vixhana."

"Oh, is he a bad person?" She put the bowl aside and directed her gaze at Jaks.

"Not exactly," he replied, then explained how their rivalry had ignited: Jaks gliding into the grandmaster's service with the threat of displacing Tavis from an apprenticeship that he had worked hard to attain. Their hostility seemed petty now, with the apprentice lying comatose.

"You people fight over the smallest of things. Come help me roll your sister to her back. Ease the pressure off her side," she directed him.

"An apprenticeship with the Academy is not a small thing." Jaks kneeled to assist the young healer with Vixhana. "People often pay huge amounts of money to gain a master. If you don't have money"—realization struck Jaks that Tavis's family probably had very little —"you have to prove yourself through tests and feats."

"Would you end him to win this apprenticeship? He is vulnerable . . ." Her eyes flicked over to the incapacitated young man.

Jaks was aghast. "No, I'm no monster," he said. "Besides, I don't wish to be an apprentice anymore. There is no reason for us to continue our conflict."

They then rolled Vixhana to her back. He grimaced with the effort but was grateful he could help her in some way.

"You speak Ascorian well," Jaks said as he retreated to the other side of Tavis's cot. The attractive woman made him nervous, and he wanted to please her.

She cast him a scornful look. "Mother says we will need to speak your language if we are to join your empire. She regrets our people tried to fight your king instead of submitting and blames herself for our exile." Xanra poured clean water from a stone jug into a tiny cup, then dripped it into a funnel and tube feeding into Tavis's nose. She did the same for Vixhana.

"She is wrong, though. We Jurns must have freedom

to rule ourselves—we would never fit in with your aggressive ways," she said as she finished her task and sat on a chair before the fireplace.

"King Silas is a just and generous ruler," Jaks said in a defensive voice, and explained how he was nicknamed the "Breadgiver King" by the commonfolk. "Our country has prospered greatly since he united it. Before him, it was a dozen small kingdoms and realms. We were forever at war with one or another for the past couple of hundred years."

At that moment, Tavis groaned loudly on his cot. He flailed his arms and kicked off his fur covering in one motion. Xanra rushed to replace the fur, but it was then that he began to retch and shudder.

Jaks froze, unsure how to help.

"Go find my mother," the young woman commanded, and leaned over the big-eared apprentice to hold him on his side. "Go. Don't just stand there."

<hr>

There was little that Jaks could do to help either Tavis or Vixhana after that—that day or anytime over the next week. He visited and helped turn them each day, but other times, he stood by uselessly as the tribesfolk attended dutifully to the patients.

Fortunately, there were other distractions as Jaks sought his part in the Jurn village. He was greeted and welcomed throughout the plateau-top by the tribesfolk. The few children amongst them traipsed after him and scattered with laughter when he drew up his arms and chased them in mimicry of a giant. There seemed to be no one parent or mother to each youngster; instead, all of the adults showed fondness for every child in some communal form of parenthood. For a population of several hundred, the eight young children were starkly few. Perhaps that was why they placed such prestige on fertile women, and particularly those who were pregnant—glowing mother-goddesses who were always with a young aide and doted upon by men and women alike.

Everyone had a duty in the Uwama's village, and Jaks's was to hunt.

Partnered up with him was Raki, the youth whom he'd met on his first day in the village. Bushy-haired and bright-faced, he beamed at Jaks and handed him a hunting spear.

"We get meat," the young man said. The grinning hunter walked over to a weapons rack and picked up another spear, along with a shortbow and arrows, then beckoned for Jaks to follow him down to the gully floor.

With that, their friendship rekindled. Over the following days, Raki and Jaks roamed through gullies and plateaus with weapons in hand and talking. Jaks became an apt student at both tossing the short throwing weapon and learning the Jurn language.

Without the judgmental and harsh criticisms of Ranger Cromer that'd had Jaks doubting his every action during survival training, his hunting instincts naturally flourished. But even with the addition of Raki's deft tracking skills, the pair only brought back about half as much meat as the other hunters each day. "Too much talking and not enough stalking," the older men would admonish them.

But despite his gradual insertion into the Jurn village, Jaks thought increasingly of Meila. He missed the easy, free talk he had with the raven-haired outworlder about anything and everything. He missed her childlike delight, as raw as someone discovering vision after being blind. Yet, it was clear that Meila did not want the intimacy he wanted with her. She had rejected him twice already, and now she was far away.

And the more he thought of her, the greater a question burned in him: Why was he here?

He had thought his self-exile was an atonement for injuring Vixhana and killing Meila's husband. And he had thought that by staying with the Jurns, he could help his sister recover, but there was little he could do— anyone could do—to bring her out of her helpless state.

So, Meila's challenge haunted him: *"Do you think she would want you to give up? Run away? Was Vixhana one to quit anything?"*

The thought nagged him that maybe he had got it all wrong.

Tavis broke out of his unconscious state several days after their return from the wreckage site.

Jaks's first exchange with Tavis did not start well.

"Here's the hero," Tavis said sarcastically from his bed as Jaks entered the healer's cottage. "I heard you were still around."

Jaks had come on his regular afternoon visit to help turn Vixhana and was surprised to see the apprentice sitting upright and alert. He had hoped Xanra would be present, as she often was, but only a toothless kaikushka sat with the still-comatose Vixhana and the thin, pale-looking Tavis. The old woman ignored him and lanced holes around the edge of a tanned hide with a bone needle.

"You're awake." Jaks ignored Tavis's jibe. "You look better."

The apprentice snorted. "For someone half-dead," he said. "What are you doing here?"

"I came to see Vixhana."

"But why are you here at all? Why aren't you out saving the world?" A sneer crossed his face. "No other family members to try to kill? Xanra told me this morning what you did." His eyes flicked to Vixhana lying on the neighboring cot.

Jaks's right fist clenched, and his left spasmed like a claw now that it was healed and no longer bandaged. The jibe pierced like a spear. He took a deep breath and spread his fingers. "Things have changed a lot since you were injured."

"Yes, I can see that." Tavis looked pointedly at Vixhana's unmoving form.

"Look, there's no need for us to be enemies—"

"Enemies? Are we enemies? You're the one who's trying to cut me out of the Academy—" Tavis began, but stopped when the elderly crone tapped his shoulder, having lowered her needle to her lap.

She raised a finger to her toothless maw and made a wheezing sound that bubbled a glob of spittle at the corner of her mouth.

Jaks silently thanked the old woman for the interruption and continued. "I'm not an apprentice anymore. I live here with the Jurns now. I vowed to never use my powers again and have left the grandmaster's service."

Tavis stared at him as though he had sprouted horns. "What? Why? What really happened? I can't remember anything from that day."

Jaks recounted the ambush at the wreckage in detail, starting from Meila's first shot with her darkcore weapon, followed by the Vor gunman's startling and explosive retaliation, and finishing with how his lightning attack had accidentally struck Anton and Vixhana. Describing the clash felt like a confession: Tavis the Pardoner, and Jaks the sinner. By the end, he was grim-faced and mired in grief.

For several minutes, the only sound in the cottage

was that of the kaikushka's needle punching holes in the leather.

The ashen-faced apprentice looked away and fumbled with the edge of the fur covering his legs. He appeared lost for words, and another emotion—ashamed. "I'm sorry, Jaks. I shouldn't have taken that cheap jab at you. I admire Vixhana. She's like one of those heroes you read about in children's books. I hope she comes out of it."

They both stared at the once mighty nightwraith.

Jaks sat down on the wooden stool next to Tavis. "I've said some nasty things to you as well. I've thought some even viler things," he said.

Their eyes met for a second, and they looked away, embarrassed by the rawness of the moment.

"We're good now, Tavis," said Jaks. Saying the apprentice's name felt alien, but somehow declared his change of heart toward the frail young man. "Let's just move on. There's no point dwelling on the past. We shouldn't torment ourselves over what we can't change."

Jaks stiffened as his own words echoed through his mind. Something twisted in the guilt-laden, troubled space between his ears. Some truth seemed to emerge like a gleaming gem unveiled in the rubble. Had he got it wrong? Were his actions forgivable, just as he had forgiven Tavis?

Although the magnitude of his own wrongdoing was at the heavier end of the stick, did it mean he had to keep beating himself with it forever? No amount of self-flagellation could bring back Vixhana. This self-exile served no purpose. It did not remedy the wrong; it was just a punishment, plain and simple. He had to honor Vixhana in deeds, not sacrifices. She wouldn't want him to quit and hide away. *She would want me to be like her —heroic.*

"Sometimes, you're not as stupid as you look," Tavis said, his face cracking into a cheeky grin to interrupt Jaks's thoughts. "Yes, let's put aside the past."

Jaks spluttered a laugh, and the kaikushka shushed him for his outburst, causing both young men to snicker. She then glared at them both until they quieted, but mirth still brightened their eyes.

Over the following weeks, Tavis continued to regain his strength and drive. And for several days now, Jaks hadn't heard the apprentice complain of pains at all. In fact, the only noise he had made recently was to plead the Uwama to clear him fit to attempt the journey back to Dunberrin.

Jaks's life with the Jurns changed with the return of Witabu.

A month after the elder tribesman had departed with Mulgrave and Meila for Dunberrin, he thumped up the stairs to the Uwama's platform on a cool, brisk evening.

Witabu leaned on his spear, puffing. *"Hodrin*

uhsaga, Uwama." He inclined his head to the chieftess as the other two tribesmen who had accompanied him appeared.

The woman replied in kind and gestured for them to sit at the low table where Jaks regularly joined her and other villagers to eat.

She laid long fingers on Witabu's forearm. "The ponies still run the plains?" she asked.

"Few. The dark wolves roam fearlessly and in packs of many dozens. Much has changed there. They are not the same grasslands we left behind."

"Maybe so, but I am glad to see that none of you were injured on the journey." She leaned forward. "Tell me. You met the Ascorian king?"

"I did, but it was a poor time to have taken him the request, Chieftess. Their enemy conquers province after province, with rumors of entire towns turned into slave camps. He says these Vors have taken all the south and threaten to burst into the north . . . if they haven't already—it's been two weeks since we left."

"But what did he say to our request?"

"Sacrifice. If we want to subserve to his rule, he demands we join this war now. All of our fighting men and . . . fighting women. Although I explained our women do not fight, he demands we provide five hundred warriors."

The Uwama slumped back and looked to the night sky. "I feared there would be a price—but not one so great as that."

Xanra leaped to her feet. "Mother, we cannot accept this. The children and kaikushkas would be left with no one to protect them," she said. "We don't have to fight some foolish war for a tyrant who drove our people from our lands. We have no duty to him. We should cheer for his death, not laud him."

And so the debate began.

The rest of that evening, arguments fired back and forth over the Uwama's deck, but with doubtful progress. It seemed to Jaks that the Uwama had already decided and was merely allowing her daughter and others a chance to voice their feelings before she declared her predetermined choice.

When Xanra eventually thundered across the rope bridge to the plateau caves, and the other dissenters lost their vigor for debate, the Uwama vowed to deliver her decision the next night, then dismissed the tribal court.

As Jaks departed for his chamber, the wizened Witabu grabbed his sleeve and pulled him aside.

"Your friend *Mee-la* said to give you this," the old man said in the Ascorian tongue. He held his horned goat's helm under one arm and extended a waxed envelope with the other.

"Is she well?" Jaks asked, accepting the crumpled package with a nod.

"I saw only a little of her after we arrived in Dunberrin. But she gave me this to give to you. She seemed bothered—pushed it into my hands and then dashed back to her forge." The man yawned. "Now, these bones must get some sleep. You should rest too." He then stepped onto the closest rope bridge and left Jaks staring at the envelope.

He extracted a parchment and studied the words under lantern light:

Jaks,
I have been trying to contact you on the communicator I
gave you. I have information you will want to know.
We need you. Desperate times.
Meila.

It had been a month since he had dropped the wrist device into a basket, along with his armor and sword, somewhere in a chamber deep in the plateau fortress. Although he had thought of Meila daily, he had never retrieved it. He hadn't wanted to talk with her until he had something good to say. But what was this information she wrote about?

He tucked the letter away into a cloak pocket, turned to the rope bridge, and gripped the sides with white knuckles. Even after traversing it hundreds of times, it still seemed to buck like a wild horse every time he walked across. Once within the caves, he wound his way through the tunnels to a storage chamber and his old possessions.

The basket stood out from the many others. The only one with a sword hilt poking above the rim. And there was the other thing, the alien device, lying under his leather armor, intact and quiescent.

He placed the gray disc against his arm, and a strange tingling prickled his skin as it had done the first time Meila placed it on him. It caused him a moment's pause before he folded its brown binding around his wrist. He marveled at the beauty of the molded metal—unlike anything he'd ever seen crafted on this world. Her planet must be beautiful if it were filled with things like this.

That first time he had worn it, though, he had pried it off within an hour of Meila riding away. She said it would keep them connected, but at that time, he had only wanted to punish and exile himself for the damage he had done, including killing her husband, Anton.

He frowned at the uneasy sensation of the alien device alive against his skin. The tingling progressed to a chill until the disc felt cold to touch.

The rim of the device lit with a copper glow and an image of Meila formed abruptly in front of him. Her oval face and almond eyes wrinkled as she frowned. Incredible. Some form of illumancy was projecting her image through the relic. She looked perfect. He gulped, not realizing how much he had missed her face.

"Damn you, Jaks. There you are. Did it take that stringy hunter all that time to get back to the village?" Meila said.

He dropped to the floor cross-legged and stared at her image, gaping and agog.

"Have you lost your voice?"

A familiar metallic odor permeated the air and filled his nose. Electromancy thrummed close by. Not the lethal lightning that he'd vowed never to use again, but something else.

He looked at his wrist and fixated on the disc, and found it was no longer an inert gray. Tiny copper-colored lines, circles, and squares glowed over the device's surface and dived into its interior. However, it wasn't his eyes that he was seeing with. Even when he closed them, he could still see the intricate paths. He was sensing them with his electromancy.

"Jaks?" Meila's voice rose with some concern. "Are you alright?"

He thought he had better say something and planned a reply that he was fine and was simply amazed to see her—but before he could even move his lips, she replied as if he had just spoken aloud.

"I was worried there. I forget you've never used a comm before. You sound strange, though. Your voice. It's different . . . sharp," she said.

"But I didn't say anything." He looked around the cave, wondering whether someone else had spoken, but his only company were baskets and shelves.

"Huh? Never mind. How are Vixhana and Tavis?" she asked. After Jaks declared the latter recovered but the former still unconscious, she shook her head grimly. "It doesn't sound good for her. If Anton had survived, he might have been able to help." She stopped, only then seeing the fault in her words. "Let's hope she recovers soon."

"Listen up," she then said. The image swayed for a moment and the background to Meila's head lit up. Workbenches and hanging lightstones of the Academy behind her gave a warmth of familiarity. "The tube we salvaged from the *Mendhelsson* was a magnetic shield generator . . . I've modified it to build a velocity cannon. I won't get into specifics, but it could be a game-changer against the Vors. Think of my darkcore pistol, but thousands of times more powerful." She paused for a breath. "The only thing is, I need you here to try to make it work. It needs an electrical generator and you're the only power station that I know of on this planet. We need you to come back to the Academy."

She wants me to kill people with a weapon she built. Is this all I'm good for? Jaks clasped his hands together and wrung his fingers. He opened his mouth to reply, but she spoke again as though he had already voiced his thoughts.

"It's not the only thing you're good for, but at the moment, it's the best thing you can do."

"You can hear my thoughts?" He brought the shimmering wrist device to his face and gazed at it, astonished.

"What do you mean? No. I just hear your voice, although it sounds sharp at times . . . and sometimes I don't see your lips moving, but I thought that was because the lighting is poor around you—"

"You *can* hear my thoughts. You responded to me twice now when I had only been thinking about what I was going to say. Or else this thing is sending my thoughts to you and turning them into speech."

"Interesting." She narrowed her eyes and scratched her head. After a few seconds, she began to nod enthusiastically. "This could be a passive effect of your electromancy."

He had an idea. *Let me test this.* He opened his memories of the past few weeks and focused them into the communicator.

"That's astonishing," he heard Meila say but continued to concentrate on piecing the past together and projecting it through the device: Learning the Jurns' language, hunting with Raki, tribal life, and images and memories of his conciliation with Tavis. His sad last thoughts were of Vixhana, comatose on her cot. He stared at Meila's unwavering projection as he transferred his memories to her.

"The comm device works as though it's an extension of you. It must be through your electromancy," she said, her face intense in thought. "I think it allows you to sense and interact with the electrical components inside the device. Although it's just a machine, your affinity to electricity must be allowing you to connect with it as naturally as the neurons in your own brain. I wonder what you can do with other devices?" She rubbed her chin in a manner that reminded him of Grandmaster Mulgrave.

Despite their fascination with this new discovery, the urgency in Meila's written note cued him to change the topic. "You said in your letter that you had some information I would want to know," he said.

"Oh, yes. We'll have to explore this other power another time." Her expression turned from curiosity to concern as she continued. "Yes, your friend Minto came looking for you a while ago. He was delivering messages to the Academy."

"He's alive? Thank God. I was worried it was him that rebel village hung from their palisade."

"I know. That's why I'm telling you. He came to the grandmaster's lab looking for you. I told him what happened with you and Vixhana. He was quite concerned about her injuries."

"He's adored her ever since he first laid eyes on her." A memory of six-year-old Minto staring googly-eyed at sixteen-year-old Vixhana flashed into his memory.

"She looked so normal back then. Probably because she wasn't dressed like an assassin," Meila commented on Jaks's projected memory from his childhood.

"You saw that? I better be careful what I think." He was amazed his thoughts were transferring so easily to her.

"He's a pleasant fellow. Anyway, he wanted to tell you he saw your *other* sister recently . . . Karisa?"

"No, he couldn't have. She disappeared after the raid. She's dead." He shook his head, confused. If she were alive, he was sure she would've been discovered by now.

"Apparently not. There was a parley between King Silas and the Vor king, where they were supposed to negotiate a truce. Turns out that damn tyrant just wanted a stage to demand our surrender."

"But what has this to do with Karisa?"

"She was standing behind the Vor king. I'm sorry, Jaks, but she was shackled by a collar . . . like how Anton was." Her gaze fixed on him, but the corners of her eyes dropped, betraying her sadness. "He said she looked well, though—glowing, in fact."

"All this time, I thought she was dead. Her body in some ditch or sunk in the sea." *She's alive?* As realization sank in, his neck tingled with joy. *She's alive!*

"A slave, though. Some would say she might be better off dead," Meila said, not as enthusiastic about the situation as he.

Jaks clambered to his feet, steadying himself against the pommel of his sword jutting out of the basket. "I've got to rescue her. It was my fault she was even at that raid."

"You can't just go up and get her. She's surrounded by an army of axe-wielding barbarians," Meila replied as she walked to another workbench, whereupon lay a long metal contraption attached to numerous wires and coils. But he was too distracted to take much notice of Meila's surroundings, let alone his own.

"But I can't just leave her. I have to do something,"

he said, the glimmerings of a plan forming in his mind. "I have an idea. We can meet up and use your illumancy to sneak into the enemy camp with a lightvoid invocation and rescue her."

"That's ridiculous!" Meila exclaimed. "For one thing, my power is very limited, and I can only conjure little fantasies—not major invocations like that. Second, you can't just wander around the Vor encampments searching for her. We'd have to interact with them to find where she is kept. And third, she's the king's prize. She'll be highly guarded."

"You're right. Both of us going in wouldn't work. But alone, I could melt into their camp as one of them. I speak Vor and have Vor blood in my veins. I just need outerwear to complete a disguise."

"You're talking suicide, Jaks."

"I need to do what's right. Karisa needs me. I made an oath both to her and my mother." As the words spilled from his lips, his resolve to fulfill them grew. "You were correct—what you said last time. Vixhana wouldn't quit. She wouldn't turn away from someone in need. If she was conscious, she'd be the first to go. I might not be a hero like her, but I can take on her courage."

"Courage or foolishness? You're so impulsive sometimes."

"I've been a fool all my life, but now I'm taking a risk that's worthwhile—it's time to be courageous and stand for what's right." Not just for his sister, but his mother, too. "They were all strong. I'll show that I can be too." He gritted his teeth.

Meila's lips pressed into a thin line, and she turned to place a hand on the contraption behind her. Jaks recognized the metal tube from the salvage site. Squares and chunks of newly forged steel sprouted from its side, but the ship part in the center took prominence. "I really need you at the Academy to help me get this thing working. It could radically change the balance of firepower in this war. You might not have heard, but we're not doing well. If Irin falls, the coasts of Finstaf will follow, and then Dunberrin."

"What does it do?" He squinted at the image of the device. The length of a ballista, but without moving parts, it gave no clue to its workings.

She lectured him on the design of the weapon—what she called a velocity cannon, or a "velocannon" for short. The barrel was the metal tube they had salvaged in the Highlands. A magnetic radiation shield. Electricity energized an electromagnetic field inside the tube, and when a darkcore pistol was fired at full power through the barrel, the plasma bolt would be accelerated to almost the speed of light. When it struck something solid, she explained, the deadly bolt would explode and destroy everything within a half mile.

"It uses the darkcore plasma and layers an additional force on top of that technology," Meila summarized. "This velocannon is the weapon that can turn the tide of war, but it needs energy."

"From what?"

"You." She smiled and held out her hand. "Watch this." A tiny figure spun to life on her palm. Jaks's eyes widened at the fine details of her illusion. The figure was him! Despite her reservations about her illumancer powers, her skill with what little she had was impressive.

Miniature Jaks stood on a stone battlement beside the velocannon mounted on a heavy steel frame. Sparks scintillated around his hands as he gripped sides of the cannon. A moment later, the weapon spat fire and shuddered in its frame. "The batteries and capacitors that I built can't generate enough electrical charge . . . but I think you can."

Although puzzled by her unfamiliar technical terms, it was clear what she wanted. "You think I have the power to use it. You want my electromancy."

She nodded, and the illusion blinked out. "We were all disappointed there wasn't a weapons locker on the *Mendhelsson*, but this velocannon, if it works, could be more powerful than a thousand soldiers armed with darkies." Her forehead creased as she implored him. "Come to the Academy and help us win this war, and then go find your sister."

"I vowed to abandon electromancy after that day—"

"Mulgrave and I have been talking. He says that you can't abandon magic—just like how you can't give up breathing. It's part of you. You might hold your breath for a while, but it'll claw its way out when you're at your most desperate."

It made sense. All those times the lightning had risen unbidden, defending him against danger.

"So why didn't he tell me this before he left?" If the old mage had known he couldn't abandon his magic, why had he let him banish himself to the wilderness?

"He knew you needed time and space to grieve. That rascal can be pretty wise sometimes. Besides, he didn't want to tear you away from your sister's side." Meila then held up a piece of shining steel in front of her chest. He recognized it from the illusion she had generated. It was the handle-piece through which his miniature self had imbued electromancy. "So, will you come back to Dunberrin now? We really need you."

"I want to help, but I'm going to trust my instincts and go after Karisa. If I wait, there's no knowing what will happen to her. If I hesitate, I could be too late. I couldn't live with that."

Emotion stormed Meila's face for a long minute, until she slowly nodded her head and grimaced. "Just stay alive. You're the only person who can power this velocannon. Promise me you'll come back in one piece?"

Jaks nodded, his thoughts already racing to the mission ahead. He'd never contemplated such a bold mission before. It would test the extremes of his abilities, requiring skills his sisters possessed in abundance—and hopefully ones he could similarly employ: disguise, determination, courage, and strength. He dismissed an unbidden mental image of the fearsome Vors from the salvage site and steeled himself to do whatever was needed to rescue Karisa. It was what Vixhana would do.

"Promise me?" she repeated.

"I promise."

Chapter 3

Crossing the Mountains

Mud splattered Jaks's leggings as he trudged alongside the engorged stream flowing through the gorge below the Jurns' plateau village. Three days earlier, a storm had rolled down from the mountains, on the same day the Uwama declared her people would go to war, like some portent of the journey to come. The mood of the village had turned grim but resolute. For despite their reluctance to fight, the Jurns were loyal to their charismatic leader. Now, at last, the rain had stopped, and the tribesfolk assembled to leave.

Could they survive the journey? Even the toughest of them feared the predators and harshness of the Highlands.

At least one villager, however, was enraptured by the promise of adventure. Jaks caught sight of the boyish face of his hunting companion, Raki, excitedly bobbing amongst the throng of tribesfolk waiting to ascend the narrow path up the cliff face to the warband's congregation point above. Hitching his backpack, he bumped and nudged his way toward Raki. Arrow nocks, spear ends, leather shields, and travel baskets of the hastily armed tribesfolk caught on his own protruding scabbard and travel gear along the way—he apologized at least a dozen times before he caught up with his friend.

"I thought you would stay here with your sister?" Raki said, his expression shifting to one of puzzlement on seeing Jaks outfitted with sword and armor.

With the hasty preparations over the past few days, Jaks had not had the chance to tell the ever-cheerful youth of his new plans. "Vixhana will be cared for, whether or not I'm here."

Although her condition had improved in the last several days—eyes opening, and making garbled sounds for a few minutes before relapsing into a deep slumber— her long-term prospects were still uncertain. *In a few days or a few weeks, Hodrin may restore her. But she may not be the mighty warrior she once was,*" the Uwama had said during her last bedside visit to Vixhana.

"Xanra will stay, and others, too. They will continue to care for her." Sixty tribesfolk, from what he saw: children, the elderly and crippled, and a dozen hunters and helpers to protect those left in the village.

Jaks clapped a hand on Raki's shoulder as it came to their turn to ascend the cliff path. "Besides, I have a task to do. I received word that my sister Karisa survives. I am going to rescue her from the king of the Voros," he said. Raki's eyes widened. The quest sounded heroic to Jaks's ears, but likely foolhardy and grandiose to others.

Raki grinned. "Adventure, my friend."

"Yes, adventure." Jaks returned a weak smile. "Come, let's join the rest of the warband," he said before his friend thought to question his sanity.

As Jaks had told Meila over the wrist communicator the day before, calling them a warband was a gross exaggeration. Although half of the five hundred making the trek could throw a spear or shoot an arrow, the rest—mainly the Jurn women, who were gatherers and crafters—had never handled weapons except in whittling, decorating, or ceremonial dance. And none had experience fighting in formation as part of an army. Witabu had told him that after the last of their ponies died over a decade ago, the Jurns had lost their greatest advantage in fighting: mounted archery. So, without their beloved animals or army training, this warband, Jaks realized, no matter how brave and committed they were, marched toward disaster.

An hour later, the warband had assembled on a stony expanse. Apprehensive faces sought last glimpses of their near-abandoned village on the other side of the gully through the treetops, and Jaks could hear scattered weeping and sobs that were quickly reprimanded and silenced.

The chieftess, bedecked in boiled-leather armor, dragon-scale helm, and bearing an iron-tipped quarterstaff, stood on a boulder to address her warriors. "My loyal Jurns, when we return, the grasslands will welcome the soles of our feet again. Our journey will be hard and fraught with danger, but one that our children, grandchildren, and later descendants will thank us for. Be proud and take courage that we walk this path together." Her voice boomed over the stony flat; Jaks had often suspected that the Uwama possessed sonomancer abilities after being spell-bound by her sonorous voice, but now, her voice projecting to him— hundreds of yards away—and to each individual as though she stood right beside them, was a clear feat of magic.

As Jaks watched the mass of tribesfolk straggle across the plateau—a sea of animal-skull headdresses and spears—he shook his head and jogged to the Uwama where she stood offering words of encouragement to passing tribesfolk. "If I may suggest, Chieftess, perhaps we should organize the warband into marching columns. And split them into smaller sections with a leader for each. It would be good training for the warband before we get to the more treacherous parts of the traverse. They will pass through the mountains far easier if they are in lines." He was thinking of the narrow gullies and cliff paths that they would surely encounter as they took the route directly west across the mountains, a shortcut that could cut weeks off their trek to join the main Ascorian army in the river city and deliver Jaks to find Karisa.

The Uwama looked down at Jaks, lifting one eyebrow. "Indeed. Your father was a famous commander, wasn't he? Maybe you've inherited something from him? You could help me with your ideas."

He nodded and stiffened from a chill that ran down his spine but decided the chieftess had no malicious intent on bringing up his father—she had no way of knowing of the evil the man harbored in his soul. If he did have some of the strategic aptitude of his father, it was the only similarity they shared. Her suggestion appealed to him. He had always fancied himself an excellent Stratega player—a board game he would play against his schoolmates and resoundingly win—and although an unexceptional swordsman, his conscript unit training and love of battle lore could be something he could use to help the Jurns.

She commanded a halt in her powerful voice, then with the help of Witabu and Jaks, selected five respected hunters as leaders. She directed the warband into sections and assigned a leader to each. "Anything more?" she asked Jaks.

"Balance the groups to have equal numbers of experienced men. The less experienced should then pair up with them to shore up their morale. I doubt they will get any preparation once you get to Irin, so I wonder whether we should begin each day with drills and training?" Some practice fighting in formation might improve their chances on the battlefield.

The Uwama nodded appreciatively and, as the first column started marching, she beckoned for him to walk alongside her and Witabu, where they discussed the transformation of the Jurns from a bunch of wilders into a proper fighting unit.

———

Hundreds of humans marching through the Jurn Highlands would never go unnoticed. A multitude of eyes, mostly bestial and hungry, but some human and cruel, prowled the high tops and cliffs overlooking the columns of Jurns—which were sometimes four-person wide but at others just single-file as the terrain demanded.

Snow carpeted the higher peaks and melted into mountain streams to join rivers already swollen with the rain of the past few days. Rockslides, crashing boulders, and towering overhangs whistled with biting winds. Not a place that Jaks really wanted to return to, but now, with a purpose and goal, the trek was simply the first of the barriers between him and Karisa that he was determined to overcome.

He shivered and thrust his balled hands under his armpits as he marched. A pair of mountain lions hunched on a vantage point halfway up a mountain overlooking their passage; he felt as though they were watching him alone, spying him out as the likeliest morsel. *Ridiculous*, he thought, *no lion would attack such a large group of armed humans.* He tore his eyes away from the carnivores.

The danger that day, though, roved even higher above. Like ice demons crystallizing from the clouds, a flight of white dragons circled the warband. Fewer than their lowland counterparts, they were larger—Jaks estimated the size of a small man—and their wings thundered episodically when they scooped the frozen air. Three times so far, the winged predators had swooped at individuals at the rear of the column—one time, talons successfully grabbed a woman by her shoulders and lifted her off her feet, only releasing her when her fellow tribesfolk fought off the screeching beast with spears and staffs. Shaken but tenacious, the injured woman bit on a stick as the Uwama stitched her lacerations and bound her wounds, then got back on her feet to march again. But, unfortunately, only to succumb to the cold a few hours later.

After that, Tavis volunteered to rear-guard with a couple of experienced hunters, and the boom and flash of the apprentice's firebolts eventually sent the dragons winging off to find some easier prey.

By the afternoon, the valley widened into highland turf dusted with snow and wide enough that the center was clear of rocks and shale. The Uwama ordered a halt, and ancient hide tents that the Jurns had once used on the lowland plains were pitched against the elements.

Campfires burst to life with Tavis's fiery touch, generating heartfelt applause from the shivering tribesfolk. The apprentice found himself the hero of the day and received the first offerings of hot soup and dough sticks of the evening. And once the Jurns learned of his ability to conjure a dome of warmth around himself, his tent overflowed with bodies clambering for a spot near this living furnace.

Angry shouts woke Jaks from a fitful sleep. His tent —the size of that of the traveling acrobats that used to visit the city once a year—was crammed with men snoring, groaning, and talking in their sleep. As the voices continued, a few light sleepers like Jaks roused and peered around the darkness. "What's going on out there?" someone asked in a croaky voice. The flickers of a campfire outside the tent greeted Jaks as he stumbled over a few sleeping bodies and slipped out into the icy night.

Curiously, he saw no sign of the duty watchmen near the fire except a couple of mugs—one tipped over, its warm contents steaming slightly—on the ground, forgotten.

He pulled his fur cloak tight with one hand and placed his other on the pommel of his sword and walked toward sounds of commotion on the outer edges of the camp. A few other men and women angled out of other tents and joined him in his investigation.

Behind a supply tent, they discovered several Jurn tribesmen surrounding three cowering figures. The watchmen poked spears and burning torches to keep the figures on their knees and barked questions and orders at their captives so quickly their responses were jumbled blatherings. A large cut in the back of the tent suggested the thieves intent, as did the scattered packages of food rations strewn on the surrounding ground. Bagfuls of dried meats, seeds, and nuts had been crushed beneath the struggle that appeared to have led to their capture. A dagger and a couple of clubs were their only weapons.

Witabu arrived and soon anger leached from his pores. "Bandits. There are probably more of them." He interrogated them in Jurn and then in Ascorian when the thieves responded in kind. They claimed they were remnants of a larger group who had ranged the Highlands for years—one of the many wild men the Jurns called "highland devils." They took whatever they could from wherever and whomever. "Thieves, in other words," Witabu declared.

The men were bound and brought before the Uwama in the middle of the camp. The sky had tinged to a steel gray of morning and the screech of a dragon echoed from some distant valley.

Jaks warmed by a campfire. The capture of the bandits had ousted what tiredness remained from the day before; with no further need for sleep, he toyed with the long-range wrist comm and explored its channels and machinations with his magical senses. The device fascinated him. Tiny rivulets of power coursing through a miraculous artifact that could transfer his voice and image thousands of leagues away to another person—and he could see and control it through a nascent sense as though the comm were a living extension of himself.

He yelped in surprise when Meila's image unexpectedly manifested in front of him. She lay on her side, only her face illuminated, tendrils of hair draped over an eye. "Jaks . . . so early. What is it?" she asked.

"Sorry, I didn't mean to wake you. I was just playing around with this thing."

"What's going on? Where are you?" She sat up in what he assumed was her bed.

He updated her on the first day of their mountain traverse and the overnight incident with the bandits.

Out of the corner of his eye, he watched the three captured thieves—pitifully thin and haggard—kneeling in front of the chieftess. She was saying something to them. Too far away to hear, he saw the men shake their heads. Then, without warning, one of the wild men slumped to the ground with a spear piercing him through the front. One of the Uwama's personal guardsmen stepped on the man's chest and tore the weapon out without hesitation. The body arched and shuddered. The other two bandits followed. Their executions were simultaneous and without ceremony. He looked to the chieftess, expecting some shock or disgust at the brutal executions, but found only an icy disdain etched across her face.

"What's wrong?" Meila asked. She drew curtains in her bedroom and a golden hue seeped in.

"She just executed those thieves. I thought she'd just cut a finger off each or something . . ."

"She's a tough leader, Jaks. I wouldn't expect anything less of her. Executing a bunch of thieves isn't going to bother her. She knows how to make tough choices and is probably leading her people to certain death." Meila bent down to pull on her boots then stood and stared directly at Jaks. "Promise me you won't fight alongside them—you'll be killed too. In fact, you should just come straight back to Dunberrin with Tavis once you get across the mountains—it's a fool's errand you're chasing to the south."

"You know I can't. I've told you. Karisa needs me. Without Vix here, it's up to me alone," Jaks said. He tore his gaze away from the dead bodies, now being dragged away for burial some distance from the camp. "I better go. We're running field drills this morning and I have to help the Uwama with instructions. I'll talk to you again soon." She said a farewell and the comm image dissipated to leave only the memory of her worried face.

Over two hours that morning, the Jurn warband trampled the valley floor with basic army unit maneuvers that Jaks had learned well from his conscript training and now taught his Jurn peers: a spear-and-shield formation and a tactical front-line retreat—the latter often yelled at him by his conscript sergeant, as being the single most important skill of a soldier—allowing the front line, as it tired, to fall back for fresher soldiers to replace them. The last thing they wanted was for the formation to flee in terror as their front row collapsed from battle-fatigue.

The tactics, and others Jaks knew of, had brought many victories to Ascorian armies in the past. Superior discipline and confidence from drills and practice translated to greater morale and lethality on the battlefield. In particular, the Ascorian victory led by Jaks's father himself during the legendary "Battle of Skulls"—the defining combat of the last year of the Unifying Wars when the Skull Clans of Cerik banded together—owed much to the ability of the infantry to hold their lines in the face of the terrifying foes while warlions and horse cavalry tore the clans apart.

The Uwama had a natural gift for command and used her sonomancer-enhanced voice to call out orders to the five sections of her warband. Jaks would instruct her on what was needed, and she would word her commands unambiguously to her warriors and leaders.

However, despite the Uwama's superb orders, it proved far more difficult for the untrained warriors to coordinate their movements. The section leaders did their best, and Jaks rushed about shouting, but learning the tactic fell to a mass of individuals whose only idea of formal movement came from ceremonial dance.

Eventually, the command trio of Witabu, Jaks, and the Uwama held their collective breath as the warband sections completed a last attempt at the drills. One section seemed to have learned the fighting retreat and transitioned their front lines fluidly, but Jaks could only shake his head as the other four groups fell over each other and tangled their spears together. Thankfully, there were still several more days to get this right.

Witabu laughed at the miserable sight while the Uwama boomed out to signal the end of the drill and instructed her warriors to separate into fighting pairs to train individually for another half hour—the first chance that some would ever have to learn how to pit spears against a human foe.

Dragging their boots and spear butts from their morning martial practice, the warband then resumed their march. Pebbles and rocks crunched underfoot. Skeletal shrubs and trees shivered in the whistling wind. Men and women gritted their teeth and shouldered their packs and weapons while staring at the back of the person in front.

***

Two days of marching mixed with exhausting morning drills delivered Jaks and the Jurns through winding valleys of cliffs and sheer slopes. Those early days seemed easy, until the valleys tapered away and Witabu was forced to lead them over high mountain paths.

Narrow, steep trails demanded they snake in single file. One mountain, one day, and then another.

Two of the tribe slipped to their deaths in this precarious passage: one youth who larked about—and thudded to his death after a wind gust—and an older man, who stumbled and then rolled down a cliff face, collecting an avalanche that buried him and stifled his cries. And yet another four tribesfolk, easy pickings on the cliff-side paths, were plucked away by predating dragons. Pragmatic and stoic, their fellow Jurns mourned as they shuffled onward.

Finally reaching what Witabu estimated to be halfway across the craggy range, Jaks stared down a ragged cliff overlooking a raging white river.

"Someone's going to swim *that*?" Jaks shouted to Witabu, who leaned over the precipice and kicked a loose pebble down into the deafening thunder of the rapids.

Earlier that day, Jaks had overheard the wizened hunter and the Uwama arguing about where to cross the river. She had favored the narrowest point to send their strongest swimmer across, for him to tie a rope and establish the first parts of a rope bridge. Witabu had countered, his deep wrinkles furrowed to dark lines, arguing that no one could safely swim this frothing barrier and that they should follow the watercourse a few days north until it calmed enough to swim safely. The Uwama, the more obstinate debater, had got her way, however, and a broad-shouldered man named Tahnn was stretching his arms and staring dubiously at his watery adversary.

"What if there was another way for someone to cross?" Jaks approached the Uwama. "Wait. Don't let him swim yet. I have an idea, but I have to talk to someone." He searched the crowd massed along the riverbank and found the sandy-haired head he needed.

"Tavis." He tapped the apprentice mage on the shoulder to get his attention. "They're trying to get someone to swim this thing."

"I heard. It's insane."

"Could you gravleap it? With a rope?"

"Me? I'm not battle-trained in gravmancy. I apprenticed to learn to make artifacts—not jump and bound into battle."

"It can't be that hard, can it? It's only about thirty yards across. Vixhana could gravleap four times that. And if you run at it from up there"—Jaks pointed to the cliff where he had been standing with Witabu—"you'd have a better chance."

"But if I don't make it, I'll get pulled under and smashed to a pulp. I don't like water, you know. I don't like dying, either."

Jaks reminded Tavis about the debt he had to the Jurns nursing him back to health from his injuries.

The apprentice yielded. "Alright, then . . . I'll give it a go," he said, all the while shaking his head at his folly.

The Uwama nodded acceptance and gratitude to Tavis's offer—the nominated swimmer slapped the apprentice on the back, grinned with relief on his face, and hastily untied the rope from his waist.

The Jurns cleared a space along the riverbank for the apprentice to practice the gravleap before he made the actual attempt. A run, a jump, an invocation of magic to negate gravity and send him into a glide; and finally, a gradual reduction of magic to land. Hurtling through the air while maintaining an invocation was not as simple as Vixhana had made it look. The first time, although Tavis leaped past the thirty-yard kern marker, he landed jarringly and elicited a sympathetic gasp from the watching crowd. The next few times, however, he soared through the air and landed as gracefully as any dove or swan. Onlookers cheered and yelled; Jaks couldn't help but join along—clearly, the grandmaster had selected Tavis for an apprentice, not only for his double-mage powers but also his ability to learn quickly.

The sun dropped behind the mountain peaks as puffy clouds reddened the sky. With a few hours of daylight left, Jaks joined the excited throng lining the riverbank and stood on a flat boulder with several others.

On the cliff ledge, Tavis bounced on his toes, pulled on the rope tied around his waist, and turned to face the rapids. People shouted encouragement, but he didn't seem to hear them over the rumbling of the whitewater monster that blocked his path.

A brief twinge of jealousy wracked Jaks as the crowd surged in anticipation. Tavis had all the attention, and he would get all the glory—if he made it across—with endless praises from the tribe.

Witabu clapped the apprentice one last time on the shoulder and stepped back.

Tavis crouched with arms crooked before him in a runner's starting position.

He rocked back and forth for a few long minutes, then burst from his crouch and dashed toward the ravine.

The clifftop offered him a generous distance to the edge, and he took all of it in rapid strides.

Rope trailing behind him, he looked heroic as he bounded from the cliff edge.

Over the crowd. Over the churning rapids. He appeared to rise even higher.

He hurtled through the air, legs pumping uselessly. Except for a few shrieks of fear, the warband quieted and held their breaths.

The waters tossed up tendrils of froth to snatch at Tavis's feet as he reached the pinnacle of his leap.

An onlooker screamed in fear for the apprentice.

He descended in an arc to the other side of the river.

Within seconds, Tavis landed on his target: a circle of smooth rocks devoid of boulders.

Jaks joined in with an eruption of cheers—

Splash.

The rope trailing from the apprentice's waist slapped down into the water behind him.

The rapids grabbed the rope.

The rope pulled at his body.

Cheers turned to cries of alarm and shouts of warning.

Jaks stared uselessly as Tavis stumbled and fell as

the river pulled him by the rope across the stones toward its crushing embrace. Fear pounded a tempo in his chest. Had he caused yet another person to take on a risky mission that would end in his death? He panic-prayed and offered his own life instead of Tavis's, but knew that Death and God could not be bought so easily.

Yelled commands from the clifftop drew his gaze to several men and women pulling their end of the rope taut—they had allowed too much slack into its length and now strained to lift the rope above the raging torrent.

Each foot the rope rose, the nearer Tavis was dragged toward the river that hungered for him.

Almost at the water's edge, his movement halted as though an anchor had hooked and fastened him to the ground. The rope around his waist tightened, but he remained motionless and stuck to the ground like glue.

Half a minute later, the rope sprang free of the rapids, lifted taut, and dripped as it hung suspended in midair.

Jaks breathed a sigh of relief and thanked whatever magic or miracle had saved his friend.

Tavis crawled up the riverbank and wrapped the rope around a tree trunk. Finally, the ordeal was over.

Not until the next day—after a rope bridge had been constructed around Tavis's hard-earned foundation, and Jaks had clambered over—did he discover what had prevented the apprentice's doom.

"Gravmancy. I weighed myself down to resist the

rope's pull," Tavis explained. But despite his self-satisfied grin, the magic hadn't protected him from a fractured rib and a flare-up of his abdominal pains where the rope had constricted him. Fortunately for him, he basked in two days' rest as the tribesfolk completed the river crossing. Two days in which Jaks never saw him alone; whether designated by the Uwama or spontaneously adoring, men and women constantly attended him in one of the great tents and plied him with food and steaming drinks.

Jaks contemplated Karisa's rescue mission during those days of waiting. Despite his brave words to Meila, he knew little of his Vor heritage or their behaviors and manners. Infiltrating her prison and freeing her without detection would rely on raw wits and daring he had never tested before. Of all the fields of magic, electromancy was of the least help. A gravmancer had superhuman agility and strength; an illumancer, disguise; a firemancer, fiery distractions; and even a sonomancer had the wrappings of stealth. Regretfully, he had no magic of practical use to sneak into an enemy war camp.

The following day, the warband amassed on the west side of the rapids—less several dropped packs and weapons but thankfully no drownings—and resumed their march. They climbed a hill of shale and then dropped into the valley below. The junction of two mountains provided a perfect drill-ground for the warband's morning training.

"Left face . . . Shield wall . . . Advance," commanded the Uwama.

"That's it, I think they're getting it." Jaks rubbed his hands together. "Can they do a fighting retreat?"

"Halt. Fall back." The front lines of each fighting section danced a retreat behind their comrades.

"Not bad. Still needs some work. A few more days and I think they'll have it."

The paired melee training afterward, however, showed Jaks the enormous steps that the warband had grown over the past days of training. The Jurns possessed a toughness and aggression that surprised him. It needed little to transform, even the female Jurns, into ferocious fighters. Having been thrust into a harsh, merciless wilderness for decades, they were instilled with a strong will to fight for survival. With confident spear thrusts, firm postures, bone-chilling shouts, and ardent battle-scowls, the warband now at least resembled a fighting unit.

A few days later, Jaks gasped as he crested the last of the mountain ridges and glimpsed brown, war-torn plains that were the Jurn warband's destination. Columns of smoke and irregular blotches dotted the flat expanse. Had the battle for Irin been fought already?

The Reynford River plunged down from the mountains and slashed through the plains until it emptied its lifeblood into the sea. Jaks squinted to resolve the City of Irin that was cut in half by the half-mile wide waterway. Two stone bridges spanned the waters, joined by a small island in the middle, and walled city sections on the north bank and south bank capped each end of the vital thoroughfare.

Over two thousand years before, Irin had once been the center of a mighty ancient civilization. The Opodic Empire had ruled the lands that Jaks's countryfolk now called Ascoria and Ellipta. And for nine generations, a lineage of Empress's held powerful sway over a terrified population, using roving priests and slayers to tax heavily and adjudicate often. However, a rebellion flared up in the third century and overthrew the rotten civilization. Now all that remained was the island of earth and stone in the center of the river that had once formed part of the foundations for the Opodic Palace that had spanned the width of the river.

Raki pointed at a wide black blot on the far side of the city. "What is that?"

"That, my friend, is war," Jaks replied, and shivered as he imagined the defenders on the city walls trembling at the enemy horde, braying to rip down every block of stone. "Tens of thousands of warriors, beasts of war, and siege machines." He spotted scores of siege towers and guessed there would be catapults and scorpions aplenty, although they were too far away to see.

"Are they still fighting, or are we too late to help?"

"I don't think they've attacked yet. Maybe the Vors are still preparing for their assault." Jaks shifted his gaze to the nearest side of the city. "Strange. Something is happening on this side of the river as well." He pointed at a dark military scar curving around the city, not as expansive as the horde on the opposite side of the city but extensive enough to blockade the road and any chance of the Jurns marching unhindered into the city to join the king's forces.

The warband came to a halt and Jaks scurried forward to join the Uwama's retinue.

"I'm sending Witabu with some scouts to find out what's going on down there." The Uwama's face had become more pinched and weary since the start of the march, coarsened now as she crinkled her forehead with concern. "We need to know who's enemy and who's not before we reveal ourselves."

Witabu and his men returned the next morning to where the Jurns were encamped in the giantwoods at the base of the mountain range. A soldier in a tidy Ascorian uniform bearing a signaler's badge stitched to his lapel accompanied him.

"The Vors have been congregating on the opposite bank for days, waiting for war groups to arrive from different directions," Witabu said. He then nodded toward the Ascorian signaler. "The sergeant here is from a warlion battalion sent to reinforce the city. They arrived yesterday to discover the Vors blockading Irin."

The signaler, sturdy and muscular, coughed to interrupt. "Signals with King Silas this morning state that Commander Nikor shall take you under his command. Commander Nikor sent me to pass on his order that your battalion is to join us immediately. There is to be a joint assault on the enemy blockade to reach the city, and there can be no delay. The opposite bank might be attacked soon and could fall if we don't reinforce them."

The Uwama shot Jaks a worried gaze.

"Don't worry, your people are ready," he said, but a quiver in his voice betrayed his uncertainty.

Chapter 4

Breaking the Siege

The Jurns emerged from the forest an hour later. Excited babbles and laughs punctuated the air, the manifestation of relief at their escape from the Highlands—even though all knew that battle awaited them on the plains.

Jaks did not share their jubilation. Instead, he rubbed his hands and breathed into his cupped palms to warm them. But no matter what he did, he could not stop shivering. The chill came from within, from the fear that what he had taught the Jurns would amount to nothing, that the Vors would slaughter the tribesfolk he'd grown to love.

As the warband squared off into sections, preparing for the march to join the Ascorian regiments, Tavis farewelled the Uwama and the tribesfolk to begin his lone journey north back to Dunberrin and his master. He pried himself away from several tearful hero-worshippers—his fawning band since the crossing of the rapids—and clasped arms with Jaks.

"I think your followers have said it all, but you made a tremendous difference along the way. If it wasn't for your bravery, more lives would have been lost," Jaks said. "A few months ago, I wouldn't have spoken this, but I have to admit, I'm envious of your powers."

"You shouldn't be. Your electromancy is by far the greater magic."

"No. It's an evil magic. It only kills. Nothing useful like what you did over the river or can do in the forge. I can't trust it. I can't trust myself to use it again."

Tavis shook his head. "Magic isn't good or evil. It's your motives that decide so. Evil intent breeds evil, but righteous intent yields good. You're a good person, Jaks. Even though it pains me to say." He looked embarrassed at the admission.

"We'll see," Jaks replied. Talking about good and evil triggered a recurring question that troubled him: Was his father's evil bred into his being? Did it yearn to escape his self-control, urging him to take whatever he wanted and satisfy any desire that took him? Was that why fear so controlled him? Preventing his inner evil from escaping?

He clenched and unclenched a fist, then hid the hand behind his back as though it offended him.

"You're an odd one," Tavis said.

Jaks laughed at the truth in the words. "Good luck

with the rest of your journey. It's a long way home," he said and smiled at the apprentice.

"Ha, you're the one who'll need the luck." Tavis pushed his thumbs into the straps of his backpack and began his trek back to Dunberrin.

The Jurn warband marched onto plains covered with the brown grass of fall. In the distance, wild horses kicked up dust, and flights of swallows darted ellipses. "We once roamed lands similar to these." The Uwama's gaze scanned the horizon. "Prairies and grasslands. They remind us we are fighting for something worthwhile."

Jaks wondered whether she would still feel the same after counting the dead and dying after the impending trial-by-battle. He would assist the Uwama with her command in the Jurns' first engagement. He owed them that much, at least. One battle, of the many that would be in this war. But after this Vor barricade was broken, nothing would stop him from finding a disguise and melting into enemy lines. Unconsciously, he scratched at his two-week beard. Rampant facial hair —a mixed gift/curse of his own Vor heritage, usually shaved away each morning—was a vital aspect of his plan.

A Jurn section leader shouted in alarm and pointed.

Swift movement from the direction of his attention

and within minutes, mounted figures dashed in from the horizon and stopped at the distance of an arrow's flight.

Warlions.

Magnificent manes billowed through vests of leather. Iron-capped skulls revealed only the tufts of their ears. Angular jaws snarled their bone-crunching power, and enormous paws hid claws that could rip open steel plate armor. Fifteen hands tall, reaching the shoulder of a warhorse, they were three times more muscular, agile, and deadly.

Riding atop, their human riders—all small and light—were outfitted in riding leathers, steel lances, and equally hardened glares. Cloaks swept from their shoulders and draped the backs of their feline mounts.

The Ascorian signaler accompanying the Uwama illumanced a pattern of flashes with his hands that brought the riders padding toward him.

The lioness-riding leader vaulted off her beast—maneless and sleeker than the males—and saluted before conferring with the Uwama. She would lead them to Commander Nikor's warlion battalion.

The warlions of the second regiment stretched and basked behind a ridge of hills. On the ridge top, sentinels and signalers monitored the Vor blockade—a mile-long stretch of enemy warriors, tattooed, bladed, and waiting—a mere half-hour's forced-march in the distance. Warlion riders readied their mounts, adjusting armor and tightening straps. Tails flicked and furred ears twitched.

Jaks shuddered at his first glimpse of this field aswarm with beasts of war. Astonished chatter, and a single enraptured shriek, burst aloud from the Jurns as they approached their bestial allies. Wary eyes in return, feline and human, however, quickly dulled the tribesfolk's excitement.

Unexpectedly, a wave of embarrassment for his adopted tribe swept over Jaks. Such an ill-equipped rabble compared to these superbly trained warlions and their handlers. Indeed, as they neared, the riders' gazes turned disdainful and wry.

"What! We were waiting for this mob?" a voice called out from amongst the handlers, and was echoed by a lion's snarl. "What a waste of time." The woman turned away and bent back down with an iron file to attack her lion's claws.

Ignoring the outburst, the Uwama called a halt to the warband and set them to rest. Delegating the warband's command to Witabu, she gestured at Jaks to follow as she ordered their seconded signaler to take them to the commander.

Several minutes later, they climbed the central ridge and approached a hard-faced man squinting at a subordinate officer.

"We mustn't delay any longer, sir," the officer said. "The south bank walls have been under assault for an hour now and the last signals from the city plead reinforcements now or the entire city could fall."

Commander Nikor, wiry and with a scar cutting a diagonal down his face, began a reply to the officer, but stopped to face the Uwama as she made final strides to reach him. He glanced over her shoulder down at the Jurn warband arrayed in an infantry square on the field below and grimaced. "Gods above. When they said a 'mountain infantry unit,' I didn't think it would literally be from the mountains. Who are you?" the man asked, his eyes ranging over the Uwama in her ornate armor.

"My lord, shall I prepare the regiment?" the officer persisted but remained ignored.

"Uwama Xandu. I command the Jurn warband," she said in the accent of a highborn Ascorian noblewoman, raising surprised looks from both men. "And my advisor," she said of Jaks, but kept her gaze locked on the commander. "We may not share your fine steel or ride fearsome beasts, but our mutual enemy waits in the distance, and we are ready to fight."

"So you are." Nikor inclined his head. "Apologies, my lady. An ally is an ally. Your arrival is timely. I am sorry we cannot dally for pleasantries."

"Sir. We must act," the officer petitioned again.

"Yes, we have no more time to lose. My lady, your warriors shall assault the left"—Nikor pointed at the distant line of enemy warriors—"my warlions will take the center, and seventh heavy battalion will attack the right." He pointed to the steel-clad mass of infantry, on the opposite side of the warlion meadow from where the Jurns had stalled, that Jaks had only just noticed a minute before as they climbed to this vantage point. The heavy halberdiers and pikemen were as uniform, disciplined, and even more heavily armored than their warlion counterparts—a far cry from the leather-armored and short-speared Jurns.

"Even with your warriors, my lady, the blockaders still outnumber us." The commander ground a thumb to the scarring over his forehead. "Pray that my riders can break their center quickly. If they do, it will be just a short step to flank and attack their rear. If they don't . . . your warriors will need to prove themselves mightily today."

The sun, gray behind clouds, hung to Jaks's right. In front of him, in clear sight of the Vor barricade, the Jurns scurried into three rows on the Uwama's command. Thick furs and cloaks, that warmed their backs in the Highlands, were left behind. With spears and shields, they faced the enemy. Their inexperience didn't show, or so Jaks hoped. It could even be said they looked fearsome with their animal-skull headdresses and lean, chiseled faces. He gripped his oval shield with the lightning-bolt insignia in his crooked hand and palmed the pommel of his stabbing sword with the other. *Here it starts.* He threw a quick prayer upward, wondering if whether some enemy soldier was praying to the same god—who would the deity favor?

A horn blared the attack. Moments later, monstrous

roars and the clatter of weapons rang down the line of soldiers and beasts. Boots and paws thumped forward, and officers shouted for a walking pace. No wasting energy until they were close enough to charge.

In response, the black line of Vors grew even darker. Behind them, the city walls of Irin, and the brown waters of the Reynford River, pinned them into a dire standoff. There could be no rout of retreat for the Vors—triumph or die. This would be a desperate battle.

Ahead of Jaks, a tribeswoman—one of the flax weavers he had befriended back in the village—fell out of formation and sank to her knees. She leaned against her shield and retched. She wiped her mouth and with an upturned head met his eyes. He spared her a weak smile as an older tribesman stooped to pull her back into the line. He wished he could go over to her and tell her she would be safe, but he couldn't lie.

"Shouldn't someone lead the charge?" The Uwama marched beside Jaks and forty reserve warriors, in addition to her ten personal guards. "Should I be in front?"

"They will charge when you command them," Jaks replied. "They need their leader to give commands and order reserves to bear up weaknesses. You are the most valuable person here. You cannot risk yourself in front." He stiffened his shaking arms and clenched his jaw. His fear wasn't for himself but for these hundreds he had attempted to train so hastily. Each death would be his fault—would any of them survive? Inexperienced, outnumbered, and poorly armed—the odds were against them.

When the three Ascorian formations marched to within a half mile of the Vors, the enemy's howls and bellows of challenge carried to their ears. Blue-tattooed, scarred, and sneering, they waved axes and swords overhead. Ditches gouged the battlefield between the two army lines, and the defenders rested their shields on mounds of packed dirt.

To signal the start of the charge, horns again blared down the line.

The warlions roared in response and pounced onto the grassy meadow.

The Jurns loped toward the enemy shield wall. But as they approached the ditches, their charge faltered. Warriors veered and pushed to avoid the deep holes, tripping and falling over each other, only to be overrun by those behind. Jaks swore aloud and shouted at his compatriots ineffectually. Picking up his words, though, the Uwama pierced the clamor and din of panic with her sonomanced voice and ordered her warriors to stop, reorganize, and then advance at a walking pace.

The warlions, unhindered by the defensive ditches, leaped the gaping holes with their riders clinging to their backs. To the far right, the gleaming Ascorian infantry maneuvered the ditches with ease well ahead of the Jurns.

Arrows clouded the sky, whistling toward the Ascorian advance. The Uwama, alert to the threat, boomed a "shields up" to the warband and ducked for shelter under her shield-bearer's barrier. Jaks's own shield bucked as an arrow splintered against steel. Wooden shafts thudded around him.

One of the Uwama's guards nearby crumpled despite his upheld shield; an arrow pierced his thigh, eliciting a pained moan from the man. Gritting his teeth, he pulled the shaft through completely. "Flesh wound," he said and grunted. A moment later, another arrow struck him in the belly, and he collapsed.

"Keep them advancing!" Jaks yelled at the Uwama, seeing the Jurns stalled under the shower of arrows. Dozens of men and women had fallen, struck by arrows, and their fellow tribesfolk dropped weapons and shields to assist them.

"Leave the wounded. Keep advancing." She repeated his command and was rewarded with a rapid reformation of an infantry line.

At the center of the Ascorians' assault, the riders of the second regiment leaped from their warlions as they neared the Vor front. Their beasts then surged forward, unencumbered, and sprang at the shield wall —those in the rear bounding off the backs of the warlions in front and then over the armored line. Swords and axes swung desperately, but the mass of muscle and claws tossed the humans aside as they tore apart the defensive wall from front and back. Chunked flesh, dismembered arms, and decapitated heads flew into the air. Following into the gap, the dismounted riders finished the wounded and wedged open the Vor center.

Several minutes later, and a dozen more dead or lame from arrows, the shaky Jurns reached the Vor line. Their spears thrust and jabbed at the Vors' shield wall but found no openings and simply rebounded off metal and wood. Several Jurns attempted to batter the wall down, bashing shield against shield, but sword thrusts from the defenders drove them back.

It was futile. The enemy was too disciplined and the Jurns too inexperienced to penetrate the defensive line. Men and women clambered up the dirt mounds and battered at the defenses, but without any progress. Several more of the warband fell as swords and axes flashed over the shields to slice exposed heads and necks.

"Send up the reinforcements. Shore up the left—the Vors may push the flank," Jaks advised the Uwama as they followed a couple hundred yards behind the warband.

He looked at his feet, stepping around a ditch. His eyes trailed into the pit and a woman's face stared back up at him. An arrow pierced the dead body through the chest. He reeled in shock as he recognized the lifeless features of the flax weaver. *Oh, God. I'm sorry.* Fighting an urge to climb down into the ditch and shake her awake, he bit his lip and continued forward.

The forty warriors yelled in response to the Uwama's command and jogged to the left, but not before the Vors on the flank surged forward and blood-thirsty axes and swords swept into the Jurns from the side. Folding onto the warband, the tattooed warriors cut and cleaved arms and necks. Already brittle, the Jurns, like startled gulls, turned to flee from the brutal counterattack.

"Keep going!" Jaks yelled at the reserves between rapid breaths. They were losing terribly. They were being slaughtered. Even if the warlions came to their rescue, they couldn't defeat this many of them. Should he shout at the Uwama to call a retreat and then run? Darkness shuttered his focus—fear, that forever demon, began morphing into terror.

The mass of flanking Vors welcomed the reinforcements with savage swathes and cut down the first dozen. The following Jurns stopped in their paces—recognizing how outnumbered they were—froze, then turned on their heels to run.

Witabu swore aloud, and the Uwama grabbed at Jaks's arm. "What do we do? I must help them. They are dying out there."

Jaks had been wrong. The warband needed a leader in front—a champion—to stiffen the Jurns' morale and stir their ferocity. Not the Uwama. She was their heart. It had to be him: he was the only one with the power to do what was needed. "Stay back. Stay away from me," he yelled at her.

White and blue flickered around the edges of his sword and shield as he ran toward the charging Vors.

Routing, Jurns scrambled out of his path, leaving Jaks facing hundreds of screaming Vor warriors.

The electromancy, suppressed for months, rushed to his bidding. The triple steps of invocation merged as one and crackled around him in a sparking, magical aura. Half-panicked, half-enraged, he willed the magic into a dazzling ball of lightning as he sprinted forward. Grass burned behind him and left a trail of smoke in his wake.

Forks of electricity leaped and blasted arrows that targeted him. The projectiles burst into flashes of fire and banged with every strike.

All eyes on the flank drew to the glowing lightning god thundering across the meadow. The charging Vors faltered and hastily formed a shield wall to meet this new adversary.

A Vor griefmaster, teeth bared and eyes rounded, pushed through the wall carrying an enormous two-handed battleaxe. He took three steps, leaped again, and then soared through the air with the crescent of his weapon bearing down on Jaks.

Jaks pointed his sword at the gravmancer. Lightning lanced down the weapon to strike the enemy battlemage. A brilliant flash splintered the axe and hurtled the charred torso backward to thud at the foot of the shield wall.

"Regroup. Follow me," he yelled at the Jurns behind him.

Jaks frowned as the shield wall parted fifty yards away. A red-robed woman marched through the gap, weaving her arms through the air. Flames appeared in her hands and grew as her arms continued their intoxicating dance.

The visage of a burning dragon flew out of the fire and flapped flaming wings above the firemage.

Jaks shuddered, fearing the powers of this woman who so masterfully conjured this draconic invocation to life. His nerve almost broke when the dragon spat a column of fire into the air and flailed its neck from side to side, hovering above her.

The firemage stared at Jaks and then thrust her arms at him.

The dragon swooped and raced across the field as though to engulf him.

An electric wall crackled in front of Jaks; a bully's sneer, a biting spider, an armored fist, and his mother's crushed skull fueled the shield into existence.

The draconic missile smashed into the shimmering barrier with a conflagration of flames. The detonation deafened and blinded him momentarily, even though he had turned away from the blast. When his sight returned, the wall of lightning stood crackling, but nothing was left of the firemanced dragon except the smoking dirt around him. Jaks staggered, fatigue sapping his concentration and focus—his lightning wall disappeared.

A second fiery dragon swooped into the air above the mage. He couldn't absorb another massive assault like the last. He would have to destroy the source.

As the firemancer's arms snaked the air, the conjuration grew with every motion. The dance focused her attention, building up another magical assault.

Jaks sprinted toward his enemy, jumped over a ditch, and dared to close half the distance to her. His electromancy had not stretched out this far before, but he had to strike now.

The dragon visage continued to grow until it was the width of a ship's sail. The red-robed woman's gaze homed in on Jaks.

He plunged down on one knee and pointed his sword tip at the firemage. Although his mouth was open and his throat shook in exhalation, he heard no sound—and saw nothing other than her scornful eyes.

Her scream only lasted a couple of seconds, before all the air burst out of her chest, and her flesh sizzled and crisped from the lightning channeled into her from Jaks. A curtain of electricity cut the field to her and then forked outward to strike the hundreds of Vor warriors sheltered behind the battlemage.

Lightning vaulted from limb to limb through the enemy flank. Weapons and shields fell from stunned hands, and spasming bodies toppled to the ground. He savored the familiar taste of metal in his mouth and poured energy into the chained lightning until every Vor warrior within a hundred yards lay twitching or still. As he stared at the bodies, a sense of power surged within, and he laughed at the thrill it gave him.

A war cry sounded from behind and a fresh charge

of Jurns, stirred on by the Uwama's rally and Jaks's devastation, pounded past him and into the Vor mainline. Drained and depleted, he leaned on his shield and watched the enemy defenses crumble under the warband's renewed assault. Satisfied that they no longer needed his help, he collapsed to the burned ground and closed his eyes as the sounds of battle faded.

Chapter 5

Finding Karisa

Jaks roused to someone shaking him by the shoulders. It was dark. Must be night.

"Wake up," his tormenter said, nudging him again.

Confused, he pushed the shadowy figure away. "Who are you?" His fingers palpated dirt all around him —a ditch?

"Friend, I knew you were around here somewhere. That stubble on your face made it hard to recognize you," the voice said. "It's me, Raki."

"What—"

"It's over." By the light of the moon and a small flaming torch, his friend's forever-cheerful face emerged, smiling despite dried blood marring his features and a bandage wrapping his head. The Jurn youth peeked out of the pit before sitting and leaning against the earth wall.

They reassured each other that their injuries were slight and then grinned at each other in relief. "After you broke the Vors, we pushed them back to the river," Raki said. "If only you could have seen the warlions rip into them! Some drowned trying to swim for their lives, but the rest threw down their weapons and surrendered."

"So, we won?"

"Not quite. Although we reached the city, the other side of the city had already been lost."

"But we still hold this side?" Jaks said.

Raki's face went hard. "The Uwama says the king commanded a full withdrawal and destroyed the bridge. Something about ships coming up the gulf. Our fight has allowed the king's army to withdraw safely from Irin, though."

"Withdraw? But this was our best chokepoint."

"Not anymore. We're all retreating to the border of Dunberrin. They say more allies are coming from Faucony and Strock to help, and then the king will be able to push back at the Vors. Come on. We have to catch up with the rest."

Jaks stood up and peered out of the waist-high pit. A column of flaming torches was snaking out of the city walls opposite to where he needed to go. "No, I've got another task to do. You leave. I have to find my sister." His eyes found what he was looking for—a dead Vor. He clambered out of the pit and dragged the corpse of the warrior back into the ditch. Raki watched him in horror as he stripped the body of armor.

"Too big. Help me find a taller, thinner one." Jaks explained his plan to the youth as they examined different bodies. "I need more than just a beard for a disguise." Minutes later, he settled on a set of armor from a wiry axeman with a gaping neck wound. This second corpse in the narrow ditch was too much for Raki to tolerate, and he scrambled out. Jaks saw his discomfort and said, "Thank you, my friend. You have been good to me. Go join the warband. I'll see you another day."

"*Hodrin uhsaga*, Jaks." Raki's eyes lingered as though seeing him off for the last time and then he fled toward the trail of torches.

Alone with the two bodies, Jaks talked to them in the Vorosian language as though to relieve some tension in the confined space. Although his Vorosian was rusty —Karisa the only person he spoke it with after their grandmother died—his ear for languages was clear and he would sometimes talk to himself just as he did now, savoring the powerful guttural sounds of the western continent. A short time later, satisfied with his disguise, physical and lingual, fatigue defeated him again and he became as still as his grave companions.

A Vor voice and shuffling above the ditch woke him some hours later. "Anyone here . . . help . . . help . . . please?"

Morning sun and cawing crows crashed into Jaks's

senses. The voice called again with a pleading, pitchy angst. Jaks shook his head—he had a plan to enact. This was no time to help an enemy, even someone who sounded as pathetic as this. But eventually, his conscience won. After tucking away Meila's wrist device within his borrowed leather chest piece and sheathing his runic-forged sword—his shield lost in the fray—he climbed out of the hole and approached the calling figure.

The Vor crawled through burned grass. Something had torn his nose from his face and turned his eyes into bloodied gouges. Warlion claw wounds—maybe the same claws that had torn off the man's arm below the elbow. Jaks pressed a fist to his mouth to counter a wave of nausea.

"Here, I'll help you." Jaks dragged the man to his feet when he realized this enemy could help improve his disguise.

He crutched the thankful warrior up to the city gates, noting a few other survivors shambling around the battlefield too. A few looted their fellow Vors while several others weaved through the bodies, ditches, and carrion birds toward the gates as well.

Four Vor sentries challenged Jaks but waved him through at the sight of the injured warrior. "Fuck, he'll be dead in a day or two, but take him up to the infirmary anyway," a red-haired one said. "Up by the bridge."

An ironwood side door swung open and Jaks guided

the blind man onto the cobbled streets of Irin. The first test of his disguise had been passed with ease.

Scores of warriors roved the streets, smashing down doors into the elegant townhouses and buildings and dragging out the few citizens who had refused to escape with the Ascorians the night before. Now chattel, men and women—most elderly but some not—were tossed onto the street to be assaulted, abused, and then clamped in iron collars. Jaks shivered and willed himself small as he limped his wounded companion to the infirmary.

At the damaged bridge—where workers were already toiling over repairs—he sighted the aftermath of the previous night's battle. A half mile away, on the opposite riverbank, fire and smoke angled over the city. Milling figures smothered the shore as rowboats, rafts, and fishing vessels, filled with Vor warriors, slid across the water. In addition, dozens of ocean-going longboats unloaded at the docks to Jaks's left and right, and more anchored mid-stream awaiting their turn. These must have been the ships that Raki had spoken of.

"Over there," a gruff veteran directed Jaks, pointing to a quaint, steepled church on the corner. Its sacrosanct interior, though, was bared to the elements: doors had been ripped from the hinges and only shards remained of its stained-glass windows. Inside, dozens of wounded lay groaning and mumbling, ministered to by several healers with bandages and thread.

"They'll look after you now," Jaks said to the blind

warrior and patted him on the shoulder. He then turned to a medic nearby and asked in his best Vorosian enunciation, as casually as he could, "Has King Harek crossed the river, do you know?"

The healer, a matron with hands nimbly stitching a leg gash, raised her eyebrows and glared at him. "How would I know? What would the king want with you?"

"Nothing. I, ah. Just small talk."

"Well, if you've got time for blathering, warrior, go empty those buckets in the gutter. Then go refill them at the river . . . upstream, mind you, don't want no piss or death in them." She nodded at several wooden buckets filled with blood-soaked rags. "Wring out the rags, too."

Scowling like a scolded child, Jaks grabbed two of the containers, cursed as gore sloshed his boots, and dragged them out into the main avenue. However, once outside, he saw an opportunity in his task. Perhaps this was no annoyance; although not in his original plan to track down Karisa, playing water-boy could at least cloak his true purpose—once he discovered where the king rested, his slaves were sure to be close.

The boulevard paralleling the docks bustled with warriors. Carts, boxes, and fishing lines were shoved into the river to make room for several mustering points. As each group of fifty men and women converged, a coarse shout would stir them to march off into various parts of the city, making room for the next unit to assemble.

Wary-eyed, Jaks toted the buckets along the edge of

the buildings, well clear of the bristling masses, until he arrived at a landing where the water ran clear, and an empty rowboat bobbed.

Two oarsmen resting on broad pilings ignored him as he kneeled at the dock edge and dipped the first bucket into the river.

A few minutes later, he leaned against a piling and pretended to rest. He made eye contact with one of the men. "How fares the king? Has he crossed the river yet?" Jaks asked, sweating, but plying a casual tone.

The men exchanged glances, and the burliest coiled a rope around his arm. "How the fuck should I know," he said, then spat into the shushing waters and returned to his length of rope.

Several more bucket trips from the church to different docks—and many more blank faces for answers —left Jaks unenlightened on the king's whereabouts. Surely, the Vor king would travel with his main army? He began to doubt the effectiveness of his plan.

His last encounter raised his doubts even more about his investigation methods. A sharp-faced archer, directing the loading of a cart with bundled arrows, narrowed her eyes at his question. "Hoo, where're you from? That's an odd accent. What's your torgue? Who's your *telsun*?"

Before he could answer, she snatched his left arm, causing the bucket to drop from his hand. Pulling his sleeve, she twisted his forearm to study each surface with painful jerks. Not finding what she wanted—

maybe the conscription brand that would have labeled him an Ascorian—she released him, and stood with hands on hips in his path.

"Well, where's your torgue and telsun?"

"Killed at the northern barricade by warlions, they were," Jaks lied, and cringed at his fabrication of a peasant's accent. "The healer sent me to take water for the wounded."

"If they were all killed, I wonder how *you* survived, then. Who was your telsun?" Two other archers carrying arrow bundles rolled their loads onto the cart and stopped to eye up Jaks.

"Rauhalik, Sicaro. Died too . . ." he said, using the first Vor name he could think of, his father's, hoping it sounded common enough to satisfy this suspicious fox.

Her eyes narrowed, but then relaxed. "Sounds familiar, but I don't know him." She turned, losing interest in Jaks. "Go on, then. When the infirmers finish with you, report to the muster commander for a new torgue."

Nodding, he grabbed his buckets and returned to the river to refill the spilled vessel, thankful she hadn't checked further up his arm.

He was drawing too much attention. There must be an easier way to locate Karisa.

Wounded warriors stumbled into the infirmary throughout the day, keeping Jaks busy with buckets while the bleeding and broken-boned were mended. No longer asking directly about the king or his entourage, he took to lingering and listening to loose tongues on the docks and streets: Yes, the craven Ascorians had fled. No, we're not to pursue them. Yes, beer and ale aplenty tonight.

Shoulders aching, and confidence sinking, Jaks hefted buckets for the tenth time that day, and ambled back to the church along a quiet side street. Shadows inched toward the last few hours of sun.

"Hey, get back here!" A shout and running footsteps thumped up behind him. For the second time that day, a bucket of fresh water was knocked from his hand as a tiny figure ran past him. Two more youths, scrawny and dirt-smeared, quickly followed the first while throwing furtive glances over their shoulders.

Jaks shrank against a wall and clamped hands around his last bucket.

A blond-haired Vor ran after the youths, leading four other warriors. "They're going down the alley," he yelled.

The smallest, lagging on the heels of his mates, turned too late and skidded into the bricks of a battered storefront. He let out a cry and fell to the pavement, but his companions vanished down the alley.

"Got you, lily-boy," the first man triumphed under a hanging sign of a gem-encrusted ring. "Find those others and clamp them in irons," he yelled at his compatriots and lifted the stunned child up by the arm.

A minute later, the men returned empty-handed, and Jaks—bucket retrieved and about to return to the river—overheard talk of the waifs escaping over a wall. "Go search the buildings. I'm taking this one inside for a while." The blond man leered at the boy, picked him up bodily, and carried him kicking into the ransacked store.

The words chilled Jaks. The boy was no more than six years old, and his captor's intent was vile. He stood for a long minute on the empty street, lips curled and jaw clenching. An unbidden memory scratched at a scarred door, stirring an inner vigilante that howled at him to act.

He might not save every child, but he could save this one. Vixhana would have.

Buckets rolling to the ground behind him, Jaks stormed into the store.

His boots crunched underfoot. He paused for his eyes to adjust to the gloom within. A mess of glass shards surrounded him, as did smashed display cases with tiny wooden drawers torn from slots.

A hallway darkened the back of the store. *Down there?*

A deep laugh came from a staircase to the right. *No, up.*

He leaped steps, three at a time, up to a room illuminated by a window presiding over a table, chairs, and three wooden cots. The boy was sprawled on the floor. The hulking frame of the warrior stood over him.

At the sound of Jaks's entrance, the Vor looked over his shoulder. "What the hell do you want?" he demanded.

Jaks drew his sword. "Leave him alone."

"Bugger off, pisshead. He's mine." The man turned and swept out a dagger with his giant paw. The boy scuttled away to hide under a cot.

Months ago, he might have wet himself and flinched from this man bulking over him, but anger, not fear, was now his prevailing current. Besides, the sword was not his best weapon by far. With an innocent in the room, his only worry was not harming the boy.

Jaks's sword crackled to life with filaments of electricity racing over the engraved steel.

"Your little tricks don't scare me." The man sneered and swung the dagger in arcs, his longer arms making up for the shorter blade, and forced Jaks backward.

Another step back and Jaks would stumble down the stairs. He jabbed back with his scintillating sword.

His opponent darted right, nimble for a big man, evading the blade—but not far enough—lightning surged between the gap to his face. He yowled and staggered a retreat.

Jaks wasted no time and grunted with a two-handed cross-swing of the sword. The blade struck the man's wrist and sliced through skin and bone as easily as paper. Although brandished in battle before, it was the first time this rune-forged sword had tasted blood—it followed through the slash and spat blood over the floor as though appalled at the flavor.

The severed hand and dagger thunked to the ground, and the knifeman screamed as blood pumped from the stump, splattering Jaks's face and further decorating the room in crimson.

Worried the noise would attract attention, Jaks switched to a one-handed grip on the weapon and lunged at the man, spearing him through the chest.

Electromantic energy seethed through the sword; sizzling sounds and smoke seeped through the man's leather tunic. The blade rammed down to the hilt.

He pulled the blade out, pushed the Vor with his crippled hand, and said, "No more little boys." The man crumpled onto a blanket-covered bed, gurgling froth and gawping wordlessly.

A moment later, short limbs scrambled out from under a neighboring cot. The scrawny boy stared at the dead body for a long moment, then his face soured and he kicked its lifeless leg.

"You got him good," the boy said in Ascorian with a squeaky voice. Eyes squinting, he edged away from Jaks. "You're not going to kill me, are you?"

Jaks forced a smile, wanting to reassure the lad. "No, I don't want anything from you . . . except don't tell anyone what happened here."

"You're not one of them." The boy stepped a foot closer. "You're talking Ascorian, like me!" Barely coming up to Jaks's ribs—and about just as thin—the lad grinned under his mop of brown hair.

He had relapsed automatically into his native tongue in response to the boy's usage. He smiled, but now glanced back at the door at the top of the stairs.

"We've got to go. His friends are around and will be back soon."

"Are you a spy?"

"In a way. I'm here to rescue someone."

The boy's eyes shone, and his mouth dropped open. "Like Gilgat!"

"I don't think so," Jaks replied, recalling popular stories of Gilgat the Great: Mighty warrior and hero from the Dawn of Steel some four hundred years before. Whereas Gilgat had no fear, children's books told—even when he fought for thirty days to defend the walls of his Empress's fortress—Jaks had much to spare.

"Yes, yes, you just saved me, and you're going to save someone else . . . is it a princess?"

Jaks laughed as the boy bounced on his toes with awed eyes gazing at him.

A shadow flipped onto the balcony outside the window; the movement caught their attention.

"It's Hugh. I knew he'd come back." The boy flicked a catch and swung open the balcony door for the youth. "Hugh . . . he saved me already."

Hugh, a pimply teen with a strong physical resemblance to the younger boy, stared warily at Jaks and leaned through the door as though to snatch the boy out. He froze when he saw the dead Vor on the bed. "Oh, God. Come on, Davey, we've got to go."

"But we have to help him, Hugh. He's going to save a princess," Davey said.

"Horseshit. This is no time for make-believe." Hugh grabbed the boy by the arm.

"He's not one of them. He's Ascorian, like us."

By this time, Jaks itched for his own escape from the building.

Too late.

A booming voice sounded from the shop below. "Krayas—you finished with the sod? Didn't find any more of them. Krayas? Ship's heading out. We gotta get back to the docks . . . Krayas?" Footsteps thumped the lower steps of the stairs.

"Follow us," Davey beckoned.

Footsteps at the top. He could stand and fight—in a narrow stairwell, he could electroshock easily—but the copious blood painted across the room dampened his enthusiasm to shed more. There had been enough violence today. Time to run away.

Hovering over a narrow alleyway, the balcony promised an ankle-breaking fall to the ground. The alternative was even less desirable: ancient vines climbing a wooden trellis.

"Come on, it's easy," Davey called down, peering over the copper spouting from the rooftop.

Thick though the vines looked, the trellis appeared dry and brittle.

"Fuck! What the hell happened here?" A tall Vor stood at the door, staring at the blood-splattered corpse.

Jaks had to jump or climb now. He gripped the woody vine strongly with his good hand but could only gain a tenuous grasp with the thumb and two good fingers of the other. Cursing his choices, he swung out and scrambled for footing on the trellis.

"Out there. Get him." The warrior began to squeeze through the balcony door as a second shadow appeared behind him.

As Jaks pulled himself onto the tiled roof, Davey grinned at him and scrambled up the sloped roof. Swearing and curses flew from below, but the Vors made no attempt to follow other than to rattle the trellis and vines.

For several vertiginous minutes, Jaks trailed the boys up and down cracked clay and over greened spouting, surrounded by brick chimneys and ever-higher rooftops. Eventually, he joined them, crouching atop a round parapet presiding over the district.

The river cut through the city below and tracked out to the distant river-mouth where the sun touched its brackish waters. Boats and ships continued their ferry work, and armed figures filtered through the main roads and boulevards. A haze of smoke blanketed the city on the opposite bank, but the fires and tall plumes of that morning were gone.

He had only visited Irin two times before, accompanying his mother, lead actress, and Karisa, child prodigy, as they toured the country with an acting troupe over a decade ago. This, the oldest city in the kingdom, and third largest—after Dunberrin and then Finstaf—contained buildings that were from an era of their own. Red-brick edifices with ornate wooden trimmings were sprinkled with towers, statues, and minarets. Jaks scanned the magnificent vista of manses and houses, and sadly reflected that stately, beautiful Irin had been subdued by a barbaric king.

"It's a princess, isn't it?" Davey craned his neck at Jaks as though wishing him to do something heroic right there.

"I came for my sister. She's no princess, but—"

"Family's everything. Our ma used to say, didn't she, Hugh? That's how I knew Hugh would come back for me. If we had a sister, we'd rescue her too—wouldn't we, Hughie?"

The older brother shrugged, staring at Jaks's deformed hand. "You climb pretty well for someone with that." He shuffled uneasily. "Thanks for rescuing Davey. We were just looking around the boats and they started chasing us. Bastards. We're going to have to hide for a while. Hopefully, our food stash will last up."

"You should have fled the city with your parents last night," Jaks said.

Hugh laughed, and Davey's face drooped. "Our ma died a couple years ago, and our da . . . well, he left to dig diamonds," Hugh replied. "Nah, us lot run the streets—well, we did before today."

The brothers were street urchins, from a gang of orphans and runaways who had gravitated to this city of wealthy merchants to leech off the rich and fancy. A naïve few, like Hugh and Davey, remained despite the siege, thinking they could blend in just as they had before, and perhaps prosper from the chaos brought by the Vors. What they hadn't counted on was for the entire city evacuating and leaving the thieves with barely anything to steal—and little food to pilfer.

Jaks listened that evening to the anxious reports of nine scruffy boys and two girls in the stained-glassed loft of a long-abandoned and partially collapsed mansion a few blocks back from the docks.

"I heard from Winny about some turnips she says were left behind in Frothton's basement. Her lot took a heap, but there's still plenty that we can have," said their leader: eldest girl, Hanna. She was stick-thin, and if not for her voice and flat neck, Jaks would have thought her a boy ripe for conscription.

Unfortunately, she didn't like Jaks.

"Why did you bring him here?" she had demanded of Hugh and Davey when they brought him through the rooftop door as the sun set behind them. Although mollified by Davey's account of Jaks rescuing him from the Vor, she wouldn't look Jaks in the eye when she said, "He has to go in the morning."

Too tired to care how a common thief felt about him, he sought some rest but dismissed the tattered mattresses and even more ragged-looking sofas, and slumped onto some cushions in a corner. Dozing, he half-listened to the urgent chatter of the youths about their encounters that day. It was several minutes later that his ears perked up when an older boy said something that triggered his attention.

"'. . . she was lovely as that statue outside Dor's Brothel,' I says to Dunny," a dark-headed youth, named Tim, was saying. "Then Dunny goes and yells at her, and everybody on the boat stares at us standing on the wall of the governor's palace. The lady and the other ladies was laughing, but the guards looked so pissed. When their boat gets to the dock, theys come after us."

"Wasn't my fault . . ." said the boy, presumably named Dunny.

"We start to run along the wall, but Dunny then goes and trips over. Feet caught in the vines, he's hanging upside down like a bat. The bastards below jumping up and down trying to grab him."

"Only fell because you were going too slow—"

"Then I see the lady bring her hands up in front of her eyes and suddenly it's like the sun landed in the middle of the governor's docks and I can't see anything, so I kneel down on top of the wall. When my eyes clear up, the lady has knifed one guard, and another is sinking into the river." The dark-haired boy continued with a grin across his face. "Two ladies chained at the neck run away through the palace gardens. But a couple other ladies just stay behind crying."

The other boy finished his friend's story. "Stupid here didn't help, so I pull myself back up, and the guards that're trying to get me see what's happening and go off after the runaways."

Jaks stood and towered within the loft. "This woman, this lady. Was she tall, like me? Slim? Did she have golden hair?" He advanced on the boy, Tim. Too aggressive—the boy and the other youths startled toward the windows and doors. "Sorry. I didn't mean to frighten you, but that lady—she could be my sister, Karisa."

He extracted more information from Tim and Dunny. Details of the slave woman and the illumancy attack convinced him it was Karisa: what other woman, so mesmerizing to men and boys, showed such daring while wrapped in nothing but silks? But despite the heartening sight, the encounter ended sadly with the two chained women recaptured on the street and forced back inside the palace.

"I bet they'll still be there," Tim said. He had quickly warmed to Jaks, like Davey, and was entranced with the idea of rescuing a damsel from an evil king.

Two accomplices for his quest. Maybe he did have a bit of Gilgat the Great in him?

"How brave are you lads?" Jaks placed his hands on Tim and Davey's shoulders and drew them in. "Here's what we're going to do."

Chapter 6

The Palace

From a rooftop nook, Jaks and his two young conspirators sheltered from the stinging weather and studied the governor's palace. Suspecting that Karisa was inside of it, they had to find out where.

Davey and Tim sought him out each day and brought turnips and keen eyes to help him locate his sister within the enormous building. He drank rainwater from jars he set on window ledges and slept in abandoned attics, never setting foot on the streets below, keeping to the "thieves' highway" and safe from confrontation.

Autumn had favored the Vor invasion, but days of hail and howling wind had now wintered down the invaders' advance and sent them into hibernation. The City of Irin was transformed into a Vor fortress as the invaders settled in: residential districts converted to barracks and slave quarters; open marketplaces to rallying grounds; and the fields outside its walls to roaming grounds for their massive gray monsters.

For three days now, they had changed vantage points, straining for glimpses of life through the hundreds of windows in the palace.

"She must be in an inner room. I'm just going to have to go in," Jaks said to the boys one afternoon. The three of them huddled in the alcove of an ornate manse as the rain eased to a pitter-patter.

Davey roused from dozing against a gargoyle carved from stone. Impishly, the small boy yearned to break into the palace himself and wander the corridors and staircases—searching, he said, but probably more likely for food or valuables than for a human slave. He would often jiggle his legs and pick his nose when forced to sit still, so Jaks usually sent him to spy from various other windows, or trees in the neighboring park. Now, though, the mop-haired boy had had enough climbing for the day.

Tim, the pimply other boy, had at first seemed as air-headed as the younger, but Jaks discovered that beneath his idealism, he simmered with anger and sought retribution on the invaders of his beloved city: heroic revenge. Jaks's mission struck at the enemy king's treasures and seemed as good a cause as any to the youth.

"I'll come too," Tim and Davey said simultaneously.

"You're too little," the older boy said. "We can't have you to worry about."

"I'll look after myself."

Jaks folded his arms. "No. I'm going in alone. There are scores of guards in there. If I have to fight, I don't want you near me. However, I do need your help to get inside. Go home, get some rest, and I'll tell you my plan when you come back in the morning." Not for the first time, he wished for Vixhana's powers, desperately. As a shadow, he could have simply leaped into a window and flitted through the hallways until he got to Karisa and then escaped just as easily.

Later that evening, after the boys had returned to their gang hideout, Jaks climbed through the attic window into his nightly hideaway. He extracted the wrist communicator from behind his chest piece and strapped it to his wrist. It chilled his skin as though stealing his heat. After a second, the alien artifact hummed alive, and offered its inner electrical pathways as it had several times before.

He sat for hours absorbed within it: following, exploring, and changing channels and corridors for no reason other than marveling in finding out how it worked.

Eventually, he reached out for the patterns of Meila's communication device with his electromancer sense. There was no response. Was she too busy to answer? Although she didn't respond to his initiating signal, Jaks smiled on discovering that he could access her device through his own.

This time, he explored the inner workings of Meila's

communicator. He infiltrated the device's storage space and found recordings of recent transmissions—not to him but to yet another device, a third communicator device.

Playing through the stored transmissions, Jaks felt a twinge of guilt, as though spying on her through a window. And well he should, because the bearer of the third device was none other than King Silas, monarch of Ascoria.

The communications were military and political: often Meila relaying messages for an advisor such as Grandmaster Mulgrave, or some other military official from Dunberrin, to the king. An apt messenger, she and the king seemed to have an easy relationship at first. The messages themselves meant little to Jaks but conveyed a picture of sound strategies that seemed to fall apart at the last minute. What should have been decisive military strikes or defenses were repeatedly subordinated by the Vors with always greater maneuvers or deceit.

But as the messages progressed, and the war had continued against him, the king's paranoia had sharpened to an edge, and he had—as of a few days ago —banned any further communication of strategic information using the device on suspicion that their transmissions were being intercepted. Indeed, Meila had barely escaped a return to prison on a charge of leaking secrets to the enemy. In the last transmission, only Mulgrave's directly spoken promises and pleadings to the king had kept her out of severe incarceration.

Playing the recorded messages, Jaks succumbed to an odd longing while he watched Meila. That opinionated, hard-willed woman had some hold over him that he couldn't stifle.

"Jaks." Meila's image materialized in front of him, startling him out of his thoughts.

"I was just trying to contact you." He sat upright and drank in her features. Raven hair tied back, she wore a tan tunic open at the neck. Her surroundings placed her in one of the Academy's workshops. Benches groaned under machinery and gadgets, and forges clanged in the background.

"Are you alright? I heard that Irin fell in the last battle. Last I heard from you, you were spouting off some nonsense about infiltrating the Vors—"

"I have. I'm in hiding opposite the palace where I think Karisa is being held. Trying to find a way to rescue her."

"What palace?" Her eyes widened. "You're in Irin? Is that where you are?"

"Yes, but I think the Vor king is in residence and the place is heavily defended."

"Oh, God, Jaks. It's far too dangerous. You can't risk getting caught. Get out of that city. I need you here at the Academy."

"She's so close. I can feel her nearby. Some boys from a local gang saw her just a few days ago." Jaks thought

the words rather than spoke them. *Still works. Best to keep silence.* He recalled the dull thuds and muffled voices that had trickled up to his ears from deep in the building earlier that evening. There might be a few people stationed below. Officials, officers?

"What boys? Never mind, you'll never get into a fortified building with the Vor king inside. Do you really think you can just skip on in and steal his prized concubine?"

Blood rose to Jaks's cheeks, and he spoke out loud. "She didn't choose to be where she is. She's clamped in irons and chains. I didn't come this far to run away now." His anger dissipated as he remembered Meila's husband had been in a similar situation.

"I'm sorry, Jaks. I know you feel responsible for her, but you and I have had terrible results from attempted rescues . . ."

"I rescued you in the forest."

"This is on a whole different level compared to two thugs in the forest." Meila frowned. "Look, I need you. *We* need you. Your electromancy may be the last chance we have to fight off the Vors. I have a velocannon ready, but we don't have a strong enough power source—we don't have you."

"I'm not turning back now," he repeated, biting his lip, remembering to only think the words this time.

"You're doing that thing again." Meila's image stilled for so long that he wondered whether his device had broken, but then she continued. "Alright, if you're being so stubborn about it, I'll send you some help."

"Huh?"

"You think you have the correct building, but you don't know where she is precisely inside?"

He transmitted a silent *yes.*

"I'll send you some eyes. A droid. Do you remember those eggs that we salvaged from the *Mendhelsson?"*

"Eggs? I didn't know they were eggs."

"They're not actual eggs, you idiot. They're Hammond-Zhang Droids. I call them zingers. I'll send one to you." Meila walked to a drawer in a workbench and held up an oval-shaped gray object that she had correctly described as the size of a chicken's egg.

The device sprang up into the air in front of her and hovered. A small fin popped out of the top and two round discs folded out of its front. A flying metal fish.

"You control it with the comm device." She showed Jaks by flitting and jigging the zinger around the workshop. "You need to place your wrist on a flat surface, like a table or desk, and the control panel will open up from its lateral port. You use your other hand to maneuver it and activate its functions."

"But why?"

"It can see through walls, amongst other things. You'll be able to fly it over the palace and see whether Karisa is actually there. And if she isn't, promise me you'll leave the city and come back to the Academy."

"But how are you going to get it here?" The zinger

sounded useful, but not if he had to go back to Dunberrin to retrieve it.

"I'll send the droid to you. I'll transfer an Ascorian language file to it first. Then, it'll take . . ." Her eyes flicked up for a second. ". . . four hours and seven minutes, give or take, depending on the wind and weather. It's designed for planetary atmospheric studies, so it's made for traveling long distances. In fact, that's all it's for, really; its sensor and sampling array is pretty basic compared to some of the other droids we had."

An hour later, satisfied with her instructions to Jaks, she rubbed her eyes and yawned. "Been up two days straight. I need a few hours to rejuve. Let me know what you're going to do before you do it." With that, the zinger droid sped out of the workshop, and Meila disconnected her comm, leaving Jaks alone in the attic.

Sometime later, Jaks awoke to a presence in the attic. Too dark to see anything except the frame of the open window. Then something hovered above him; his electromancy sensed an oval object glimmering in his magical eye, dense with silver and gold. *Has it been four hours already?*

He sat up and grasped the flying device in his hands. Like the wrist comm, it chilled his skin to touch. Jaks examined the device under the moonlight at the window. The same gray metal as Meila's ship, a similar ovoid shape except for the dorsal fin and two eyes that seemed to return his stare. *It looks curious. Does it blink?*

He frowned. Meila had said something about giving it orders. He delved into the droid's electrical interior and lost himself to his magical senses as the device lay in his hands. Vastly more sophisticated than the wrist comm, many pathways and compartments made no sense to his naïve brain, and he withdrew confused and astounded—the device seemed alive.

"*Standby. Awaiting instruction,*" the zinger messaged into his thoughts.

"Fly around the room," Jaks whispered. It flew a circuit of the room so quickly he barely registered its movement.

Touching the droid's cold exterior, he repeated the instruction wordlessly, activating the device's circuitry through his electromancy. Again, it darted around the dark attic, dodging the pile of furniture atop the trapdoor leading to the lower floors.

Next, Jaks manipulated the wrist-comm device with his powers. Far more effective: he could control the droid directly.

And in addition, by doing so, he found he could look through the droid's eyes. Amazed, he saw an overhead view of his body, unconscious on the attic floor—a quick lesson that diverting his mind to the zinger rendered him senseless to anything but the device's sensors.

With electromancy, he didn't need the control panel as Meila had; instead, he could communicate with the droid through the wrist comm as though controlling an extra eye—an incredible one that could fly around and spy.

Dawn light filtered through the window when Meila interrupted him from his experimentation with the zinger. Her image materialized in front of him, refreshed but for her mussed hair.

She quirked an eyebrow. "Well? Have you found her yet?"

"I haven't sent it out yet. I've never used this thing before, remember."

"You're not using the control panel? Damn. What I'd give for that ability. Mental manipulation of tech."

"At least it's useful for something other than just killing people," Jaks said.

"Here, let me . . . the building over the avenue? Impressive-looking place." Meila had her arm planted on a desk in what looked like the grandmaster's library.

The zinger droid sped out the window. Jaks closed his eyes and followed the device's path through its sensors. Mind-locked to the droid, his forehead bumped down against the attic floor as his body fell senseless.

"I'm switching to a gamma scan. Then we can look inside for biologicals."

Jaks's mind reeled as images returning from the zinger swirled and distorted. Colors vanished and the facade of the palace building dissolved into a depth of grays and whites. He cast his thoughts to Meila. *"How can there be so many people in there?"*

"If it's the Vor king's residence, you don't think it'd

just be him and a few women to keep him entertained, do you?" Her voice sounded in his mind, but his vision remained focused through the zinger. "Also, some guard dogs."

Jaks grimaced. *"Only way they can detect nightwraiths."* Even so, Vixhana would still have had far better chances of infiltrating this place than him, judging by the number of soldiers he would have to elude.

"I'd say most of those we're seeing are guards, although many on the lower floors are probably servants. I don't know what your sister looks like, but if we sweep through the building, tell me if you see anyone who resembles her, and we can focus in on the face."

"How about you let me have the droid back? It's easier for me to see if I'm controlling it," he said.

He directed the droid in a circuit of the palace, achingly slow, stopping to zoom in on tall, slender figures, not that there were many of them, and the ones he saw—each time his heart lurching in hope—were all strangers.

"Get an angle from inside the courtyard," Meila said. "We'll get a better view of the inner rooms."

Jaks soared over the five-storied palace and into the central garden. Nausea rolled in his gullet for a moment but was soon replaced by exhilaration. *"It's like I'm flying. Is this what it's like in your ship?"*

Meila laughed but didn't reply. "Hover in the branches of those trees there. Best to keep hidden as much as possible." A bird fluttered from a tree as the device descended into the leafless branches.

The palace was well awake now. The bottom floor, especially the kitchen, teemed with figures, while the grand hall was busy with servants and guards. And in a chamber on the third floor, yet another gathering assembled. All the while, dozens of armed silhouettes roamed or sentried the building. But it was on scanning the top floor, in a room overlooking the gardens facing the river, that Jaks thought a triumphant, *Yes!*

"It must be her. I need to get closer." Within a few seconds, Jaks had the droid hovering outside the balcony window, peering through a slit between closed curtains. Could he make the droid talk if he could get close enough? Inside the room, two figures lay side by side. Although he couldn't see furniture well with the droid's special vision, he guessed they lay on a bed.

"Is it her?" Meila asked.

Jaks studied the angular face, turned toward the window. Her eyes still closed, she breathed steadily, as did her female companion behind her. A gem-encrusted collar connected to an iron chain tethered her to a granite column at the center of the ornate bedroom. His heart skipped a beat as his sister's features resolved in the faint morning light and his shuttered eyes squeezed out tears.

It was her. He had found Karisa.

"Can I talk through this?" He directed the thought to Meila.

"No, it doesn't generate sound."

"What about a light?"

Activating the droid's light beam, Meila highlighted the internal pathway for Jaks's attention.

Directing the zinger's light through the part in the curtain, he focused the beam on Karisa's closed eyelids. He switched the light on and off several times.

Her face crinkled, and she rolled away from the light.

Not giving up, Jaks directed the beam to the back of her companion's head and weaved it around, hoping the moving light would wake his sister.

A minute later, Karisa stirred again and lifted her head as though watching the bright dot weaving over the bed.

With one hand grasping the chain dangling from her neck, she sat up in the bed and turned to the window.

"I'll try some basic signaler's code." Jaks directed the beam to her chest—too bright to shine in her eyes—and flashed the droid's light in a sequence that he racked his memory to recall.

J . . . A . . . K . . . S.

Was that right? Would she realize the short and long flashes were a code?

Karisa squinted, as though confused. She walked to the curtain, her slave chain taut by the time she reached an arm to pull the fold aside. She stared in astonishment at the device with silver eyes flying outside her window.

Again, Jaks flashed the signaler's sequence at her, hoping he was doing it right. At the same time, a few distant thumps registered on the edges of his hearing. Something out of sight of the droid's vision —unimportant.

Her astonishment turned to surprise. She mouthed something back to the droid through the glass. It looked like she was saying his name. "Jaks?"

Another face appeared beside her to stare at the device; a shorter, buxom woman, wrapped in similar colored silks. The two women looked at each other and back to the zinger and spoke energetically.

He watched as Karisa stretched out a hand toward the droid. The chain around her neck kept the window latches out of her grasp. She then held up her palm and illumanced a light at the droid. **J.A.K.S.**, she signaled back his sequence, and then mouthed his name again— but instead of her voice, he heard a boy's. It sounded familiar, but not Karisa's.

"Jaks!" a boy's voice cried out again.

And then pain. His eyes flicked open.

The attic was full of people.

Chapter 7

The Thieves' Highway

Jaks grunted and rolled to his side, dazed as he transitioned back to his surroundings. A shadow stood over him, the whites of its eyes menaced him, and a huge paw reached down to grab his arm.

"Stay down or I kick you again, fucking roof rat. Got you now," the shadow yelled at him. A Vor voice. *How did they get up here?*

The attic door, inlaid with the floor, gaped open. The piled furniture he had thought would hold it down was shoved aside. Their hideout had been discovered.

"Jaks," Davey shouted. It must have been he who had yelled before. The boy was standing half out of the attic window. The older boy, Tim, had a hand on Davey's shoulder, looking as though trying to pull him along. They must have arrived while Jaks was senseless. Before or after the Vors pushed their way up through the attic door?

A second shadow stomped past Jaks, boot barely missing his head in the narrow room. "Come on, lads. We're not going to hurt you. Just want to talk." The shadow stepped into the light streaming through the window and revealed a greasy-haired man trying to sculpt a reassuring smile despite a mouthful of rotten teeth.

The hand clasping Jaks yanked him to his feet, aggravating the stabbing pain in his ribs. He cried out as his captor, a heavyset warrior, ripped open his collar and exposed the Ascorian conscript brand high on his arm. "A spy. Thought so," the warrior said in the guttural tones of Vorosian.

An open palm smacked him across the face, and Jaks fell stunned to the floor.

Angry voices, deafening in the attic, shouted and yelled at each other, and stirred Jaks out of his mind fog.

Thumps and thwacks of a frantic struggle threw chaos into the confined space.

Jaks pushed himself up on his arms, but a body bounced against him and knocked him back down. Wetness splashed his face.

"Fucking runt stabbed me." Greasy Hair said as he clutched at his bleeding leg. He pulled himself up and staggered into a corner of the attic.

Little Davey trembled at the other end of the attic, brandishing a thin stiletto blade that looked as long as a sword in his small hand.

Tim stood behind him, also flashing steel but

displaying annoyance rather than the obvious fear of the younger boy. "Shit, why'd you do that? Come on, Davey, we got to get out of here."

"No." The mop-headed boy continued to bear up his stall at the two Vor warriors. "Jaks needs us."

The heavyset warrior rounded on the two street urchins. His bulk dominated the triangular room, and a shortsword appeared in his hand. "You're the little runt that face-planted the wall the other day. You're too small to have killed Krayas . . . was it your bumtoad here who killed him?"

"Kill him, Stug. The fucker stabbed me. Just kill all three of them," the injured Vor said.

Fear paralyzed Jaks. He couldn't risk a lightning bolt. Tim and Davey were too near; a lethal invocation could kill the swordsman, who was an easy target with his back to Jaks, but could as easily transmit through him and kill the boys as well. It had to be a shocking touch, hopefully stunning the man until he could draw his own sword to stab him. Restraining the electromancy was the hardest part.

"Put down your knitting needle, boy." The Vor named Stug dipped his sword tip under Davey's nose and grinned as the stiletto blade fell from the boy's trembling fingers. Neither boy understood what he had said in Vorosian, but they understood his meaning. "You, too, bumtoad." The sword moved toward Tim.

Jaks reached out with his good hand, dimly aware that the other Vor was shuffling up against the wall behind him. Grabbing the left leg of the swordsman above his boot, he dampened his fear with thoughts of angrily stabbing the man to death and then invoked a jolt of lightning to his fingertips.

"What the fuck?" The swordsman kicked away from Jaks's grasp. Underpowered, the jolt had merely stung the warrior. Half-turning to look down at Jaks, he said to the wounded Vor, "Finish the spy. We'll keep these other two."

Jaks rolled onto his back to look up at the greasy-haired Vor. A fresh wave of panic urged Jaks to retaliate as harshly as he could. Electrocute these damn Vors to a crisp. No, he couldn't. Davey and Tim were still too close.

Greasy Hair snarled and flourished a long knife. He bent down on his good knee, one hand tipping Jaks's chin to expose his neck as though to shave his beard; however, the tip angling toward his throat told otherwise. "Hold still. Won't take long."

Jaks grabbed the attacker's wrists. His crippled fingers were weak around the man's knife-hand wrist, but his good hand grappled the man's other hand away from his chin. The evil tip of the blade wavered over him in the struggle—

The knife plunged through the outer part of his left shoulder, piercing skin and muscle. Jaks screamed in agony.

As it had done only a few times before, his power surged to his defense without thought.

Boom! A lightning blast launched Jaks's attacker upward and threw him against the tiles of the slanted wall and breached a hole through the roof. Slate fragments clattered through the attic and light poured through the shattered lining.

The Vor lay broken across the gap; he twitched for a few moments and then went still.

The pain in Jaks's shoulder forced his attention to the knife impaled there. He grabbed his arm below the wound and groaned.

Pain clouded his vision, but out of the corner of his eye, he saw the remaining Vor, still with his back to Jaks, suddenly drop to the floor with a thud.

A small, gray ovoid object clattered to the wood next to the swordsman's head. The zinger droid. Had it attacked the Vor?

Davey's small face appeared over Jaks. "Don't die! You can't die." He stared at the knife.

Voices shouted from below.

More Vors on the way. They had to get away from here, but he couldn't bear to move with the steel in his shoulder. Jaks knew from his conscript training that he should wait for a trained medic to remove the knife—someone who could stifle the torrent of blood that might follow. However, more warriors were coming for them, and he needed to run and maneuver to escape. Wild movements would grossly widen the knife wound—especially if he knocked the blade or handle. The risk of worsening the injury by extracting it now was less than stumbling with it in place. Besides, even now, the slightest movements were like shards of glass grinding in his arm.

"You've got to pull it out of me, Davey," Jaks said, staring into the boy's terrified eyes.

Davey wrapped trembling hands around the handle and hesitated.

"Pull it. You can do it," Jaks said, gasping between the words.

His shoulder lifted slightly as the boy heaved on the weapon and rolled onto his backside with the effort of pulling out the knife. Jaks let out an involuntary yell at the spear of agony.

He clapped his hand to the shoulder wound, squeezing blood through his fingers despite the pain. Thankfully, the blood seeped rather than gushed. Gritting his teeth, he staggered to his feet.

"Come on, Davey. We've got to go. Through the hole." Jaks flicked his head toward the jagged opening he had blasted. It would be faster than running to the window, where Tim had already disappeared.

Davey scampered over the dead Vor and out the makeshift escape route, slowing only to tear off the man's coin pouch—too much of a temptation for the little thief to resist even in the height of danger.

A steel-helmeted woman's head popped up through the attic door opening. "Crap, Stug. What a mess." The new Vor planted her elbows on the attic floor and pulled herself up.

Too pained to focus an invocation—although it would have been an ideal opportunity to take her down, without either boy in the way—Jaks squeezed himself through the opening behind Davey.

Tim was on all fours beside Davey on the sloped slate roof. The two boys pulled on Jaks as he clambered up to join them.

Thankfully, the slope ended in a gutter that joined with the adjacent building rather than a steep drop to the road below. The gutter gave them a flat surface to follow. In fact, knowing the rooftops as well as Tim and Davey did, a thief could travel for entire blocks of buildings without pause.

Under a clear morning sky, Jaks scrambled after the fleeing boys as fast as his damaged body could take him.

Minutes later, the helmeted Vor climbed up onto the roof after them.

Jaks's neck itched under her glare. When he dared a glance back, he swore as several more warriors appeared next to her. He had hoped all Vors were as phobic of heights as he had been—before those months of crisscrossing the Jurns' rope bridges—however, these ones seemed to have no fear of the vertiginous terrain. They followed Jaks and the boys, slowly but steadily.

"They're chasing us," Davey shouted. He had a habit of stating the obvious.

Slate to clay tiles, sloped and flat roofs, around chimney stacks and lightning rods, Jaks climbed and shuffled as Tim led them across the Thieves' Highway.

The wind felt fresh and the sun warm on his face after the confines of the attic; however, there was no time to appreciate it in this snail-and-slug pursuit.

He would have laughed at how ridiculous their pursuers looked—lumbering warriors swearing and cursing as they slipped on and cracked tiles underfoot—if the stakes had not been so serious. Blood oozed between his fingers, and every movement clouded his mind. At that moment, he wished he had some of Meila's pain-dulling pills.

In a mere three-quarters of a mile, the buildings changed from majestic mansions of minor nobility and wealthy merchants to workers' lodges and boarding houses that teetered upward like children's blocks. Each floor slapped haphazardly on top of the last, with little thought to aesthetic or safety.

"In here. No one's lived here for years. It's condemned," Tim said, dropping to a rickety balcony that creaked under his weight.

It was clear why the building was uninhabited. It was so poorly constructed that misaligned floorboards gaped wide while rotted ones bent underfoot of even the malnourished boys.

"Can't stop here. They would've seen where we went," Jaks said, despite wanting to pause to apply some first-aid to his bleeding.

"Careful, the stairs here have collapsed in places. I'll lead. Follow in my footsteps," Tim said and took to the poorly constructed stairs.

One flight down and Jaks stared through a raw hole where the steps had collapsed in a fragmented mess to the flight below.

Foot over foot, he reached for jagged remains of the steps jutting out from the wall. His head spun and vertigo flared for a moment. He froze and breathed deep breaths for precious seconds while he recovered his nerve.

Deep voices sounded from the top floor, where they had been minutes before. A sharp crack was followed by voluminous swearing. Would the heavy-footed oofs dare this death-trap? No sooner had the thought framed in his head than a plate-sheaved leg crashed through the ceiling above. The steel-capped boot on the end of the foot dangled pathetically as its owner cursed, and rotted wood thunked around Jaks's head.

"Keep going," Tim called to Jaks, from where he stood on the landing below.

The leg pulled up and out of the hole, and a face glowered back down. "Damn runts. Stay where you are," the woman yelled at him.

Jaks breathed in relief as he made the last step and joined Tim on the landing.

"Look out!" Tim cried out and pushed Jaks to the side.

Thud. A wooden shaft quivered in the floor where Jaks had been standing. The vanes of a crossbow bolt glistened green and brown. His gaze flew to the hole where the warrior's leg had smashed through. A pair of eyes peered through it over an expended crossbow.

"There's an entrance to the sewers in the courtyard. Let's go." Tim pushed Jaks toward Davey, who was already fleet-footing down the next flight of stairs.

The last two sets of stairs groaned threateningly as they continued their descent, but eventually released them to the ground floor with nothing more than a few blisters from gripping the railings too hard.

"Do you think they're still chasing us?" Davey stared up the staircase.

Jaks listened for a few seconds, but what voices he heard were remote. "They're persistent, but I don't think they're coming down this way. They'll probably look for another way down. It'll give us time to get some distance. Where are these sewers?"

They stumbled out of a doorless entrance into a courtyard. In a distant past, the square space might have been filled with carefree voices of children circling the tree at its center; however, the only residents now were lizards and crawlers, and the only things that grew on the skeletal tree were cobwebs.

Tim shuffled along the wall to the bush-covered northeast corner of the courtyard. When Jaks joined him, the boy pointed down at a stone-lined hole edged with brown algae and slime.

"Davey, you go first. I'll go last," the older boy said. The smaller boy slid down the sewer hole as Jaks looked on with open disgust. "It's not so bad down there. Use the holes in the side as you go down."

Jaks wanted to clutch his shoulder to prevent it from scraping the sludge, but he needed his good arm to climb. He gulped and swung his legs into the hole, poking his foot around for purchase. Although his boot found the first hole, the next failed and his planned descent turned into an uncontrolled slide. He yelped in panic and landed with a splash. Pain shot through his buttocks and shoulder all at once, and he lay in the ankle-deep water, not daring to move.

A presence brushed up to him in the narrow tunnel. "Are you alright?" Davey asked, barely visible in the semidarkness.

"I'm okay." When the pain subsided, he palpated his legs and was relieved to find no lasting injuries. A broken ankle would have been disastrous. "Let's go," he gasped. His strength was fading. He needed to rest, but Tim dropped down beside him and urged him along.

"Not here. We have to keep moving," the youth said.

The sewers wormed away in every direction: stone tunnels and drains filtered away the city's filth and kept it from drowning in the storms. If he had been alone, Jaks was sure he would've been lost within minutes. Fortunately, Davey was as knowledgeable of the network beneath the city as he was of the one above it, and he led them without faltering for over an hour. From time to time, marching boots or coarse Vor voices echoed from above, but they encountered no one and nothing other than the occasional scuttlebug or rat.

"We need somewhere to stop for a while. I have to tend to my arm," Jaks said eventually, guessing that they were nearing the river. The air was brisker here, and a seagull cawed through an iron grate overhead.

"Almost there," Davey replied over his shoulder. "This is the timberyard. It has the best hideaways. It's huge."

Indeed, he was not exaggerating.

The three fugitives scanned the expansive timberyard from atop a long wall. Their tunnel had opened out to a walled stone channel that sloped down to the main river some yards distant. From there, they had climbed green-stained steps to their current observation point.

The timberyard stretched a mile along the riverside, right up to the outer city wall. At its busiest, Jaks imagined it would have been a miniature town within the city. Hundreds of workers, ant-like, would have unloaded logs from river barges, cut and prepared planks in deafening sawing sheds, and swung them on cranes to their store piles. At the moment, thankfully, the complex of buildings and yards was as still and silent as a graveyard.

"I think they took most of the wood to the south city to build up the walls and barricades," Tim postulated after Jaks remarked at how little lumber there was around. "But even before that, they say the yard was low on logs trying to supply the army's weapon smiths and armorers. The foresters couldn't keep up."

"To the big storehouse?" Davey fidgeted as he quizzed the older boy.

"The old bargehouse is better. It has running water, and there might be some dried fish hanging up there."

Several minutes later, Jaks stood at the door of a sturdy bargehouse. The wooden building stood low over the water on heavy columns, with its rear section resting on solid ground. He stopped at the entrance, his gaze drawn out to the river. Anchored ships and boats bobbed against the current but showed little life onboard except the occasional guard. The city bridge, arcing from south to north, on the other hand, teemed with activity; even at this great distance, light glinted off shields and blades under the late-morning sun.

Shoulders slumped, he entered the building. A refuge. But was it a place to recoup for another rescue attempt, or a place to launch an escape from the city?

Chapter 8

The Bargehouse

In the bargehouse, a walkway surrounded three boats and two flat barges floating in the middle of the building. At the top of a ramp, out of the water, another barge rested on wooden supports. A pair of river gates, lower edges rotted, were all that separated the building's wet-space from the river.

Empty workbenches lined the walls of a workshop that filled the dry end of the building. Loops of hessian rope lay in coils whilst others stretched across the ceiling, from which hung dried husks of cod and trout.

It was a good space to recoup and decide what to do next.

With a sense of relief, Jaks walked to the solid ground of the workshop and sat cross-legged before peeling off his leather tunic to examine his shoulder wound. Pain returned afresh as the adrenaline rush of escape faded.

Davey stared at Jaks and wrung his hands, while Tim paced about the walkway.

Blood clots and smears obscured the wound. Although it was less alarming without the knife sticking through, he couldn't trust that it would heal without further treatment. It could fester. Vixhana had told him about a dragon handler she knew that died several weeks after one of his beasts nipped his wrist. Infection had set in and they didn't amputate his arm in time. If only Meila were here; he needed her able hands, miraculous bandages, and pain-dulling pills.

As if his thoughts had summoned her, the wrist communicator vibrated against his skin and a yellow light swirled around the disc edge. He electromanced the device with the tiniest of invocations, barely requiring a thought, and accepted the connection.

An image of Meila's annoyed face materialized, hovering over the comm. "You've got to stop giving me such frights. I saw what happened after I flew the zinger back to your attic," she said.

"I'm sorry, I thought the attic was secure with the furniture holding the door down—"

"Clearly, it wasn't." After a pause, her voice softened. "You have to get out of that damned city. It's far too dangerous to carry on with this fool's task. I got the droid back into the air after I used it to knock that warrior in the head. And I can tell you, there are hundreds of Vors searching the buildings and rooftops around the palace after that fiasco. Guards have doubled. Your sister isn't getting out of there any time soon, even with your help."

"I've got to try again." Jaks's stubbornness persisted, even though he knew the truth of her words.

"You tried, and you have to accept you've failed. Come back to the Academy and we'll win this damn war. And *then* we can rescue Karisa. She's probably as safe there as anywhere." Then, as a consolation, she added, "At least you know she's alive."

He chewed on his lip. He'd discovered his sister's prison but couldn't get near it. Frustration tore at him like clashing tides. Damn the Vors who'd found his hiding spot.

A minute later, air swished through a cracked window high up in the bargehouse. The zinger darted inside, its owl-like eyes homing in on Tim and Davey. The boys squealed in panic and took refuge behind the dry-docked barge.

Jaks laughed despite it aggravating his shoulder pain and called out to the boys, "Don't worry. It's not dangerous."

"This is the gang you were talking about? They're just children. Where are their parents?" Meila asked.

"They're orphans," he said, then grimaced in renewed pain.

"Jaks, I didn't realize you were wounded. What happened?" She maneuvered the zinger to hover by his shoulder. The boys crept back to Jaks and ogled the flying wonder.

Jaks described the desperate fight in the attic to her, what little he remembered of the chaos. Although she had observed part of the standoff through the zinger's sensors—after she had flown it there to investigate his abrupt communication loss—the zinger had shut down temporarily after smashing into the Vor's head.

"No telling how deep it is with these scanners. The zingers aren't designed for wound analysis. Pity we didn't recover a medical droid. Anyway, you need to open it up and wash it out." She fumbled about her workshop bench and drew out a second droid identical to the other. "These zingers have a compartment we usually use for drawing environmental samples. Let me see if I can fit a gel bandage inside and fly it to you. It'll take a few hours, like last time. Stay put."

Her image blinked out.

"I need some water and rags for this, boys," Jaks said, clutching his arm below the oozing shoulder wound. He'd be lucky if anything were remotely clean here, let alone approvable by a real healer.

"I'll find a bucket." Davey padded off to search the workshop.

"I'll look for some rags," Tim said, heading for stairs leading up to a second level of the building.

Jaks blinked away a tear at the boys' loyalty; the bond bought on the promise of heroism was shattered, but persevered now in friendship. An even more valuable attachment, given the help he needed.

His thoughts drifted back to Karisa. She had been so

close, just a glass pane away. He fought further tears at the memory of her face, beautiful even without her illusions, and of seeing her shackled by the neck like a common criminal. They had connected through the droid: she had recognized his signal and responded. So close.

He kicked his heel in frustration against the side of a nearby boat, rocking it on its supports. In this wounded state, he couldn't climb, couldn't fight effectively, and couldn't attempt any semblance of a rescue. But could he hide here until his shoulder was healed enough to try again?

The boys returned with water and rags, and despite their squeamishness, they helped Jaks clean his wound. Davey pried the skin edges apart while Tim tipped water from the bucket into the wound.

Stars circled Jaks as the pain ravaged his arm. With gritted teeth, he watched the bloodied water wash away. When it ran clear, he grunted for Tim to stop.

Tim handed him a ragged piece of sailing cloth he had found in an upstairs room and helped Jaks crudely wrap his shoulder. Hopefully, Meila's second zinger droid would arrive soon with her miracle bandage. The last one had saved his hand; if this one had similar effect, his shoulder would be healed in just a few weeks—or even just a few days. They could stay holed up here in the meantime and then make another attempt to rescue Karisa. He perked up at the thought and even forced a smile for Tim and Davey.

"Thanks, boys, you've been good to me. You're real heroes in my eyes," he said, eliciting a grin from both.

Remembering a sentinel function that had intrigued him during his previous explorations of the zinger's internal circuits, Jaks glided his hand over the droid's sleek fin and activated the pathway to *guard and watch*, centered above the bargehouse for any intruder larger than a mouse. The metal owl turned and flew back out the cracked upper window. It glowed green around the disc edge and would continue to do so as long as the perimeter remained "safe." It boggled his mind to think of how anyone, even Meila, could create something so incredible.

He frowned, remembering her comment from months ago, about her people following after her—that she was just the first of an entirely new colony. If they controlled such powerful artifacts, like this droid and the darkcore weapons, was this war just a roach fight before the victor was squashed by an invasion of invincible flying machines? He shook the thought out of mind. Regardless of the distant future, it didn't change his resolve or immediate goals. Life could not stop because of ifs and maybes.

Tim had chosen well. The old bargehouse was an ideal hideout. Jaks learned that, except to dry fish, it was long disused since two newer, larger bargehouses had been built further upriver. The only things left upstairs, where a couple of boat-repairers once dwelt, were damaged sails, dirty mattresses, mugs, rat traps, candles, matches, and a single laceless boot. Boys and girls from the street gang would occasionally visit to "borrow" dried fish and sometimes hide if chased from other thieving activities around the timberyard.

Jaks sat restlessly as he waited for the other droid that Meila had sent, imagining it flying across the plains at tremendous speed.

"I wonder if Hughie is okay," Davey said, as daylight dimmed outside, obviously worried about his older brother. "He was going to check out some of the travelers' inns today. Yesterday, he scavenged a bag of dried mushrooms and reckoned there could be more stuff around there. He was mad at me 'cause I kept coming to help you and said I wasn't doing my share."

Tim, the older boy, was asleep upstairs—the morning's escape had taxed him to exhaustion. So, it was up to Jaks to reassure the younger boy. He shot him a smile and ruffled his mop-like hair.

"Let's check on him, shall we? I'm sure he's okay," said Jaks. He flicked an electromantic instruction to the zinger, via the wrist device, and sent it skimming toward the gang's den, a mile and a half away through the evening sky, and angled the projection of the wrist-comm image for both of them to see.

The zinger arrived in less than a minute. If only he himself could fly like this, his quest would be over in minutes. He would fly into the palace window, grab his sister, then return to Dunberrin in hours . . . but all Jaks could do was sigh in envy of birds and dragons.

Outside the old mansion, he instructed the droid to circle and survey the building. It was oddly bereft of activity. He had expected some activity on the top floor at least; however, only one human-sized biological object inhabited the building. But staring at the gamma scan returning through the wrist comm, it looked like nothing he had seen before.

The droid zipped to the balcony doors at Jaks's command. Heart pounding, he realized the twin doors lay shattered and broken. He switched the scan to regular vision and activated its light beam. He wished he hadn't.

Davey gasped and whimpered beside him.

Transfixed by the zinger's image-feed display, Jaks felt his breath freeze in his throat.

The object was a streak of blood. A dark rivulet smeared the floor and ended at a pair of glowing red eyes. Rat eyes reflecting the light.

The vile creature was hunched on the chest of a body. It stared into the light for a moment, then leaped away and scurried into a dark corner. A dagger protruded from the body's neck. The slender neck of Hanna, the leader of the gang.

The zinger continued its survey of the room. Blankets torn from cots were strewn about. Shelves, once laden with the gang's loot and forage, lay askew with their contents scattered over the floor. Bloodied boot prints, too large for any of the youths, tracked out of the balcony doors. There had been a struggle here. Hanna hadn't gone out without a fight.

"They killed her." Davey sniffed and ran a sleeve across his face.

Jaks wrapped his arm around Davey and held him close. "Well, Hughie's not there. He might be alright." He couldn't be sure, though. The mess around the room looked far more than just one orphan's fight. "I'll search around for any sign of the others."

The droid circled widely for a couple of hours, gamma scanner penetrating buildings, searching for survivors. Disappointingly, Jaks could only conclude that the Vors had brutally combed out all the buildings in the palace's vicinity. No sign of Hughie, the street gang, or any free civilians whatsoever—only dead ones and a few dozen chained up in a warehouse by the docks.

It was true, what Meila had said. Around the palace, troops garrisoned every building, inside, outside, and on rooftops. Guards manned nascent barricades blocking the streets, and several neighboring buildings were being pulled down for materials—it appeared that gravmancers were even better at demolition than construction. Anything to separate this fortified area from intruders. They might even dig a ditch and flood it for a moat, Jaks mused. The Vor king had reacted strongly to discovering a spy so close to his residence. The chances of rescuing Karisa were bleak.

One last sweep of the palace took the zinger back to the courtyard, even though it was dark now. He had to know.

Again, the droid hovered outside the curtained room that was Karisa's prison and revealed the inhabitants of the room, but only the buxom slave woman from that morning was present.

As he squinted at the wrist comm, about to instruct the droid to scan the rest of the palace for Karisa, the image feed spun wildly and then blacked out.

A few seconds later, the image returned, revealing a sleek head and talons raking the zinger's sensors.

"Damn. A dragon attacked the zinger," Jaks said to Davey, but the boy, distraught after seeing his gang leader dead and left to the rats, was curled at his feet on a thin mattress and sucking his thumb, eyes closed.

The wrist-comm image flashed a red light and strange letters appeared. And then, just as he was fearing the droid had been destroyed, the images revealed the zinger speeding upward, faster than any dragon could fly, directly toward the night sky—as though escaping into the stars.

A minute later, he sighed with relief as the droid continued skyward without further attack. As it pivoted its sensors down to the city, streetlamps and firepits appeared as tiny dots far below.

But relief turned to disappointment as he realized

the zinger couldn't be risked near the palace anymore. He instructed the droid to return to him and resume guarding the bargehouse.

Turning away from the wrist comm, Jaks squinted into the dark interior of the building. He should go find a candle upstairs, he thought. Instead, however, he stayed seated on the steps. Succumbing to fatigue, he nodded off beside the younger boy.

A buzzing noise woke Jaks from a nightmare of his father's giant hand looming toward him through the dark. Eyes flicking open, sweat soaking his garments, he found the sky outside the window as dark as midnight.

In the few seconds it took him to shake off the specter of his father and orient to the shadows of the bargehouse, his wrist comm buzzed again and flashed red.

Sentry warning.

He activated the image feed from the zinger and smiled as the pictures highlighted an incoming droid similar to the first. It could only be Meila's delivery. If it was midnight, as he was guessing, this delivery had taken thrice as long to get here as her estimate.

A few seconds later, the delivery droid flew in through the cracked window. It was encumbered with a bulky package, making it look like a flying ball of string. No wonder it had taken so long to fly here.

He cut and pried the bindings away from the droid to reveal one of Meila's medigel dressings half-stuffed into a cavity in its underside. A few green pain-dulling pills accompanied it within a stoppered vial. He popped one into his mouth and welcomed the immediate dismissal of pain and the sense of invulnerability that followed.

Davey sat up on the mattress beside him, rubbing his eyes.

Feeling guilty that he'd woken the boy, Jaks nevertheless enlisted his help to peel the medigel from its protective wrapper. Then held against his shoulder, it clamped over the wound like a limpet. A wrap of bandage and it was secure. He thanked Davey and patted him fondly on the head.

The next morning, Tim received the news of their gang headquarters' discovery by the Vors and Hanna's murder with difficulty. He blinked rapidly for several seconds, then, with veins thick in his neck, stormed out into the timberyard. On his return, although his eyes were red, he seemed otherwise back to his usual self and toted a sack of loot that he had scavenged from nearby shacks. He then disappeared upstairs to sort his find.

For the next two days, they stayed in the bargehouse, pondering their next steps. Should they remain in Irin hoping for another opportunity to rescue Karisa, or stay to spy on the enemy army, or flee this wasps' nest and return to Ascorian lines?

As Jaks monitored the timberyard and city around

them with the zinger droids, Davey and Tim wandered the timberyard, looking for supplies abandoned by workers to fill out their rations beyond just dried fish.

Jaks, however, only traveled outdoors in those days through the eyes of the zinger droids; his electromantic connection with them became second nature. He flicked between both devices, sent them instructions, and received image feeds with minimal conscious thought.

Although directly receiving droid images into his mind gave him the most clarity—as though he were the droid himself—he dared not fall into the trance the electromantic connection required. Instead, the wrist-comm projection sufficed. Projected against the wall gave the best view; otherwise, the image hovered in midair—great for depth, but poor for detail.

An endless influx of Vor warriors and beasts of war trickled into the city from the south. The many thousands repaired damaged buildings and moved in as though to settle for a long while. Beautiful mansions and estates became military outposts, market squares transformed into distribution centers, and gardens and fields were stomped over as practice grounds.

And as more Vors arrived and space within the city diminished, incoming torgues moved into buildings closer and closer to the abandoned timberyard. Within a few days, they would surely move into the site itself, and Jaks and the boys would need to find a new hiding spot.

Other than to spy on the enemy—though valuable in itself, feeding information to Meila and King Silas's advisors—the next days did little to aid Jaks's personal quest. Indeed, the longer he spied on the Vors, the more he realized how impossible it was to reach Karisa.

Stubbornly, he lingered in the captured city despite Meila's forceful pleas to leave while he still could. Eventually, they devolved into angry commands.

And in the end, she was right, as usual.

On the third morning in the timberyard, Jaks startled awake as his wrist comm vibrated and constricted his wrist. Immediately, he identified the electromantic alarm of the droid he had renamed "Slasher"—marked by the scratch on its side from the dragon attack—signaling down from its patrol circuit two miles above the bargehouse.

The disc flashed red, but before he had time to project Slasher's image feed, a series of coarse voices yelled to one another outside the building's river door. From the number of verbal exchanges, it sounded like a large ship coursing along the river. However, bending his neck to gaze under the rotted wooden barricade, the closest ship was moored a half mile distant.

Frowning, he returned to his wrist comm and flicked on the image feed. The bird's-eye view clearly showed the bargehouse—familiar from days of examining the city from above—and the timberyard as still as always. But there in the river was a small ship, crewed with warriors.

Impossible. Nothing had been there a few seconds ago.

Davey came running down the stairs, his hair crumpled where he must have been lying on it, calling Jaks's name in a panicked voice and rubbing one eye at the same time. "Ship . . . ship, there's a ship in the sky!" He pointed toward the cracked-glass window above them.

"It can't be—" Compelled by the waif's fear, Jaks arced his neck up to stare and gape as the prow of a gray-colored mass edged into view several yards above the building.

More shouting sounded through the window, and he caught a glimpse of a wide-browed woman leaning over the side of what he could only describe as a "skyship." She pulled on a rope until a metal pulley clanged against the side of the vessel and looped it several times around a mooring bit.

The ship continued to pass over the bargehouse, a wooden hulk with patches of red and many more ropes dangling off the side.

Hairs on the back of Jaks's neck rose. He felt tiny under the massive object, fearing that at any moment it would fall out of the sky and crush their bargehouse.

Seconds later, Tim leaped down the stairs, three steps at a time. "Do you see it? Are my eyes playing tricks on me?" His voice trailed off as he followed the gaze of his two friends and confirmed the reality of their shared vision.

"It *is* flying," Jaks reported as he examined the pictures from his wrist comm. The vessel resembled the timber barge in the workshop behind him that he had slept in over the past days. Rectangular and flat-hulled, it was built to carry heavy loads, but more than that, this magical object—for it had to be magic to fly—was three times larger, bore a couple of small sails, and brimmed with warriors and weapons. Scorpion bolt-throwers, crossbows, spears, and crates of square blocks with no obvious purpose.

The fore-and-aft sails seemed too small to guide the giant ship, but when Jaks magnified the droid's sensors onto the deck, he suspected that its actual propelling force came in the hands of four people seated beside large sourcestones at the corners of the ship. Indeed, when the ship changed course and glided downward, a communication seemed to transpire between these navigators that only finished when the warship settled on a central lumberyard a few hundred yards from the bargehouse.

"Alright, that's it. We've got to get out of here," Jaks said to the boys and looked around the building for an escape route.

"We could go back to the sewers?" Davey suggested.

"No, you rat-brain. That ship is between us and the entrance." Tim screwed up his face, then turned his back as though looking through the walls.

"Are there no other ways to the sewers?" Jaks asked.

"Sure, there are, but we'd have to hunt around for them. I only know the big one because that's the only one I've ever needed."

"They're too close for us to sneak out and start searching around . . . I've got another idea." Already, Jaks thought he could hear the coarse shouts of the crew getting nearer to their hideout. Glancing down to his wrist comm, his pulse quickened as the overhead view revealed warriors spreading out from the skyship to enter nearby buildings.

Davey spluttered another suggestion. "I could run out and get them to chase me through the yard while you and Tim sneak to the sewer entrance? I know the place real well and they'd never catch me." The boy held up his head, lip trembling but bearing an otherwise courageous face.

"Brave, but unnecessary, Davey." Jaks patted the smaller boy's shoulder. "No. There's a better option." He nodded toward one of the rowboats moored just inside the river gate. Missing a rudder, oarlocks, and thwarts, the thing was nothing but the husk of a boat.

"That wreck? It's so bare, it doesn't even have anywhere to sit."

"We're not going to sit. Quick, go upstairs and bring down those old sails. Davey, you help me open this river gate."

A couple of minutes later, they had cranked the wooden gate up a yard, and Tim had dragged down a tattered sail.

"Grab some food and we're out of here." A glance at his wrist comm showed warriors at the building next door. "Forget it. No time. Get in the boat. I'll cover us and push us out."

He threw the rotted sail cloth and a bargepole onto the rowboat and beckoned for the boys to climb down; the old boat rocked wildly as they clambered in one after the other. "Tim, untie us. I can't do it with one arm."

Once the boat drifted free from the mooring, he needed Tim's help again, this time to maneuver the bargepole and push them out into the river while half-covered by the sailcloth. As they slid under the partially raised river gate, a light breeze swept over them. Feeling exposed, Jaks hastily pulled in the pole and then tucked the cover over them, hoping their rowboat looked uninteresting and abandoned.

Holding his breath, he listened for the outcry of anyone who might have spotted them. Daring to slip into an electromantic trance, he accessed Slasher's sensors. Back on shore, there were no efforts to chase them, nor any sign that the warriors had even seen the rowboat.

But on the other side of the river, something else seized his attention.

Several more skyships skimmed the buildings of the south city, gliding toward the river. Swarms of dragons accompanied the flying ships; some perched on the railings, while others flew in a multitudinous cloud of red, bronze, and silver.

Not just the one skyship, but an entire flotilla.

The odds against Jaks's countryfolk seemed abysmal. The gargantors dominating the ground war were bad enough. But they had nothing to match these marvels of the sky.

Something jabbed him in the chest, and he snapped back into his full body senses.

"Wake up." Davey poked him again in the chest. His worried face then softened as Jaks's eyes regained focus. "You looked like what you did in the attic."

"It's not good, boys. But we got away just in time. There were lots more ships on their way." He grimaced at the two pairs of eyes looking back at him under the sailcloth.

"The princess . . . we're not going to rescue her?" Davey whispered over Tim's head.

"Sorry, Davey. We can't. It's impossible. Our opportunity, if we ever actually had one, is truly lost. I think we were lucky to have remained hidden for as long as we did." Jaks sighed as the river sloshed their boat downstream and beyond the city's borders. "No. There's no way we can get back without getting caught. We're going to Dunberrin."

"Dunberrin? Never been there." Davey paused for a moment, then added, "Maybe me and Tim can find a new gang there."

But Jaks was already lost in thought and didn't reply. Did he regret entering Irin on a quest that, in hindsight, was a disaster? No, he had to attempt that rescue, for Karisa's sake. The regret would've been if he had not tried at all. Should he damn himself for failing? He snorted. He had tried his best but had been a fool to think he could rely on his wits and a magic so volatile that he still feared it like a tempest inside of him.

Yes, he had been wholly unprepared, but his only regret was not having the grandmaster's training. Strangely, he felt more focused now than ever before: he needed to master this electromancy; he needed to return to Mulgrave—and Meila. Although it was a curse and a gift, he was determined to tame it, especially now that he saw a use for it beyond just lightning bolts and destruction.

He grimaced as his thoughts returned to Karisa. *Sorry, Karisa. I'll come back when we win this war.*

Chapter 9

The Engineer

Meila—The Academy of the Arcane, Ascoria

Meila Tahn ran her thumb over the runestone of her welding torch and blinked as a thin, white flame shrieked from its nozzle. Sweat beaded her brow as she flipped down her welding mask and crouched behind the steel frame of her latest build. Although she hid any outward excitement at Jaks's imminent arrival—following his escape from the City of Irin three weeks ago—she welcomed the distraction of uniting steel to steel to calm her anticipation. Bemused by a childlike giddiness, she attributed the feeling to relief at finally being able to trial the velocannon using the young man's electromancer powers. If it worked, it could destroy thousands of Vors in an instant; if it failed, the Ascorians would remain greatly outnumbered.

The runic furnace, at the center of the square courtyard, roared at her back. *Hell, it was hot here . . . and noisy.* The only reprieve was a constant cool breeze blowing in through the ocean gate and out through the main gates leading to the land bridge and the main city. With the slightest of thoughts, her auditory implants selectively dampened out the sound of dozens of other magesmiths and their assistants hammering and welding. She sighed with relief, wondering why she hadn't thought to muffle the sound earlier.

High above, the underside of the bronze dome of the building curved around the furnace's chimney like the hand guard of a thrusting sword. Sparrows and other small birds flitted about and nested in the corners of the high ceiling.

Built over six centuries ago, when the city outside was burgeoning as a shipping hub, the Academy was an imposing castle. Besieged several times, it had fallen only once when Duke Dunberrin's griefmasters gravleapt onto the walls from assaulting ships. The victor had renamed the locality after himself, built a gravity-defying palace on the peninsula nearby, and was then invaded by the Ascorians a day before the last blocks were about to be laid. Out of respect for the overwhelmed Duke's valiant attempts to lay the last stone before he died, the Ascorian king allowed the city name to remain unchanged. Now, the castle was The Academy of the Arcane—the kingdom's center of magical studies and the forging of sorcerous weapons and devices—and the palace housed the Ascorian throne.

Focusing now, Meila returned to her task. Other

than her protective visor, she wore little more than a leather apron over her sleeveless top, shorts, and boots—similar to the men assisting her: Grandmaster Mulgrave and Apprentice Tavis. Anything more and it would have been intolerable working so close to the two-thousand-degree heat source for so long.

She nodded to the apprentice, trusting him to gravmance the heavy steel tube into place while the older man steadied the base.

"Righto. It'll just take a minute." Unlike the plasma-welders she had supervised during her spacecraft-manufacturing days, this dual-runestone device amalgamated fire magic and grav magic into a supra-heated torch as efficient as any welder she had seen. That it was being used to create an even cleverer device of her own design, a gravfire mortar, brought a smile to her face.

Meila the engineer, once was, was again. It had been over forty years since she had designed and built anything lasting. Too long . . . the pleasure of creating. Why had she ever abandoned her engineering career? Invention had been in her essence since the engineers' playground of the UWF orbital factories where she had begun her working life. There, she had refined quaternary engines and stardrives until her promotions peaked with designing fighter-craft and atmospheric flyers. But for a born "engine head," it was the decades of building starships that had sparked her desire to fly the damned things.

It had seemed natural back then to submit to the implant modifications, flight school, and years of scraping her way up the UWF hierarchy in pursuit of snagging her own command. Although her lack of aggression kept her from a Juggernaut, or any of the other coveted military helms, they had never been her goal. Instead, a tiny science vessel, like the *Mendhelsson,* had been ideal for her.

And although she still grieved the destruction of her ship, the past few months of engineering devices for the Ascorians had revived a childlike thrill of design and construction. These war machines were not the sophisticated starships she had once built, but magic certainly led to innovative designs under the guidance of crafty magesmiths like Grandmasters Mulgrave and Hazeldine.

Several minutes later, she set down the welder, lifted her visor, and signaled for the mages to stand aside. As the metal cooled from yellow to gray, her eyes traced over the completed weapon.

Her visual implant calculated each exterior angle of the weapon. The measurements didn't need to be exact, but she would have judged herself harshly if the tolerances deviated by more than a quarter of a percent from her blueprint. Finally, she grunted and nodded to herself. Almost perfect.

In twenty-four hours' time, after it had cooled and then passed her second inspection, the weapon would be ready for battle—its embedded runestones channeling compressed air through a variable-angle tube to lob incendiary bombs onto enemies up to two miles away. A powerful weapon, of which they had built ten after experimenting with different-sized prototypes.

"That's the last of them, lass," Mulgrave said. He still spoke to her like she was a girl. Of course, it didn't help that she looked half his age. She couldn't help but smile back at the mage, withholding a chastisement over his error, unable to rebuke a man who resembled her great-grandfather's age: five centuries old.

"When Jaks gets here, we should trial the prototype," she said.

Tavis shook his head. "Not that again. It doesn't work. We're wasting our time on that thing. Jaks doesn't know smithing; he can't do anything that we can't."

A week ago, Mulgrave's big-eared apprentice had staggered into the Academy one midwinter's eve. Unkempt and stinking from his journey, having left the Jurns behind in Irin, he spoke little of his travel except to mention accompanying one of the many convoys bringing stores of food and grain back to the capital. Of the recovery from his head wound, he also made light explanation. But to Meila's surprise, when the grandmaster asked after Jaks, instead of the dismissive reply that she'd expected, Tavis slumped and made a sincere confession to the old mage. He begged forgiveness for the antipathy and maliciousness he had subjected Jaks to in the past. What had triggered this change of heart, she didn't know, but she appreciated that he was less prickly and snarky than before.

Ever graceful, the grandmaster had granted his apprentice the forgiveness he pleaded. And since then, the two had returned to master-and-apprentice; together, the three of them were a constructive force spitting out weapons and inventions at a pace second to no other Academy workshop.

As such, Tavis's turnaround against her velocannon, and dig at Jaks, surprised her. Perhaps Jaks's imminent arrival had rekindled the apprentice's fears of being usurped. "Sure, Jaks doesn't know the workshop or forge as well as any of us," Meila replied, "but it isn't his knowledge that we need . . . it's his electromancy. You only saw the velocannon when I tried to energize it with the sheet-metal capacitors. They weren't anywhere near powerful enough. But I've seen what Jaks's electromancy can do and I think he can easily generate enough voltage to make it work."

Mulgrave interrupted as Tavis stared at the floor moodily. "She knows what she's talking about, lad. Why don't you go assist Master Doeg and Shazair this afternoon while she and I meet with the Lord Defender? It doesn't need all three of us to discuss the best locations for these mortars and organize training for the crews."

"Sorry, master. You know best." The junior mage bowed and shuffled off after draping his leather apron over a nearby bench.

"Let's clean up before visiting his lordship. Meet me in the library in a half hour," Mulgrave said, as he arched and pressed his hands against his back.

Waylaid, as he often was, it was two hours later that the bald magesmith appeared again. Shaking his head, he jabbered some excuse involving Grandmaster Hazeldine and her "flying-ship folly."

"Ever since those images of the Vors' skyships came back, she's been obsessed with getting her version to work. I've told her we don't have large sourcestones to spare, like what those blue-stained barbarians have. But that stubborn mule is going to use Doeg and Shazair's sourcestone packs instead," Mulgrave said. "They're still quite unstable."

Meila nodded. "I did offer, months ago, to help her out. Maybe I could have a look at her plans later on. I've a lot of experience in engineering systems to compensate for poly-drive concepts. Math can solve a lot of things."

Mulgrave stared at her for a few moments before his brow unfurrowed and he laughed. "If only I could steal your brain for my own."

"Your brain is fine. It's my memory implants you want. Come on, the lordman awaits." Returning his laugh, she took his proffered arm, and they exited the library into the main corridor.

As they crossed the land-bridge from the Academy to the city, dodging horse-led wagons clattering under loads of coal and timber, Meila gasped as a tall, bearded man lunged into their path.

Mulgrave reflexively thrust a hand in front of Meila, but she pushed past and cried out, "Jaks!" Although his face was weathered and his clothes disheveled, she knew the figure was him. She grabbed his wrists. Cold to touch and thicker than she remembered.

He looked a decade older than last time she had seen him in the flesh. She plied her memory for anything that had happened over the past weeks that could account for his appearance.

After Jaks and his two new wards had fled Irin by boat, they drifted until nightfall, then poled their vessel to the river's edge and continued their escape on foot. Through vales and copses of trees, the zinger droid had traced a path that evaded the episodic Vor patrols. And after two days of sneaking north through wine country, surviving off charred rabbits that Jaks would zap, and sleeping in abandoned vineyards, they finally left the Vors behind.

Once in this neutral zone, Meila and Mulgrave had cajoled the sullen Cromer—in Dunberrin, training ranger apprentices—to order a ranger patrol to bring the three escapees into safety. The wiry hunter had no love for Jaks. Pity and anger, yes, and at least enough loyalty to Vixhana to have stirred him into arranging a signal transmission to the frontline.

From there, rangers had found and escorted Jaks and the boys back to the border of Dunberrin and King

Silas's encampment: a little village transformed into a defensive line between two mountain ranges. Comprised of a hastily built fortress and two miles of wall, it was the last barrier between the invaders and the Ascorian capital.

Tim and Davey had been reunited at the border camp with Hughie, the latter's older brother. The older boy had escaped the raid on their gang's hideout. Hanna, sacrificing her life for her gang, had slowed the Vors long enough for Hughie and a few others to fleet-foot to the sewers and eventually to safety. Jaks had insisted the boys rejoin their friends, who had been repurposed from their light-fingered work to running errands for soldiers in exchange for food and shelter. He had departed for Dunberrin days later, sad at losing Tim and Davey's cheerful banter but also relieved at not having to worry about two dependents.

"You look terrible," Meila said, releasing his wrists and restraining an impulse to stroke his cheek. "You look like a Vor. That beard, I'm surprised no one has tried to cut it off you . . . head attached."

The intense look didn't shift from his face. Instead, he took her shoulders and tipped his head down to her face. This time, she didn't resist. Couldn't resist. The hunger in his eyes was unstoppable. Their lips met with such electricity, she feared his magic had stirred. But it wasn't electromancy—it was passion that flowed from his lips to hers.

"Enough, enough," Mulgrave's voice clamored

behind them, a few seconds later. "Every carter and his horse is staring."

Opening her eyes, she pushed away from Jaks, and her breath steamed between them in the cold, still air. His eyes still pursued her. She stiffened her back and shook her head. "What's got into you?" she said, then laughed lightly. "That was some greeting. Come on, let's get off this bridge before we get run over."

She pulled him to the end of the bridge and found a space on the busy wharf. In the distance, a coal freighter groaned against the dock and poured dark nuggets down an iron chute into a bin. Dockworkers, blackened with dust, shouldered shovels up and down, as they transferred the load to awaiting carts. Closer, though, a merchant eyed Meila from the prowl of his ship as his crew rolled empty barrels up a gangplank.

Ignoring the stare and the activity behind them, she turned to embrace Jaks briefly, then inquired after his shoulder, hand, and legs, frowning as he responded. She then palpated his arms and chest to assess his health.

"He's fine. Stop acting like an old ma'am," the grandmaster said, shaking his head imperceptibly.

Her face turned hot, and she stared up into the air.

Stealing the opportunity, Mulgrave interrogated Jaks. "Any news from the highway? Anything of the thaw?" he asked.

"A ranger with my caravan thought the chill will stay awhile yet. He said he'd been in the mountains a week before and the iron mines were laden with snow, and the ice dragons were bolder than ever—a sure sign of a long winter, he reckoned."

"The weather could side with us, then. Let's hope for at least another month before the Vors shake off their winter crust." The grandmaster then smiled, as though he had just remembered who he was talking to. "It's good to see you, lad."

"And you, Grandmaster." Unkempt, sour-smelling, Jaks clasped the mage's extended hand.

Mulgrave then nodded to the avenue of workshops leading toward the inner city. The ringing of iron on anvil sang throughout the district. "Come. We're going to visit the City Lord Defender. We need to discuss training up crews for a new weapon we've invented, as well as other matters to discuss. You look like a felon and stink like a beggar's blanket, but you should attend all the same." He exchanged a glance with Meila.

"Lord Defender? I've not heard that title before," Jaks said.

"One of King Silas's most trusted generals. The king designated his lordship to review and tighten the capital's defenses. But most significantly, the Lord Defender was tasked with raising mercenaries from the Pact countries. Indeed, he has been quite successful in his negotiations with the embassies, and apparently, a few legions are already on the march as we speak." Mulgrave paused and shifted from foot to foot as though weighing his next words. "You've met him before, his lordship."

"Lord Castias? Welsford? I don't know that many lords personally. That was . . . my father's thing. He rarely took me to functions and usually sent me away when he held them at our estate." Jaks lowered his gaze as his voice trailed off.

"Yes. It was your father's thing." The grandmaster placed a meaty hand on Jaks's shoulder. "The king's delegate *is* your father. He's asked for you to attend him personally on your return."

Chapter 10

City Lord Defender

Jaks—The City of Dunberrin, Ascoria

Jaks sagged under the mage's hand. Lord Sicaro Rauhalik, City Lord Defender, and the dark hand of his nightmares. Here in Dunberrin. Tiny claws scratched at the sealed door in his mind, tearing at the edges, threatening to release the terror it hid.

"Are you alright, lad?" Mulgrave asked as he gripped Jaks's arms.

"It can't be so. My father?" Jaks reached for a dock post and slumped against it. "He was down south when the Vors landed. They started with his province and castle. I thought he was dead." Or so he had hoped since first learning of the invasion. Never voiced, but strongly wanted.

"As alive as can be."

"He should be dead—"

"It is said he escaped wounded with a handful of his garrison. Lost an eye to the cause. You do know he was one of the king's staunchest supporters during the Unifying Wars. He's been here since the fall of Irin," Mulgrave replied. "Done an excellent job scaling up the industrial district's production and bolstering the city's defenses. We've had little to do with him so far, but with the gravfire mortars completed, we need him to give us soldiers to crew them."

"I can't go. I can't see him—not now."

A gentle hand took his and Meila crouched into his view. "I know it's a lot to take in. It'll be okay."

"You know what he did. What he's done. I told you about him."

Taking both of his hands this time, she drew closer and locked his gaze. "He's highly stationed now, the king's man. Has done a lot for the city. People can change. Maybe he regrets his past?" She took a breath. "He seeks you out. Perhaps he wants to make peace with you?"

He glared at her as though her words dripped with poison. How could she side with him? Make peace with the man who beat his mother to death in front of his eyes?

"You don't know what you're asking," he said, and yanked his hands away from her.

Meila's face furrowed in worry. "Sorry, Jaks. If it's just going to churn up bad memories, don't come."

Jaks gritted his teeth and muscles corded his neck as he girded himself against the storm of anger and confusion inside. Maybe he should see the monster?

Publicly expose the past, demand he admit his crime and face the executioner's blade? No, it would be futile. He had no proof. His father wouldn't admit a thing.

However, the least Jaks could do was confront him and show that he was not afraid of him any longer. The past months proved he could be courageous: fear no longer defined him.

He made a decision. "I'll come." Jaks flipped a nod and stood. Not because his father requested it but to prove to himself—"I'm not scared of him."

The City Lord Defender held court on a floating fortress moored in the naval yards. Accessible only through the Army District and down a lengthy pier, it was gated and guarded as though protecting the king himself. The giant ship, bedecked in painted carvings of sea sylphs and tritons, bristled with guards.

Around midafternoon, Jaks followed the grandmaster and Meila up the ship ramp, wishing he hadn't come. He was flustered from the last checkpoint, where the guards had removed his sword and dagger and left him with only his coin purse and the zinger droid—a harmless bauble to them—treating them like criminals being brought before a magistrate. They forced even the grandmaster to spreadeagle like a common thief.

A man sneered down on them from the floating fortress and motioned for them to walk up the gangplank onto the ship. Onboard, yet another contingent of guards awaited. A gesture from the man allowed them to pass without challenge.

"Grandmaster, apologies for the inconveniences," said the man, hands concealed beneath his cloak, and the sneer unshifted from his face. "One can never tell from appearances alone, with illumancers and disguises all about."

He looked familiar to Jaks. Similar of age to Ranger Cromer and cast from the same craggy mold, the man triggered some memory from the past.

"Understandable," Mulgrave replied, his face unreadable.

"I am Lord Sicaro's humble servant, Master Kyle Halwoth. His lordship has been waiting." He pivoted and walked to a tower below the quarterdeck of the ship.

Halwoth. Of course. One of his father's veteran retainers. Often slinking after his father and staring at the children, licking his crooked lips. However, it was by a different name that he recalled him—Sneer.

They entered the ship's tower, passing beneath a doorway carved with cavorting sylphs and mermen.

The door closed behind and Jaks's eyes struggled with speckled beams of red and green within. As his eyes adjusted, and he dismissed the kaleidoscope projecting from the colored-glass bricks along the outer walls, a chamber unraveled before him, and he discovered it partitioned by shadows and curtains.

Several guards he mistook as statues, until one

turned his head, dotted the vast room and at its center stood a giant of a man.

Sneer tiptoed to whisper in the man's ear and then swept a hand at the awaiting trio before retreating into the shadows.

"Mage, how many years . . . was it at the scorching of Trillian Castle?" the giant boomed.

"No, my lord, I was not at Trill when it fell. Master Iver, perhaps?"

Behind the grandmaster, Jaks couldn't move—his limbs rigid, then trembling, as a thieving darkness rose. His father's voice alone, enough to seize him with panic. Frozen in place, he could only listen, even though his core screamed to run and hide.

Lord Sicaro laughed. "Of course . . . it couldn't have been you. That one died inside the castle with the rest of the traitors."

Mulgrave tensed but continued. "Three years past? Our king's jubilee. His highness shared his table with us. We sat left and right, if you recall. The day his highness named you Castellan at Sanford, I believe."

"So, it was. Well-remembered, Grandmaster." Sicaro stepped into the light. A patch tied with a string covered his left eye, but nothing else had changed. Black hair and beard bordered features that would have befitted a bear as much as a man. Penetrating eyes lifted over the mage's head and fell on Jaks.

To his astonishment, the Lord Defender surged forward, nudging Mulgrave and Meila aside. His hands gripped the sides of Jaks's head as he studied his middle child. "Who is this? My son? Mirror of my image. The beard makes a man of you."

Locked into the bear's grip, fearing the hands would crush his skull, he gaped at his father wordlessly. Skeletal flashes, like hands clawing out of a grave, tore through the door of his memory and unleashed a flood. Jaks's eyes glazed over as the past rushed back—

He trembles, brandishing a knife at his father. On the hallway floor beside him, mother shields her bruised face. She scrambles for the stairs. His father bats the knife out of his hand and shoves him aside. She descends the stairs on the threshold of escape, but the giant snatches after her. He must be stopped. In an instant, a snap of light and a thunderclap splits the air: lightning sparks from his hands and strikes his father and his mother—their bodies spasm and tumble. Her head strikes a step, then another. Hard. She slides to the bottom of the stairs, neck at an unnatural angle.

"Shocked to see your own father?" His father laughed, releasing him and disrupting the deluge of memories. His one eye then fixed on Jaks's crippled hand. "Seems we have much to catch up on."

Finding his voice, Jaks whispered, "I killed her—"

"What's that? Speak up."

"I killed her," he murmured.

"Master Halwoth, bring my son a drink. He sounds parched. Traveled far today. Bring him a stool to sit."

The grandmaster coughed. "Yes, apologies, my lord.

He arrived just this hour. I should have sent him to rest and present himself later."

Sneer led him to a three-legged stool. Behind it, a man with twin daggers at his waist slipped further into the shadows, but not before Jaks glimpsed rings of tattooed ink around his neck. Surrounded by his father's men and reeling from the flashback, sweat beaded his face, and fear—he had thought conquered—gripped him hostage.

Had he remembered true? Doubt seized him. Who was the monster here? His father or himself?

Unheeding of Jaks's turmoil, his father returned to the center of the room and looked at Mulgrave and Meila.

"So, this is the so-important prisoner I've been hearing about." Sicaro traced his gaze over her. She crossed her arms in response. "Silas is beguiled by her, it seems. But what is to stop her from escaping?"

"Ward. Not a prisoner. She is promised her freedom in exchange for passing her knowledge to the Academy," said Mulgrave. "As to her running away—"

"I have nowhere to run to," interrupted Meila. "You may have heard that I have no way of returning to my home."

"Indeed, the king himself believes you're cast here from another dimension," replied Sicaro.

"Planet. But for all purposes, it may as well be another dimension, as I cannot travel to either."

"Remarkable. Perhaps you would stay and tell me

more of this 'planet' after we finish our business today? Master Halwoth would return you to the Academy this evening."

Meila's face creased, and she firmed her lips, but she was saved by the grandmaster.

"A shame, my lord. I cannot spare my ward today," Mulgrave said. "Even now, Grandmaster Hazeldine awaits her otherworldly knowledge to assist vital calculations in constructing a skyship. A most critical counter to the Vors' own—if we can master its flight."

Darkness clouded the Lord Defender's expression fleetingly. "Another time . . . let us tend to your petition then, mage."

Their discussion faded from Jaks's ears as the grandmaster and his father retreated to an oak table recessed in an alcove. Meila dragged her feet after them until only her back was visible to him. Left alone to his thoughts, even the lurker behind him fell from his consciousness.

He bent forward and stared at the floor.

How that memory had shuttered itself away for these past years, he could only guess. It was that day when he had faced his father with Vixhana and Karisa at their family estate, that his shield of self-delusion had begun to peel away. At the bottom of the very stairs she had died on. And it was today, when his father had held his head as though to crush it, that it had collapsed.

It was guilt he had barricaded himself against, deceiving himself into blaming his father for the murder to cover his own guilt. His rampant imagination was an escape, a guardian against horrors that threatened to drive him insane. Perhaps this was how he dealt with secret pain. What other memories had he lied to himself over? Bolted doors to secrets he hid from himself. Too painful to open.

The stairs. It was an accident.

Electromancy, maybe the first time ever, had risen in the panic to save her—but had instead killed her, just as it had injured Vixhana. Twice now to his family. Would there be another? Would he end up killing Karisa? Or was he destined to kill his father? Weren't these things fated to occur in threes? He needed to escape the situation. Leave the city.

No, not again.

He had descended this spiral once before after he injured Vixhana. He'd fled responsibility for months. No, it couldn't happen again; guilt and self-blame wouldn't smother duty again. He would not flee. He had debts to pay. Still had to rescue Karisa.

His father's muffled voice crept into his ears. "Ale?"

Jaks's eyes rose, and he flinched from the bear of a man standing in front of him, holding a mug in each hand.

"Ale?" his father repeated. Perhaps misinterpreting Jaks's horrified look as puzzlement, he continued. "I sent them off. The mage and the girl. Give an old man time with his son."

Indeed, the grandmaster and Meila were

silhouetted against the reddening sky at the door and then vanished as it closed behind them. How could they have abandoned him?

"My thanks, my lord," Jaks said, accepting the drink as though the head of froth might turn into acid.

His father gestured, and a guard brought him a chair. He sat and drained his mug, his one eye never leaving Jaks.

Jaks sipped the ale, then realizing how thirsty he was, downed the remaining liquid with one long draw. A small boy appeared and hastily removed both of the empty mugs, bowing as he disappeared back into the shadows.

"I brought you up the way my father raised me. And his before that," said his father. "The rod and the fist are the best teachers. Your warriors will only respect you if they know you can beat them down at any time."

Jaks stared, not finding words to respond. The realization that he himself had caused his mother's death made his father's beatings and abuses seem almost trivial.

"You're the same as me. We've both done what others call evil." His father pulled his chair closer. Jaks resisted the urge to lean away. "I covered for you . . . when you killed her. Using magic to kill your own mother—it would have been a witch trial."

Jaks kicked the stool back and stood. "I didn't mean to. Didn't want to hurt her. I was trying to . . ." He could hear his voice rising, but couldn't finish his sentence.

"Sit down, boy." Lord Sicaro nodded, and a firm hand from behind guided Jaks back to his uprighted stool. "Your sister, too. I hear you killed her, too. That oversized bitch."

"I didn't kill her . . ." Jaks replied in a voice barely a whisper. Indeed, Vixhana was still alive; he had sent a droid a week ago to check. Although he had seen her only for a short time through the zinger's owl-like sensors, he had shouted with joy at finding her conscious and hobbling around the Jurn village on crutches. However, to tell his father that would not remove the fact that he had nearly killed her.

"It seems this power of yours is a rare one, my sources say." Sicaro loomed over Jaks, who sat on the stool like an obedient schoolchild. "Perhaps it's time you did something useful with it."

"I was apprenticed to Grandmaster Mulgrave before—I think he will have me back. Then I'll be able to learn the magic properly."

"Nonsense. I heard about how you broke the barricade at Irin. Defeated a gravmancer and then a firemage. Summoned lightning to decimate a formation of warriors." His father raised a finger and Halwoth the Sneer materialized to receive a private instruction. The henchman then departed, and his father continued. "You don't need further tuition. You need a role that befits your ability. And a mentor who will grow your power, not stifle you in some forge, turning you into a smith."

"Ever seen a gargantor, son?" Sicaro asked abruptly, his gaze drilling down into Jaks's.

Without waiting for an answer, he continued, "Monsters! Big as a house, with claws and tusks like sabers, and the head of a tiger with teeth like daggers. The things can leap as high as they are tall. Few places they can't get to. We fought one in the Unifying War when the Heran rebels brought it over from Voros. Routed an entire regiment before it could be brought down with ballistae and fire." His father's eyes gleamed with almost worshipful intensity.

Jaks nodded, wondering how the topic had changed so quickly.

"Born killers. Like you." His father leaned forward in his chair. Jaks leaned back, intimidated by the huge presence. "When gargantor pups are ready to be whelped, they don't wait for the mother to push them out. They tear at the birthing sac and claw their way out. The mother falls into throes of agony as her newborns rip up her insides. She eventually collapses from the savaging and the pups tear their way out and take their first feed off their mother's corpse."

Jaks felt sick. "I'm no gargantor. I didn't tear her apart."

"Alas, you are a born killer, boy," his father persisted. "Born with the power to kill anything in your way."

"I don't enjoy killing people," Jaks began, but then stopped as he remembered the exhilaration he had felt on seeing the field of dead Vors he had killed. He had laughed with the thrill of exerting his power.

His father grimaced. "The world is changing, son. The old ways don't work. Uniting Ascoria under one crown was a start, but Silas lost his way. We need to start anew."

"But it means nothing if the Vors win—" Jaks's head spun with the turn of topic from gargantors to crowns.

His father stared at him as though waiting for him to understand something.

The back of Jaks's neck tingled. Something significant had been said, but he couldn't grasp its meaning. There were too many thoughts and emotions clattering in his mind.

The Lord Defender continued, "Started but stalled. That's why Voros invaded. Ascoria had gathered a great harvest but failed to protect it. Instead of solidifying Ascoria's might, that fool Silas disbanded the armies and allowed good warriors to soften and lose their edge."

"Why are you telling me this?" Jaks asked, fearing that the more he heard, the more he would sink into some trap.

Sneer appeared at that moment and passed an object to his master before settling back into a shaded alcove.

His father weighed the object in his hands and then presented it to Jaks. "Here, take it," he said.

It was a rod of cold metal. His arms sagged under unexpected weight in the three-foot-long object. At its midpoint, steel twisted around an octagonal, black stone that he would have mistaken for a cylinder of coal if not for the engraved runes. Similar spiral cages at each end of the rod bound equally dark runestones. A sense of doom radiated from all three—danger dwelt in each. He clenched the artifact around the grips between the runestones.

"What is this?" Jaks's voice took on a high edge.

"It was crafted by the last electromancer in known history, a Grandmaster Vinton. You heard of him?"

He nodded, recalling a copy of the personal account left by Vinton in the Academy library. The electromancer had embodied the spirit of a true battlemage and was a legend. Jaks often marveled at the power the mage must have commanded, such as summoning a storm that sank half of the Ranilan fleet a century ago and thereby ended their religious crusade. Yes, he even remembered mention of Vinton's rod of lightning piercing the clouds to draw down forked tentacles of electricity.

"I thought you might like it—a loan from me to you."

"Me?" Jaks stared slack-jawed at the artifact and trembled at the thought of what power it contained. Unable to form a sentence, jumbled words fell out of his mouth. He couldn't recall his father ever giving him anything of value in his life before, certainly nothing as valuable as this.

"On one condition," the enormous man said. "Join my retinue. Develop your power under my tutelage.

With the rod and my guidance, you might eventually be as powerful as Vinton himself."

The idea both appalled and appealed to Jaks. Fame like Vinton? Ever since the siege of Irin, he had felt a strong desire to weave electromancy once again. What if he could do far more? Alter weather and summon clouds of lightning? What a spectacle. No one could dismiss him any longer. They would lower their eyes in respect and beg favors from him.

Jaks studied the rod and felt a thrum of power course through the artifact as though welcoming its new owner. "I can sense its power," he said. He knew he wanted it. But could he accept it at the cost of kowtowing and submitting to his father, who, up until this day, had been the person he most feared and despised?

"Other things, too, of course—wealth, women." He snapped his fingers and Sneer pulled back a curtain to reveal a recessed alcove. Three thinly clad women lounged on settees and cushions. The henchman stroked the braided hair of one; she arched her exquisite neck like some exotic creature.

Jaks fumbled for words, but nothing other than mumblings came out of his mouth. Of course, he wanted power, money, and companionship. Didn't everybody? His eyes connected with a particularly curvaceous woman. He turned away, painfully aware of his aching need, worsened by Meila's casual dismissal after he had kissed her that afternoon.

"Go and think about it. I return south within the next few days. I would have your response by then. Son. The world is changing faster than a swift on the wing. What you see is only the tip of what all that is happening, and you would do well to be at the center of it all—with me."

"Yes, my lord . . . Father. I will think on it," Jaks said. He stood and reluctantly dropped Vinton's Rod back into his father's extended hands.

The tattooed man stepped out of the shadows and guided Jaks off the ship into the dark of evening.

At the end of the jetty, beneath flickering torches, the swordsman looked at him sideways. "Your father is a great man. Many of us have followed him for longer than you are old and would die for him without pause. You would do well to accept his offer. If you did not, an offense would be created that could not be ignored." He then turned and simply vanished as only an illumancer could.

Chapter 11

Firing and Testing

Jaks shuffled through the city, savoring the solace of the darkening streets despite the nip of winter at his face. Hours later, as bells rang the night curfew, he arrived at the Academy and a familiar guard bid him through the night door. Although he glimpsed Meila and Mulgrave with a few others in the ground-floor laboratory, he slipped past unseen and found his old room. Collapsing onto the bed, he fell asleep and was haunted by black hands proffering a glowing bar of red-hot steel.

"Come on. Wake up. We've got lots to do today." Meila's voice pierced his slumber. The light of dawn silhouetted her against the doorway. "*Blah.* Go and wash first, though. I've lived for decades in tight spaces, but this is the worst I've smelled for a long time. Come down to the lab after you're done."

"Wait." He threw his legs over the cot and rose

unsteadily. "What did my father say to you yesterday?" He had awoken confused, not from the tendrils of sleep but from a dilemma. Perhaps she could help.

"What? He didn't say anything to me. First time I've met him. Stared at me as though I were curio at the museum. Even when I explained the firing process for the mortar crews, he wasn't really listening."

"Nothing about big changes taking place?"

Meila quirked an eyebrow at him. "Well, there is a war going on. So, something will change . . . win or lose. What are you on about?"

He shook his head as he sifted through his thoughts. His father's invitation had not been a peace offering to a neglected son—it had been a bribe and a threat. It was becoming clear now, with fear and fatigue no longer buffeting his mind like a pair of mad ravens as they had the night before.

Lord Sicaro had not changed at all since the days he had frothed at the mouth as he beat his son and his wife. *Mind games. I'll not have any more of this.* The death of Jaks's mother from panicked electromancy was his father's fault, not his.

He clenched his jaw and moved toward the door. Meila stepped back, her nose crinkling.

"He's planning something. He's *always* planning something," Jaks said. "I don't know what, but it's always about power. He must want more—"

"More than he has now? He is in charge of the

largest city in the kingdom. The capital, nonetheless. What's more?"

Realization crept across her face. Jaks nodded at her. The unspoken inference thrummed in the air between them like a hideous portrait that should be trampled and destroyed.

"But if he wanted the Crown, why would he do it in the middle of an invasion?" Meila said, thinking aloud. "The disruption would allow the Vors to just walk in while the kingdom reels in chaos."

"I don't know. It's just some things he said . . ." He trailed off, unable to pin hard evidence to his suspicions.

"Do you have any evidence?"

"Nothing I can show someone."

"Then we have to leave it be. There's no point slinging around accusations without proof. It would do more harm than good." Meila stood back from the doorway as though ending the conversation.

He nodded, seeing that he needed more proof before he could convince anyone with enough power to do anything. He might possibly even need to go to the king himself. "I'll get evidence. He's not just a danger to me, but to everyone."

"Just don't do anything stupid. I'll see you downstairs when you're not stinking like rotted tripe." Meila wrinkled her nose and left.

An idea gathered momentum as he grabbed clothes from the shelf and then went to wash in the water room at the end of the corridor. The beard came off with flicks of a shaving blade and was flushed down the drain. Dashing back to his room, dripping and slapping wet feet, he retrieved his carry pouch and extracted the zinger bot.

Minutes later, the droid sped off to carry out its orders. The plan now in motion, Jaks went downstairs to find Meila and the grandmaster.

"Better," Meila remarked when he came across them in the downstairs lab. She slid a hand over his clean-shaven chin and slapped it lightly. "Follow us. We're doing the rounds."

The morning shot by in a haze after he joined Meila and Tavis traipsing behind the grandmaster like subordinates tailing a general. Keeping to some schedule that only he knew, Mulgrave attended meetings with other grandmasters and roamed the lab and workshops, inspecting and barking instructions at his journeymen and master magesmiths. Everywhere within the massive building, in whatever corner or room they could find, men and women found space to work magic and muscle on all sorts of weapons, armor, and contraptions.

By midday, Jaks was ready for their primary task of the day. They stood at the Academy's sea gate, the huge iron barrier leading out to the abandoned wharf. Ocean air whistled between the gaps of the gate to counter the immense heat of the runic furnace.

Inside, off to one side of the sea gate, a large object lay beneath a ragged shroud. After they peeled away the canvas, Jaks gazed upon the creation that had been awaiting his return.

Sturdy steel legs and frame grasped a long metal cylinder with a metal box capping off one end. Jaks realized he had seen the device before—back in the Jurn caverns when Meila had projected her nascent illusion of the device. It had looked smaller then. What stood in front of him would not be easily carried on a battlefield.

"The barrel is the magnetic radiation shield that we recovered from the *Mendhelsson*. It used to generate a constant double field, but I've modified it with parts from the escape pod and one of the darkcore handguns to create an old-school velocity cannon."

"Looks interesting," he said, intrigued by the weapon's eclectic manufacture.

"Velocannon for short. The finish is rough, but the principle is sound. Darkcore particles become unstable as they approach the speed of light. In a normal darkcore weapon, the plasma bolt is limited, so it doesn't damage the weapon. But in a velocannon, as soon as an over-charged bolt leaves the primary weapon and enters the magnetic field inside the secondary barrel, it is accelerated to a point that hyperexcites the particles—but all the while keeping it from contacting the interior. It's bloody marvelous." She then smiled as though he should be equally impressed by her explanation. Seeing that he wasn't, she continued, "An agitated darkcore bolt is so powerful that they are usually only fired from space where the target is hundreds or thousands of miles away. It can vaporize anything within a half mile, while the blast will carry even further."

Now Jaks's eyes widened. "Is it safe?"

"Don't worry. It's *old-school,*" she replied dismissively. He frowned at her peculiar phrase.

A loud clank drew their attention to the sea gate where Tavis had been hand-cranking a cog and chain. The gate racketed to a stop and the passageway to the old stone wharf stood wide open. Out in the open, a couple of dragons screeched overhead. A breakwater, a half mile out, whisked up ocean foam as it buffered the sea's incessant pounding. Several dinghies and fishing boats bobbed in the waters of the harbor and a frigate flying Ascorian colors sailed past and made its way to the city's naval yard.

The grandmaster walked along the slime-coated wharf with a fan of fire spewing from his hands, searing the slime until it was blackened and devoid of its slippery growth. Both gravmancers then carried out the velocannon and positioned it facing the open sea. "Let's hope it works this time," Mulgrave said and stepped back. Tavis shot Jaks an irritated look and followed the grandmaster back under the archway.

Meila withdrew a handgun from a satchel she carried and inserted the weapon into the steel box from the bottom. Her hands inside the device, Jaks couldn't see what she was doing, but it was a quarter hour before she finished and called him over.

"I've unlocked the darkie to your neuronal

signature. Don't trigger it more than once. There is only enough ammunition for perhaps six or seven of the hypercharged shots."

Jaks nodded. "How do I use it?"

"When I tell you, take the left grip and hold on to the gun inside. Aim it above that breakwater." She demonstrated by placing her left hand on a metal handle on the side of the box and sticking her right hand into a hole at the back. "Then you're going to have to channel your electromancy through the handle."

"That's it?" Jaks stood behind the weapon as its creator stood aside.

"See the fins on the end of the barrel?" She pointed at short, thin pieces of metal lying flat. "If you generate enough field, they'll spread out like flower petals, telling you it's charged enough to fire. That's when you pull the trigger."

Suddenly aware of the power in his hand, Jaks released the weapon, fearful of accidentally firing it.

"Okay, I'm going to go hide in the archway. Listen out for me to give you the go-ahead." She darted away and left him gaping as she went to join the grandmaster semi-hidden in the archway. After a minute, she shouted out for him to proceed.

Palms sweaty, it was hard to keep a firm grip. He looked at the velocannon and then back at Meila several times. She waved him on. Was this how Karisa and his mother had felt on stage, pressured to perform exactly how the audience demanded? Sweat beaded his brow.

Emotion. Visualization. Will. The chain of power was second nature to him now. It took little effort to trigger the spiral of fear: always violence, the threat or memory of it. Today, he drew on the memory of seeing his father the day before, heightened at knowing he would have to answer to him, worsened with imagining the consequences of denying him his fealty —the fist and backlash that would surely follow. Shaking with the emotion, he imagined lightning coursing through his hands and then furrowed his forehead to will the magic to life. He closed his eyes to concentrate.

A loud humming sound startled him back to the present. The metal fins at the end of the barrel vibrated erect. Strangely, their tiny movements reminded him of little fish dancing rather than of the flower petals that Meila had described.

"Now, Jaks. Aim with the scope over the breakwater and fire," Meila yelled from behind.

Sighting down the magnified lens tube, he inched the orange dot in the center over the top of the wave-swept outcrop. A few seconds later, he squeezed the trigger.

The weapon shuddered and emitted a coarse scream. A white line seared his vision but was gone in an instant. In the distance, the horizon disappeared as the ocean was tossed into the sky and became a billowing cloud folding in on itself.

Another cry sounded behind him, but it was one of

delight from Meila as she ran up hooting and calling out, "Yes!" and, "That's it!" repeatedly.

Her excitement contagious, he caught her up, and the two jumped up and down, staring at the cloud that seemed even now to be growing.

A roar grew from the ocean, killing the laughter on their lips. Moments later, a booming gust of wind and water blew Meila and Jaks to the ground. And as they struggled to hands and knees, a giant wave crashed against the harbor's seawall and swamped it from view. Broken but still angry, the wave slapped at the boats on the other side and threw itself against the Academy's dock with one last effort.

The pair watched uselessly as the wave surged against the velocannon and knocked it off the dock into the water.

Meila swore aloud in a foreign tongue.

The mist blew away minutes later, and the harbor settled into choppy waves. Thankfully, most of the larger boats were still afloat, but Jaks was certain there were fewer rafts and dinghies than before.

Meila ran to the edge of the dock and stared down at where the cannon had disappeared. Seconds later, she sighed in relief, touching the side of her eye socket. "Thank God, it looks mostly intact and is just a couple of meters under the surface. Shouldn't be too hard to retrieve."

"It'll work again?" Jaks asked.

"I hope so," she replied. "Once we fish it out."

Mulgrave and Tavis appeared beside her, the old man shaking his head, muttering and cursing at the harbor as flotsam bobbed to the surface. "Gods, there's going to be a lot of explaining to do."

Sure enough, dismayed faces soon jammed the archway and shouted a hundred questions. Grandmaster Hazeldine, clutching a forge hammer, stomped out to the dock. "What the hell, Mulgrave?" She stared out at the harbor as it sloshed like a bowl of water in a toddler's arms.

Sheepishly, Mulgrave pointed first at the seawall, then at the patch of harbor where the velocannon lay submerged, and then shrugged as he spread his palms.

Chapter 12

The Bribe

The rest of that afternoon, Jaks clung distractedly to the slippery ropes that Tavis—grumbling and spluttering each time he resurfaced—tossed up from where he ducked and dived to bind the velocannon in its watery grave. Despite the apprentice's protests, Mulgrave had decided the task was a great opportunity for a lesson in gravmancy and ballasting. But despite the shouts and splashing of the pair in the water, Jaks gnawed his lip, thoughts fixated on his father. Should he vow allegiance to him or risk creating an enemy of him?

"What's going on?" Meila stared at him from where she stood holding another set of ropes several feet away.

"What—"

"Yesterday, you grab me on the bridge, and since then, you've barely said anything except to ramble on about some conspiracy. And now, after we've successfully trialed a weapon that could change this stupid war, you're as glum as if you were at your own funeral."

Jaks returned her gaze, as the two gravmages gulped and dived again. "I'm sorry I grabbed you yesterday, but I was so excited to see you . . . although it may not seem so, I've missed you more than anything. You know how I feel about you."

"I thought you'd be over that by now," she said. Did he catch a glimmer of affection in her eyes? She then shook her head, and her face was unreadable again. "We've no time for that sort of thing at the moment. We need to focus on our mission," she said with finality.

It was best not to press the issue. She did know his feelings, but he couldn't pressure her into reciprocating his love.

The divers resurfaced with a splash, then sunk away again, thankfully breaking an awkward silence.

Jaks stared at the ripples they created as his thoughts returned to his original dilemma. "He wants me to join him," he spurted out, in a sudden impulse to share his problem with Meila. "My father, that is. He wants me to go into his service."

"Your father? Is that what's stirred you up?"

"There's this artifact. A true magical artifact—I could sense the raw power it held. He's going to give it to me, if I vow fealty to him and join his retinue."

"Sounds like a bribe." She paused.

"Isn't that what I should do? Forgive and join him— like a proper son should?"

"That's taking it a bit far." Doubt clouded her face. "Maybe it wasn't such a good idea for you to have seen him on such short notice."

"But if I get the rod—I could kill him. I'm sure of it."

"What? I can't believe you'd even think of that. What sort of person would you be? Vow loyalty to your father—even for a bribe—and then murder him with the very thing he entrusts you with?" Meila shot him a look of disbelief. "That is vile. I thought I knew you better."

Jaks's shoulders slumped. He wrapped the rope around his hands, not knowing what else to do with them as they waited. "You're right. It'd make me a monster as much as him." He sighed and shook his head. "You're right. I wasn't ready to deal with him so soon."

"Say no to him and stay here with us. You know the old mage will do anything to keep you around," she said, looking down to where Mulgrave submerged. "I know nothing about the artifact your father offered you, but I doubt it can affect the course of this war as much as the velocannon. And because you're the only one who can power it, you're more important than anyone else in Ascoria at the moment. Even more than your father."

Jaks eventually nodded, seeing some truth in her words. "Do you think Grandmaster Mulgrave will take me back as an apprentice—after I said I'd given it all up?"

She chuckled. "He knew you would come back eventually."

"Did *you* think I would?"

"Probably . . ." Her face was blank and unreadable again.

At that moment, splashes and splutters signaled the divers' surfacing. Tavis paddled to the dock, swearing between breaths, as the half-naked grandmaster stroked to the wharf with rope in tow. Their conversation interrupted, Jaks and Meila bent to grip slippery arms and assisted the swimmers back up the ladder. The velocannon resurfaced too, soon after, dragged back to dry land. Meila sighed in relief and ordered the gravmancers one last task: return the device back to the lab. Once back with her tools and bench, Meila tended to the velocannon as though it were an injured and long-lost child—chastising it for its scrapes and blemishes.

Chapter 13

Father and Son

That evening, Jaks stood on the rooftop of the Academy, gazing over the city. Dunberrin was renowned as a cultural center in the Pact Countries. Opera houses, theaters, and festivals drew merchants and visitors from faraway lands to see talented performers like Karisa, and their mother before her, on stage. Colored lanterns, illumanced skyworks, and street performers had once festooned the streets, celebrating the city's brilliance. But now, shadowed with war, it looked nothing like the multicultural oasis of that past era. Instead, it was dull and lifeless.

The winter sun had fallen to dusk and cast a red-rimmed haze over the horizon lined with building tops. As vestiges of sunlight vanished, a full moon illuminated the rooftops and streets. Heralds sounded the curfew with horns and cries, and the last remaining citizens dashed home to avoid a fine or a night in jail.

But throughout that eerie transcendence, Jaks thought of nothing but his father.

He was somewhere out there. On his capital ship, or in some hall within the army district, or perhaps visiting some official. There had been more to Lord Sicaro's words yesterday than mere arrogance or wishful thinking—they hinted to disaster within a spiderweb of subterfuge and deception. Or so he thought. Just as well he had a spy that might help him refute or confirm his suspicions.

Hugging his cloak tighter, he ignored the twinge in his shoulder—thankfully healed, with only an occasional pain to remind him of the knife wound that had sunk to the bone.

He plodded past the huge bronze dome and descended a corner tower to spiral his way down to the hallway and finally into his little room. Mulgrave and Tavis were nowhere to be seen, nor Meila.

He closed the door and lay on his cot, wrapped in darkness, eager to meld with his droid and see what it had discovered.

During the weeks returning from the river city of Irin back to Dunberrin, Jaks had become well acquainted with the zinger. Within the safe confines of the Academy, while he tranced out, it was second nature now to subsume the circuits of the wrist comm: to see and hear through the droid's sensors, while flying it like a bird. And in the inner workings of the device, he had discovered how to instruct it to complete certain tasks.

Circling a hundred yards up, the zinger scanned the Lord Defender's ship. Under lightstone lamps lofted about the vessel, dozens of sailors scurried about the deck as though preparing for sailing the next day; working into the evening surely meant an early departure. Perhaps, Jaks hoped, his father was being called away and he might not have to encounter him again. Of his lordship, though, there was no sign—even with the droid's gamma sensor to pierce the deck and walls of the ship.

Fortunately, the zinger had not wasted the day. Deducing that his father's business revolved around the ship's tower, Jaks had had the droid record hours of images and sound. It only needed Jaks to review them—and surely, he would find evidence of his father's traitorous machinations.

Barely sensate to his body lying on his cot, Jaks spied on ghostly recordings of his father from earlier that day. Images played through his mind as voices accompanied the figures and revealed their secret discussions. However, after the first hour of a dull meeting with the royal quartermaster, he fell asleep.

Sometime later, he awoke to a shout nearby—but a few minutes of quiet dispelled that idea. Slightly refreshed, he returned to the zinger's memory bank.

Picking up the replay, the quartermaster finally departed with a dour look. Next, a flurry of courtiers and messengers proceeded before the Lord Defender. A late shipment of coal from Zura; Strockian mercenaries delayed; Fauconian allies questioning a request to sail east instead of west; the merchant union begging for tariff reductions; and a city physician reporting a cluster of disease. Hints of trouble, but unclear of what.

Around midday in the recording, the flow of visitors halted for a notable character: his father's man, Craeg Vesenira. The blue-tattooed swordsman from the deviant island of Ellipta sauntered in from the deck and bowed. And Kyle Halwoth, with a sneer—as always—plastered to his face, lingered by the Lord Defender's side to complete the sinister trio.

"My lord," Vesenira began. "The woman reports that she could not access the nightwraith barracks last night."

"But the rest?" Sicaro asked.

"Except for that one, all the packages have been delivered."

"Plenty enough. Three-quarters of the nightwraiths are down south, anyway. The few remaining will make little difference," Jaks's father replied to the Elliptan warrior.

"We have done all we need to do here. You've messaged the king, Master Halwoth?" Sicaro queried.

"Yes, my lord. The tower signaled the report this morning. As you say, the capital is as well-prepared as it can be. A competent commander of the Guard has been appointed. And now that your role here is complete, you return to his majesty's presence forthwith."

The Lord Defender nodded, then strode out onto

the middeck with his two lackeys behind. "One last inspection of the city, then our final task tonight, and our time here will be done." A squad of soldiers clicked to attention and turned to break a path for the Lord Defender. A whistle sounded, and sailors ceased their tasks to stand and salute.

As his father walked out of the droid's scanner focus, Jaks pondered what he'd heard. What were these "packages" they spoke about? Where were they delivered? And to whom?

He had to find out more.

Jaks refocused on the zinger and sped through the rest of its memory banks. As the shadows stretched and the sailors tired around the quarterdeck, Lord Sicaro finally returned to his ship.

The bearlike man walked without hesitation to a curtained alcove. Opening a chest with a velvet lining, he wrapped a huge paw around an object and slung it to his belt. A weapon with three runestones bound in steel spirals—Vinton's Rod.

"My lord," Sneer said, as his master shuttered the curtain and returned to the main chamber. "My man in the Academy reports that the foreigner and your son have not left there this full day. Apparently, they have been causing a great disturbance in the harbor." As he spoke, he assisted his master out of his fur coat and into a black leather jerkin.

"How so?"

"That king wave that struck this afternoon? Not

some freak phenomenon but a result of a weapon that the magesmiths and the woman built. Fired out to sea, it created enough of an explosion to send a wave rushing back. Said to be made from parts created on her world."

Jaks's father stood motionless for a moment. "That mage mentioned nothing of the sort. How could he keep this from me?" His tone was more melancholy than angry.

Sneer shrugged.

"Large weapon? Siege or hand?"

"Said to be the size of a ballista. It was thrown off its perch into the harbor but was retrieved. Maybe damaged."

"The woman is the main prize, but if the weapon is not too sizeable, we will bring it back. Otherwise, I'll destroy it. Stay here. We'll be back soon." Sicaro swept out to the ship's deck, and with Vesenira behind him, vanished into the night. *The bear and his shadowdancer.*

His father's last words stabbed a sense of dread through Jaks. It must have been his father who had sent those men to kidnap Meila at the river town. He was after her again.

She was in danger.

Jaks flicked a return instruction to the zinger and then snapped out of communication with the droid. His father might even be in the Academy now; the recording was several hours old. He sensed it was near midnight; Meila would most likely be abed already.

His mind spun as it recovered from the prolonged

connection with the droid. Groggily, he threw his legs over the edge of his cot, stood up in the darkness, and stumbled to the door.

Thumping noises in the hallway outside his room. Scattered light under the door. Someone was out there.

He trembled as he reached for the handle, but then pulled away, fearing what he would find. Unbidden, electricity sparked along his fingertips. His subconscious was readying his defense; electromancy had awoken like the talons of a guardian owl.

The light under his door flickered as though someone stood outside.

Jaks stepped backward until his legs struck his cot and stopped his retreat.

The door swung open, pushed inward on well-oiled hinges. A giant stood silhouetted in the doorframe.

"Here you are. I've been looking for you, boy," his father said.

More thumps sounded from the hallway, but his attention was only for the intruder looming over him, a mere two strides away, as though he were a child again cornered in his room.

"Put it away. There's no need for that. It's just your old papa," Sicaro said. No eyepatch covered the older man's eye as it had on the previous day. Both eyes, intact and undamaged, stared at Jaks. Of course, the eyepatch had been a ruse.

As though suddenly ashamed of being found out, the crackling energy at Jaks's fingertips disappeared.

"Why are you here?" he said. "What's going on out there?" He squinted into the glare of the hallway but couldn't see any sign of what was making the sounds.

"So full of questions. But I asked mine first, remember. Only yesterday—surely, you've not forgotten." His father hefted the artifact that was Vinton's Rod and waggled it toward Jaks like a chew toy to a dog. "You owe me your life, son. If I hadn't covered for the foul murder of your mother, you would have hung by the neck. Everybody hates a mother-killer."

"That's a lie . . ."

"A lie that everybody hates a *mother-killer*?"

"I didn't kill her on purpose." He stared at the long shadow of his father, unable to look into his face. Meeting his eyes would shatter his nascent courage. "It wasn't my fault. You were beating her, and I tried to defend her . . . the bolt stunned you both. It was an accident. She fell down the stairs."

"Yet, still the same result." Lord Sicaro thudded the tip of Vinton's Rod against the stone floor and planted both hands on the top. "She was an adulterer, you know. By rights, I could have had her tried and imprisoned—you just did the job first."

"More lies. Lies, lies!" Jaks glared at his father, angry enough now to look at him directly. His fists clenched into balls. How dare he malign her like that—his mother, who had given everything to raise them. "She wasn't like that. You twist everything. She used to be famous, and you couldn't bear the attention she got. But she never strayed from us . . . or you."

"How the pup loved his mother," Lord Sicaro quipped. "She was a pretender. Deceitful and lying, like them all. If only you could see through the masks she wore. Not like you and I, boy."

"I'm not like you. I would never be a tyrant." Jaks needed to unveil this beast. How could his father wrap himself in so many deceits? "I know what you used to do to Karisa . . . she was just little . . . your daughter, of all things. You're the monster. You beat your wife, you tortured me, you abused your daughter—*you* are the liar here."

Lord Sicaro stood rock steady; the air seethed with tension—ready to burst into fire. But when he spoke, his tone was level and calm. "If we're talking monsters, son, you need only look at yourself, boy. It was you who killed your mother."

Jaks panted for several breaths, ignoring the accusations, true as they were, and then continued, "I also know you're planning some treason. I don't know what it is, but I heard you conspiring with your men. I will tell the king."

Lord Sicaro shook his head slowly. Then, as though disappointed at Jaks's outburst, he said, "This little room is far too small for this. Come out into the hallway." He turned and walked out, still clutching Vinton's Rod.

Jaks balked, swaying and grinding his teeth as his anger dissipated, to be replaced with fear. Despite his earlier bravado, he saw no way out of this situation. Cornered and desperate, his electromancy was his only ally, but his fright spiraled tornado-like, sucking away the focus and imagery needed to invoke the magic. He just wanted to slide under the bed and hide.

An exchange of voices in the hallway, out of sight, refocused his attention. His father and his henchmen? Did they have Meila? Or were they still searching for her? Maybe she had worked late into the night in the maze of labs downstairs. She had little need for sleep. He had to find her before they did.

Jaks fumbled for his sword where it lay nudged into a corner and pulled it from its sheath. He sidled out of his room. The doors were all closed down the hallway, except for one.

Outside Meila's room, three figures faced him. And there she stood, immobile.

A blindfold, a gag, and ropes around her wrists bound her, while a muscular Vesenira clamped thick fingers around her arm. Blood trickled from a split in the shadowdancer's lip; he spat and smeared red over his chin. Meila, too, showed evidence of violence: grazed knuckles and a severe lean as she held her weight off her bare right foot.

In her lightweight flightsuit—that she still often wore, swearing it kept her warmer than any other garment—she cast a tiny figure against the two warriors detaining her.

As Jaks stepped out of the doorway, Lord Sicaro

tapped Vinton's Rod to Meila's chest. "Your friend here is quite the battler." She twisted against Vesenira's grip and shook her head as though to rid herself of the blindfold and gag.

Jaks stopped in the center of the hallway. "Leave her be . . . I don't want to fight you. But I will if I have to." His knuckles whitened around his sword. "I won't let you hurt her—not like every other person I've loved."

"He loves her? Isn't that nice," Vesenira said, then laughed.

"Let her go."

"She doesn't need your help," Sicaro said.

"Let her go." Jaks raised his sword an inch. To fully brandish a blade at his father would be unreconcilable.

"Who is in the right here?" Sicaro asked. "What is she really, son? . . . nothing but a ward of the state. I am merely taking her back into custody. I have rescinded her captivity and am taking her under the king's protection."

Jaks faltered. It was true. His father would bear all rights in his position to do what he wanted with prisoners in the city. Blocking him was to impede a royal agent. It might as well have been the king standing here. The tip of his sword dipped to the floor.

"Now, put it away." Sicaro lowered the rod from Meila's chest.

But Jaks wasn't finished. He looked at the stump of his missing finger—one of the many "punishments" from his father. "But this isn't about *your* privilege. This is about right and wrong." Anger burned like a naked flame. "Your twisted words bare your corruptness. You cannot confuse me with them any longer. I know what you are. And I won't stand for it." He raised the sharp point of his sword at his father. "Now, I'm telling you again, let her go."

"Take the prisoner. Go find the device." Lord Sicaro half-turned to Vesenira. Wordlessly, the swordsman tossed Meila over a shoulder like a sack, opened the door at the end of the hallway, and vanished into the darkened library. "Uh-uh," his father said when Jaks took a step toward them.

Sicaro's eyes then drooped. Sadness etched his face like lines of bark.

Jaks's sword tore away from his hand, suddenly heavier than a block of granite. When it struck the floor, it didn't bounce or rebound, but clung as though glued by an extraordinary force. Then, Jaks sagged uncontrollably to his knees, succumbing to a weight that pressed down on his head, his shoulders, his arms—the over-bearing heaviness of gravmancy.

"I never hated you, boy—you just had nothing worth taking notice of. A thready runt with no backbone," his father was saying, as Jaks's face remained plastered against the cold stone floor. "But after hearing about how you broke the siege at Irin, I thought you might finally have something worth bringing in."

Jaks fought for breath, barely hearing his father's

monologue crushed beneath the tyrant's gravmantic invocation. Too much longer and he would suffocate.

"But it's clear your backbone is as stiff and inflexible as that of your bitch sister. Obsessed with rules and lacking ambition. The two of you have been of no use to me. If only you were more like your little sister—such a pleasing and progressive creature."

Jaks growled in this throat but emitted little more than a mewl. Intolerable, to hear this monster spewing more lies, talking about Karisa as though she craved to please his vile whims.

Although he hoped Grandmaster Mulgrave might come to his rescue, he needed to regain control, himself.

Immobile under his father's gravmancy, he reached for the only thing he could think of—remembering how Meila had distracted the warrior in the attic.

The zinger droid was hovering in the freezing night outside Mulgrave's library, awaiting instructions. At Jaks's command, it smashed through a painted glass panel and zipped through the bookshelves toward the light of the open door. It centered on a giant, silhouetted figure and darted forward—its tiny but powerful motivator transforming it into a dangerous projectile.

"What's that?" Sicaro said, a few moments after the glass broke. He inclined his head to listen.

A thud, followed by a grunt, granted Jaks release from his father's control. Like a marble slab lifted from his back, the magical weight dissipated and once again

Jaks could lift his head. His father was bent with one hand on his knee: stunned by the zinger's blow.

The giant reached down to the droid lying inactive by his foot and picked it up. Inspecting it, he grunted again, and then dropped it to the stone floor and crushed it under his heel.

Jaks felt a pang of anger and loss, as though his father had murdered his pet. He pushed up onto his hands and knees.

Another object lay in the hallway, halfway between them—Vinton's Rod.

The zinger's strike must have sent the artifact flying from his father's hand. Whichever of them possessed it would have an advantage. Jaks had felt its dormant power; he didn't know if his father could use that power, but either way, he needed to get to it first.

Jumping to his feet as his father continued to grind the zinger underfoot, he sprinted for the rod.

But, with his hand almost on one of its runestone spirals, his father was already there.

Sicaro landed from a leap of jaguar speed—that, as a human, only a gravmancer could achieve—and kicked aside Jaks's hand.

A gauntlet followed, an uppercut that smacked into his forehead and sent him flying backward down the hall.

Stunned from the blow, his vision clouded, Jaks staggered, pushing against the wall. A framed painting of a past grandmaster lay fractured nearby, knocked down by the fracas.

"Too slow, son—"

A hesitant voice called from behind his father's back. "My lord . . ." The voice came again, in an even higher pitch. "My Lord Sicaro, is that you? What is going on?" The speaker stood in the doorway from the library. Tavis, wrapped in a nightgown. "A noise awoke me . . ." His voice petered out. Jaks hoped it was because the apprentice had comprehended the violence before him.

"You should have stayed in your bed," Sicaro said.

Jaks's head cleared in time to witness his father turn and strike the blurry-eyed Tavis with the end of the rod. The apprentice's head crumpled. Blood and brain splattered the wall as his body fell to the floor. *Oh, God, Tavis. I'm so sorry.*

"You shouldn't have done that. He wasn't involved," Jaks heard himself say, astonished that his voice held up despite his bowels twisting like snakes. Tavis's corpse continued to trickle blood from its shattered skull. Blood dripped from the tip of the deadly rod. Did it seem to glow in his father's murderous hand?

"You're all involved. Sadly, that's what you don't seem to understand." Sicaro kicked aside Tavis's body, imprinting the pooling blood with his boots. "If you are not my servant, you are my enemy."

Face still throbbing from the earlier slap, Jaks backstepped two paces from his father. Fearful of being gravmanced to the ground again, he had to use the advantage of distance.

Sicaro strode toward him, rod half-raised, face curled as though he regretted the violence to follow.

Jaks punched the air at his father and threw his fear along his arm and transformed it into lightning. He yelled as jagged lines of electricity cracked through the air. Metallic odor filled his nostrils. The hallway erupted with brilliant light.

And lightning struck Vinton's Rod.

Silence spanned the distance between them in the corridor. Lord Sicaro and Jaks froze and stared at the magical artifact that the older man held in front of him. Two of the once dark runestones glowed emerald green in their steel spirals after absorbing Jaks's lightning bolt. Dreadful realization stabbed at Jaks. Vinton's Rod stored electromancy, just as a common lightstone stored an illumancer's power.

Sicaro sighed as the rod dipped to the floor. "Such a waste," he said. The runestones colored the giant's face in a sickly green glow. The rod then angled toward Jaks. "How does this go?" Electricity then scintillated the cages of the runestones as though seeking an escape.

Anticipating his father's next move, Jaks invoked the one defense he knew. Electromancy sprung into a cocoon around him, dancing and circling in a protective shield. Over the past weeks, he had refined the invocation to a point where he could now see through this shield while keeping it reactive enough to repel any regular weapon. Although confident it would shield him from an elemental power of his own creation, he was uncertain whether it would repel the attacks of a gravmancer.

The tip of Vinton's Rod leveled. His father, unperturbed by the scintillating shell around his target, mouthed words and thrust the glowing artifact at Jaks.

The rod blasted out lightning, filling the hallway, probing the walls and ceiling. Drawn to Jaks's shield, as though thirsting to rejoin its source, the power returned. The shield pulsed and absorbed the electricity, but his doubts grew as his cocoon grew hotter and brighter—blinding him to anything outside his invocation. Over the sounds of the crackling magic, another sound—deeper, more ominous—drew his sightless eyes upward.

Then the shield exploded.

Hard fragments peppered his head, and dust filled his throat. The overhead noise became an aching groan.

His shield overpowered, and his vision clearing, Jaks gasped at the sight of tremendous blackened cracks in the curved ceiling. They riddled the stonework from above his head down the hallway to where his father still stood.

"I'm still here . . ." Jaks croaked in defiance.

Stone fragments fell around Lord Sicaro, repelled by a cocoon of his own gravmantic power. With a snarl, the giant raised Vinton's Rod to the ceiling—and *pulled* it down.

Chunks of granite, placed by gravmasons and

supported for centuries by mortar and sheer weight, tore from the ceiling. His last glimpse of his father was of the man turning away before disappearing behind the veil of falling rock.

The ceiling buckled toward Jaks in an avalanche. Panic spurred him to scramble backward. He turned and ran, one arm above his head, as though he could hold back the massive blocks of stone.

At the end of the hallway, he flung open the door to the water room, but the small alcove yielded no exit. A dead end.

Jaks climbed up on the washbasin, feeling the press of the brass tap against his back, and turned to face his doom.

A wave of dust blew over his face and all light blinked out. Half-deafened by the smashing of stone, and blind to approaching death, he held his breath until the burning in his lungs forced them open again.

Several more breaths . . .

He coughed. If not for that spontaneous act, he could've believed himself dead, such was the quiet and darkness around him.

With extended hands, he probed the alcove's walls and traced the surface to the door. But instead of open air, his fingers found only rough, unyielding hardness. Cupping his hand, he concentrated, and a tiny ball of lightning spun into life with flickering light.

Blocks of granite piled against the doorframe. Bizarrely, amongst the settling dust lay broken lengths of wood and leather-bound books. The Academy's main library had rested above the hallway; now, parts of it lay within. Although alive, Jaks couldn't budge anything but a few torn volumes and small rocks from the debris.

He was trapped.

An hour passed and, with each minute, Jaks felt fragments of his soul go with them. Meila was in the grips of his father and Vesenira, bound and restrained. Each second seemed to seal her fate as much as he was sealed in this veritable tomb.

With nothing else to do but wait in hopes of rescue, Jaks sought to make sense of the events. What did his father want with her? An object of desire? He had seen the gleam of interest his father had in her; that, he could understand, but not the lengths his father had taken to kidnap her. It could not be a salacious need. He must have another reason to possess her. They said knowledge was power. Perhaps that was his motive. But for what ultimate purpose?

He wondered whether he should be sad that his own father had tried to kill him. Perhaps in a different lifetime, but not this one.

He had never doubted the man could murder without remorse—whether it be a warrior on a battlefield, or his own son in his bedroom. The attempts today merely consolidated Jaks's suspicions of a monumental deceit cranking in the hands of an evil man. Although he had no grasp of his father's plan, he had to convince the king that he was in danger from his most-trusted nobleman.

After another period of shouting and useless shoves at the rubble, he finally heard voices yell back at him from above. Another half hour passed before Grandmaster Mulgrave and several other Academy gravmancers found him and lifted away enough debris for Jaks to scramble up to what was left of the main library.

"It was my father—" Jaks began as soon as he clambered up beside his rescuers. Several incredulous faces stared at the dust-covered Jaks, not at his appearance but at his accusation.

"Come away," the grandmaster said, pulling him to a desk and chair away from the collapsed pit of shelves and stone. All the Academy staff seemed to be in the library, helping with the damaged floor or hindering with pointless instructions. "I found Tavis dead. We haven't found the lass. Tell me."

Jaks recounted the confrontation and fight with his father and then described the suspicious conversations he had witnessed in the zinger's recordings. He left nothing out, and by the time he finished, he was out of breath, having spoken so quickly. "We might be able to save her. We have to go after her."

The grandmaster rubbed his chin and then his head. A habit of the mage when mulling over a hard decision. Eventually, he shook his head. "It's been over three hours. If what you say is true, and I do believe you, he'll have her wherever he wants by now. If it was to his frigate, it would be impossible to get to her without a fight. You must remember that he has all the city garrison on his side." Mulgrave's face sank with a sadness that Jaks had never seen in him before. "The Lord Defender marches to his own beat. I do not doubt your suspicions about him, but there is nothing to evidence his actions or intent except your word."

"If we can prove he has Meila, it would show that he came here and killed Tavis . . . and tried to kill me."

"But would not prove that Lord Sicaro intends to kill the king or contest his crown—which is what you're saying. Alas, your father is a powerful man. Not one at which you can casually point the finger of treason. I'm sorry, Jaks, but thin accusations from an estranged son will convince the king of nothing."

"I have to do something." Jaks hammered the desk with a fist and several books bounced. "I snuck into a captured city. I can sneak into the docks. That has to be where he's taken her."

Mulgrave shook his head. "You'll get nowhere until the curfew lifts. Your father has turned the night guard into militant thugs and the gate-men into prison keepers —all in the name of keeping the city safe." He paused as Jaks's agitation sidled into desperate futility. "Once the curfew lifts, I will see what I can do. Besides, I will need the time to rally Grandmaster Hazeldine and the rest of the faculty. I'll need them to accompany me as witnesses. From what you say, I dare not audience with him alone."

Jaks nodded as though to join him.

"Yes. But *you* must stay behind. I would not risk what might happen if he saw you still alive, even with us all there. There cannot be a fight," Mulgrave said. "Based on your report, I will confront the Lord Defender at his naval yards and demand he explain himself. Although, I don't think he will willingly give up Meila. Considering the efforts he's made to take her, we can at least confirm the situation. And after that, we can seek the king's favor for her return." The grandmaster then sighed and rubbed his eyes. "But first . . . I have a dead apprentice to take care of."

Jaks followed the grandmaster down to the Academy morgue—nothing more than a small basement —and stood next to Tavis's draped body for several minutes. Responsibility for his death dragged like a millstone around his neck. Although they had clashed over apprenticeships, his tears for the big-eared youth were as genuine as any he had wept before. Tavis's life would have been so much better without Jaks around.

"I am in need of a new apprentice . . ." Mulgrave raised his eyebrows inquiringly at Jaks.

"I'd be honored, Grandmaster." He bowed awkwardly, all too aware of the proximity of the dead apprentice he was replacing. "I shouldn't have abandoned your tutorage in the first place. I hope I can serve you as well as he did."

"I'm sure you will. Maybe not in the same capacity, but I'm sure you will."

Leaving the morgue, they passed through the lab, looking for Meila's velocannon, checking on his father's threat to steal or destroy the weapon. Jaks sighed in relief, finding it standing untouched where he had last seen Meila working on it, although now covered by a sheet and tied with rope, as when he had first seen it.

However, what was out of order was an over-sized prototype of a gravfire mortar that Meila had decided was too cumbersome to use. Flattened and crushed to pieces, its tubing and frame were destroyed. Meila had outsmarted her captors on at least one thing, fooling them, at least temporarily, into believing the lesser weapon was what had upended the ocean. Jaks smiled at her cleverness.

"Not all is lost. At least we still have her inventions." Mulgrave nodded. "Get some rest. Use Tavis's room if you need," he said, reminding Jaks of the demolished hallway leading to his own room. "I'll go round up the faculty now."

Jaks returned to the grandmaster's library and slumped into a chair. He sent an instruction to the droid above Irin City to return, and then, still wide awake, drummed his fingers over the central desk as he awaited the rising sun.

Hours later, the horns blew an end to the curfew, and dawn colored the lead-lined window.

Seeking to examine the weather, he walked over and

peered through the break in the windowpane made by the zinger that last evening.

But at a sight that drained his last hopes, he stiffened and bellowed a cry of anguish.

Too late.

At full sail, Lord Sicaro's frigate was far out at sea.

He thumped his fist on the windowsill, mindless of the glass fragments, and emitted a sob.

He knew exactly where Meila would be. There was only one place. And that ship was sailing.

Chapter 14

Ascension

Meila—Sicaro's Frigate, City of Irin

The sound of chanting roused Meila from a restless sleep. The chain attached to the iron cuff around her ankle scraped against the floor of her prison. Unnecessary because of the locked ironwood door and guards outside, but Lord Sicaro, she had learned, insured his cargo several times over. And, it seemed, she was his most precious.

Even after a fortnight of sailing, and the ship having docked two weeks ago, she remained confined to the brig with only a thick, smudged portal to tell her day from night. And even then, her knowledge of the blurred, but majestic, buildings through the glass came only from overhearing the chatter of her prison guards: they were docked in the Vor-conquered City of Irin.

To combat hours and days of tedium, she sought comfort from her memories over the past weeks. She called on visual and auditory recordings of her daughter, engineering school friends, Anton, and, strangely, Jaks.

No opportunity for escape had presented, but she would not give up hope. She had escaped worse situations before. They knew nothing of her implants or illumancy. Those and her wits. She would use them to escape, somehow.

She pushed aside her blanket and sat up on the thin mattress—the one piece of furniture they allowed her, other than the chamber pot in the corner.

The chanting and shouting continued, and she bolstered her auditory implants to clarify the distant voices. Thousands of voices. Adulatory and excited.

"Trumpus, nai garn. Trumpus, Garn Sicaro!" enthusiastic crowds repeated throughout the city. Whoops and yells accompanied the mobs.

"What are they saying?" Meila called through the bars in the door at a guard, who also oriented her head to the noise.

"Glory, the new king. Glory, King Sicaro. Or something like that," the pig-nosed woman replied. "Our leader is finally at the station he deserves," she stated without any lick of sarcasm. An idolatrous smile and insane glint twisted her face—clearly one of the many sycophantic minions who infested this ship. She cuffed one of the other guards on the shoulder and pulled him into a circle-dance as they both laughed in delight.

The words, however, burned like molten lead in

Meila's stomach. Disbelief dissolved into dismay. What dominoes had fallen in the past weeks to dispose of the previous Vor king? So quickly? Her captor was even slyer than she had ever imagined. Jaks had thought it was the Ascorian king who was in danger, but it was the Vor king who had been dethroned.

Later that evening, several Vor warriors led by Sicaro's head minion, Sneer, clanked into her prison cell. He motioned and the largest of the goons kicked Meila in the shin until she stood up.

She said nothing, ignoring the pain, and stared daggers into the man's head.

"Put this on her," Sneer said. The warrior obeyed without hesitation, snapping a leather-lined collar with a chain around her neck and cuffs around her wrists. The female guard then sidled past and unlocked Meila's leg-iron.

"I understand congratulations are in order," Meila said to Sneer as the man tugged on her chain, leading her up through the ship. She was glad to escape this floating prison but couldn't resist a jab at one of her kidnappers. "Your esteemed leader . . . now a king. Who would have thought? It seems these barbarians will follow any hairy swine."

Kyle Halwoth paused mid-step and stiffened at her taunt. He tugged on her chain, snapping her head back, and glowered. "Behave," he chided her, wagging a finger. He resumed the climb up the stairs that opened to the middeck and moonlit night.

The Vor thug behind her planted a hand on her backside and shoved her up the hatch.

The buildings of Irin, lining the river, flickered and wavered in the light of thousands of torches, pulling away as if horrified at the riotous celebration seething through the streets and avenues below them, their grandeur mocked by warriors and followers drunkenly vomiting and pissing over centuries-old fences, porches, and hedgerows. Bookshelves, paintings, tables, chairs—anything that would burn—were dragged from mansions to fuel great celebratory pillars of fire.

Meila, thankful for the clearance given her by her armed escorts, trudged behind Sneer through the chaotic corridors of the city. Her experience of Vor natives was limited to her interactions with the captives they had taken at the wreckage of the *Mendhelsson*. Their behavior, albeit as prisoners, had suggested none of the potential for the debauchery that raged around her now.

Despite the chill winter night, nakedness danced with abandon around bonfires, and lust humped and grunted within the doorways and recesses. Fights broke out with fists thrashing in the semidark. And everywhere, barrels poured out mugfuls of froth and ale to sate the staggering crowds of merrymakers.

A barricade of stone blocks ended their march through the wild night. Sentries ushered them through to a makeshift courtyard that, in contrast to the streets outside, was disciplined and tense. Vor warriors and ex-

Ascorian soldiers—presumably traitors from Sicaro's retinue—stood guard together. They eyeballed one another as though, at any moment, this armistice would fragment.

Before her, the palace, for it could not be called anything less, wore the majesty of the surrounding city. Several stories high, it was crowned with palisades and fronted with towers at each corner. The upper windows were punctuated with flower racks beneath each, but no balconies were to be seen.

And inside, all glittered with gold. Statues, orbs, vases, and even sitting furniture glistened with luxurious yellow under lightstone chandeliers.

Meila balked at the opulence. Back on Earth, such waste of precious elements was rare on the homeworlds. The United Worlds had dealt with such class-bound maldistributions of wealth many millennia ago. Here on Planet Maya, despots, dictators, and their nobility still hoarded their riches—while their peasants scrapped the ground for sustenance. At least the UWF were good for some things.

Sneer tugged on her leash again, snapping her head back and yanking her from her thoughts.

They arrived at an antechamber before an ornate pair of doors. Two guards, both tough-looking women, straightened to attention as the trio approached. A hound behind them growled menacingly.

"This is King Rauhalik's new prisoner. She is to join the others," Sneer addressed the tallest guard. Although he spoke in the Ascorian tongue, the woman comprehended his instructions. She nodded and turned to the doors while extracting an iron key hung from a pocket.

Sweet scent and perfume escaped the doors as they swung open. The guard captain vanished into the chamber beyond. Seconds later, the room flooded with light; a central lightstone sconce reflected light off mirrors and golden surfaces and illuminated the far reaches of the room.

Her heart raced; her senses absorbed the sensuous fabrics, languishing settees, and the fragrant air. Was she to be a pleasure slave once more? A rare creature to expand a collection? A flashback from her year of slavery returned to her—defiled and hopeless on an orbital station, an object of a depraved cult—filling her with panic until she stamped out the fear with a tweak to the implant in her amygdala.

"What do you want at this time of night, captain?" a young woman's voice called out in Ascorian. Several figures, tucked under fine blankets and lying prone on stacks of velvet and sateen, were scattered around the chamber. A few stirred and groaned in their bed-places, covering eyes with a hand or a cushion.

However, the woman who spoke was already on her feet next to a long, plush settee against a pillar in the center of the room. Wrapped in red and white silks, her limbs were naked and her hair tousled and wild.

Meila stared, wide-eyed. A tingle of déjà vu

unsettled her as she regarded the woman's face. Thick locks of yellow hair framed a face of cosmic beauty. High-cheeked, wide of eye and mouth, and plush of lips. The type of face that would draw stares from men and women, no matter which planet they colonized. Meila squinted, as the initial sense of recognition—she would not have forgotten this face if she had ever seen her before—shifted to envy. She snorted back a laugh at herself. She was losing her mind. Jealousy? Ludicrous in the circumstances. How could she begrudge a courtesan for her attractiveness in a harem?

"And who is this?" The woman stared back at her while tightening the impractical silk shifts around her torso and waist.

"Ah, lovely Karisa," interrupted the rat-faced Sneer. "You must remember your father telling you of our new guest?"

Looking Meila up and down, she replied, "Your new prisoner, you mean."

"Karisa . . ." Meila said, choking back her surprise. The woman's gaze narrowed in return. "You're Jaks's sister."

That was the source of familiarity. The doe-like eyes, high brow, and straight-edged nose. Like brother, like sister. But what cast him handsome for a man, sculpted her celestial as a woman.

"You know my brother?" Karisa turned to Sneer. "Is this some sort of trick?" she demanded as she stepped forward until a chain halted her. She hooked fingers under a slave collar wrapped in soft leather around her neck.

"No tricks. Why would I play games with you?"

The guard captain interrupted, "My lord, is the new one to remain collared and chained?"

"Release her. She is no mage," Sneer replied, tearing away a wolflike gaze he had fixed on his master's daughter.

Not that you know of, thought Meila.

A few minutes later, with the restraints removed and both Sneer and the guard captain retreated from the harem, Meila rubbed her neck where the collar had chaffed.

"Turn out the light," a woman's voice croaked from the shadows, its owner a figure lying on a mass of cushions.

Karisa slid a hand over the lighting sconce, and the room plunged back into darkness. Seconds later, dim yellow and red flames danced along the top edge of the centerpiece settee as though it were on fire—illumancy, for the fabric remained unsinged.

The blonde-haired courtesan sat down on the settee, heedless of the flame illusion behind her head, and pulled a blanket around her shoulders and knees. She looked at Meila. "How do you know Jaks? Does Father keep him prisoner too?" Pushing aside a cushion, she patted an empty spot beside her.

Knowing the risks and dangers that Jaks had taken in attempting to rescue this young woman, and knowing the abuses she had suffered as a child—and presumably now—Meila brushed aside Karisa's contained manner and was overwhelmed with a need to comfort her. She reached for Karisa and wrapped her arms around her, pushing aside iron links hanging from her slave collar. Her eyes moistened, and she replied, "No, he's no prisoner."

Karisa stiffened at the embrace but soon relaxed into her arms.

Meila broke the hold and sat back with Karisa's hand in hers. "They fought. Your father and him—Jaks was trying to stop him from taking me. There was violence. Thunder. The inside walls of the Academy collapsed. It couldn't have been anything but his electromancy . . . but then your father emerged with no sign of Jaks."

"I'm sure he's alive. I would know if he was gone." The young woman looked uncertain, as though trying to convince herself of the denial.

"I hope so. He would have fought his hardest."

"What is he to you?" Karisa asked, her blue eyes turned down at the outer edges, reminding Meila of Jaks's face when he spoke of his mother. "I haven't seen him for a long while. Were you lovers—"

"No. Nothing like that," Meila cut in. Guilt twisted her gut at the memory of how she had spurned his romantic advances. How it must have shattered his heart. "He tutored me in prison and helped petition my release to the Academy under Grandmaster Mulgrave."

"I can't place your accent. Is it from the south . . . the Isles of Ranila? No, that's not right. I've never seen your like before. And one thing I know is faces."

"I'll tell you, but keep an open mind . . ." Meila began, and then shared with Karisa deep into the night, trusting that this sister of Jaks and Vixhana would keep her secrets from their captors. She described her homeworld and her flight career. Conjured scale-model images of the starship *Mendhelsson* and pictures of a dying Earth to an intrigued and wide-eyed Karisa. And finally, she recounted the journeys and encounters that she and Jaks had endured.

It was the first time she had spoken so fully of her exhilarating adventures on this planet with another person. It was cathartic. Enthralled by Meila's origins, the young woman was an attentive audience and, unsurprisingly, saddened to hear about her sister rendered unconscious by Jaks's electromancy.

Meila ended her story and said, "I don't know what your father wants with me. But I didn't think it would be for this kind of thing." Her eyes darted around the chamber decorated with colored silks. "He went to a lot of bother to kidnap me, but I haven't seen him since that day. Just that sniveling minion of his eyeballing from time to time."

"Everything he does has a purpose. You are pretty . . . he takes what he wants," Karisa said, wringing her fingers together until she looked down to them and smoothed out her palms.

"I'm sure I'll find out soon enough," Meila said. "Unless we can find a way out of here before then. But first, tell me what has been happening here."

Karisa folded her legs on the settee and described the recent events. A week before Lord Sicaro's frigate had docked, the Vor king had fallen ill with a mysterious ailment. By the morning her father arrived, King Harek had been dead for two full days. "I'm sure my father had something to do with it . . . probably some plan to coincide with his arrival. He must have planted an assassin close to the king," said Karisa.

"The king had no heir? Isn't that how these dictators plan their succession?" Meila asked.

"A child the age of seven. Back in the Vor capital. But she's of no consequence, apparently—the Vor way is only through combat."

"I should have guessed."

"It was chaos out there. The one time I was glad to be locked away safe. We could hear clashing in the streets, and a few times, even in the palace corridors. Continuing even until this morning. One challenger would win, with peace and quiet for a day; then another would arise the next."

"So, what's different about your father winning today? Won't there just be another challenger tomorrow?"

"Possibly. But he has already eliminated two other contenders, even before they challenged him. The last had been Voros's most powerful pyromancer. A legend, so the chambermaid says. Thought to be undefeatable. I didn't witness the duel, of course, but apparently father easily bested him with speed and lightning."

"Lightning. I thought Jaks was the only one around who could do that?"

Karisa shrugged. Chain links rustled with her movement. "Perhaps it runs in the family? Maybe . . ." She stared wishfully at her hands. The next moment, tiny lightning bolts sparked to life and danced around her fingers—but without the crackle or presence of real electricity. Disappointed, she folded her fingers into a fist.

Their discussion turned to details of the palace, from what little information Karisa had garnered from her shackled excursions to the gardens and to and from King Harek's bedchamber before he died.

The courtesans' chamber itself comprised three rooms: the lounge where they lived and slept, a bathing room with a pool of flowing, warm water pumped around the building, and a toileting closet that the women used—except Karisa, always chained, forced to use a lidded pot that a chambermaid would empty and scent daily.

There were several entrances and exits around the palace. Kitchen-workers, servants, and guards accessed various doors and gates around the building, while the main entrance was only open to guests and officials. However, escape would not be easy, for even the lowliest of portals was highly guarded.

"Rope these silks out the window?" Meila speculated.

"No. Guards on the ground and dragons in the air. We wouldn't get far."

The outworlder continued thinking out loud. "Jaks escaped the city through sewers to the river."

"The chambermaid complains about odorous sewers," Karisa said.

"Can you find out if there's a connection from the palace?"

"Yes, if anyone knows, Rasish will know. I'll find out from her. Even though she has to empty my waste, she says I'm the only person who talks to her."

"It's a start. Getting rid of that collar is going to be a problem, though. Does it nullify your magic as well?"

Karisa shook her head. "Just plain iron. It's all it needs to be." She sighed, pulling at the device futilely.

"If only we could get a key," Meila said, wondering who else other than the guard captain could unlock the padlock on the collar.

"Do you know how to pick locks? None of us know. Maybe you do?" Karisa's eyes lit with hope as she fingered the metal restraint.

"We don't have mechanical locks like that where I come from. Our neuronal signatures are our keys." Meila bent closer to examine the device. "I could try to figure it out."

Sunlight edged the window curtains, and a few of the sleepers stirred. A woman on a plump sofa nearby propped herself up on an elbow. She yawned, then her face wrinkled as she studied Meila. "You must be the new girl . . . what is that you're wearing?"

The topic of her flightsuit, worn for almost a month, and her unwashed state became the focus of the five women who comprised the late King Harek's harem—and so presumably the new king's—as they each awoke and descended upon their new companion.

Meila needed little encouragement to strip off her flightsuit and sink into the steaming waters of the harem's bathing pool. Three of the courtesans, including Karisa, scrubbed her back and lathered her hair. Meila laughed in surprise when one woman, a buxom brunette named Takola, bucketed water over her head. When the last drops trickled down her face, they teased her about the layer of scum that her bathing had left in the pool. Fortunately, a ready supply of hot water replaced the first, gushing from a bronze tap shaped like a lion's mouth.

Refusing to wrap herself in one of the ridiculous silk swathes that the courtesans wore, Meila hand-washed her flightsuit and slipped it back on, knowing that its advanced material would leech out moisture and be dry within minutes.

The following two days passed with no further challenges to the Vor crown, and Meila learned every detail of her ornate prison. In their daily routine, the courtesans—except for one girl, prone to spontaneous weeping, torn from her family's farm only a few weeks before—would craft a joint fantasy of courtly grandeur within their prison: serving tea to one another, reading out poetry, and singing. In efforts to keep up the illusion, Karisa would illumance away the chain around her neck, even though its weight could be seen to drag on her. "We know it's a farce, but it's the only way to not end up like her," Karisa explained, glancing at the timid, red-eyed girl clutching a cushion to her chest. "Harek had her only once, but she was a virgin up to then. She has the curse."

"Curse?" From afar, Meila studied the girl's face for flaws but found only perfection.

"She has the look of an angel. For as long as she possesses beauty, she will be pursued by men driven to own it."

Meila laughed ironically. "Yes, this world and every other. Only where women are treated the equal of men, is it curtailed. And, even then, it is only by wafer-thin layers of civility that keep men from falling to their desires."

"Not Jaks, though," Karisa defended her brother.

"All men," Meila asserted.

During those two days, Meila made many attempts to unlock the padlock around Karisa's neck, kneeling beside the young woman as she lay on a divan patiently. She guessed that as a start, the pins inside the device needed to be manipulated exactly to activate the lock. However, the hairpins that they had were too stiff and broke at any attempt to bend them into a helpful shape. They needed something more flexible.

The only people to visit the courtesans were the harem guards, who delivered food and drink twice a day, and the chambermaid. The girl, Rasish, visited each morning and completed her duties, cheerily carrying an empty chamber pot when she arrived, and still smiling even as she left with a used one.

Despite her unenviable job, the girl's joy was constant. "Only when I come here, miss," Rasish said, when Meila commented about her demeanor. "The princess is so lovely, and she is always nice to me."

She looked at Karisa, who smiled back at her and replied, "Thank you, Rasish. You're beautiful too. I hope that one day, we can all be free and happy like you."

Then, on the second day of their frustrated attempts to manipulate the padlock, Karisa leaned to the girl's ear and asked, "Will you bring us some nice hairpins, Rasish? Ones that will bend and won't break."

The girl agreed with a nod.

That afternoon, Sneer was back with his personal guards. Without explanation, they escorted Meila by the arm along the corridors and stairways of the palace until they stopped in a round chamber.

A pair of guards stood before a single iron door.

With no other exits, whatever lay behind that portal must be important. Was this her new holding cell? A few minutes later, Sneer's guards clattered to attention.

"Trumpus, Garn Sicaro," they chanted in unison, as a giant figure with several more Vor warriors approached.

King Sicaro claimed no adornments with his new title, looking much the same as how Meila had first seen him on his frigate and every time after. His dark eyes pierced into her soul from within his bearded face. He wore a black bearskin draped over his shoulders, a black steel chest-piece, and banded armor over his arms and legs. A sheathed sword hung at one hip, and a twisted spiral of iron at the other.

Sicaro approached the door and pressed a dimly glowing runestone to a panel; the slab of iron then slid into a slot in the ceiling, revealing a tunnel beyond.

"No interruptions," he said to his men and disappeared inside. Sneer nudged Meila into the room.

A lightstone flared to life in its sconce. Three doors, similar to the first, awaited. The king paused before the furthest and again applied the runestone key to the door.

Another lightstone ignited within a chamber filled with shelves that sagged with gold and silver bars, golden ornaments, and chests that, too, must be filled with riches.

"I have heard stories of your kind," Sicaro said to Meila. Without waiting for a reply, he strode to a steel chest and bent to manipulate its lock. He continued, "Someone had Harek believing your people fell from some distant star."

Meila stilled herself, a sense of dread rising into her

chest. It could only have been Anton who informed the late Vor king of their origins. Her dead husband might have volunteered the information at first, but their subsequent treatment of him—enslavement—suggested they wanted more. And, that their last meeting was at the crash site of the *Mendhelsson*, told her he had most probably bartered the promise of high-tech salvage in exchange for his life—just as she had.

"What you're wearing seems to reinforce your oddness. However, fanciful myths don't draw my interest, and frankly, I don't really care where you come from," Sicaro said. "What does interest me, though . . . is this." He reached into the chest and lifted out a beautifully engineered object. Familiar to her eye and training, it was a darkcore rifle.

"What is it?" Meila played dumb. She knew exactly what the UWF12MW Standard Darkcore Rifle was. She just didn't know how he had acquired one.

He pointed the barrel at her.

She flinched. *Damn.*

"You know very well what it is and what it can do." With the weapon still pointed at her chest, he pulled the trigger. This time, she forced herself not to react. She knew it wouldn't fire. Only she, as the ship's commander, had authority to unlock a rifle—whether it be to a specific individual with implants or to a specific neuronal signature as she had for Jaks. Only *in extremis* would she remove all the protections that prevented it from firing by the pull of the trigger alone.

"This is my disappointment," he said, releasing the trigger. He sighed and lowered the weapon barrel to the floor. "However, I was told that, similar to how a key unlocks this vault room, you know the key to unlocking this artifact."

"I don't know what you are talking about," Meila replied, frowning.

Ignoring her reply, the giant moved in front of the steel chest, nudging it closed with his leg, and continued. "Some trickery, I presume, to unlock it. The previous one of your kind, with great confidence, said that you could do so. You being his superior and such."

Meila scowled at the mention of Anton, but then swiftly relaxed her facial muscles, reprimanding herself for revealing her emotions so openly. She couldn't feel antipathy toward her dead husband for revealing the information. She wouldn't have been surprised if they had tortured it out of him.

"Whoever said that was wrong. I know nothing about unlocking that thing." She would never authorize the release of a darkcore rifle to this tyrant. However, if she could gain control of the lethal weapon, she would gain the upper hand. All she needed to do was get ahold of it.

Pain smacked the side of her head as something hit her.

"Lies," said Sneer. "Liar. You will obey the King." His gloved hand slapped her a second time.

Her head hung limp and stars spun as she sucked up

the pain. She had forgotten about Sicaro's rat behind her.

"This doesn't have to be difficult," Sicaro said. "Simply do what I ask and then you can go back to the women's quarters to stay in luxury. Then, after everything settles down, I'll free you. All you have to do is activate this—along with the others in the chest behind me."

Of course, there were more. Since the first moment she had set eyes on the rifle, she had assumed that Anton had brought the rifle down with him in his escape pod; just as she had assumed of the captured pistol at the salvage site. The pistol was a standard survival weapon in every pod, but the rifle was not. He would not have brought the rifle, would not have brought something he could not activate.

There must have been another wrecked section of the *Mendhelsson* that had made planetfall. Untracked. And the Vors had found it first.

A few seconds later, the pain subsided. "Maybe if I have a look at it, I can figure out how it works. I have a knack with mechanical things," she said in a quiet voice, with an obsequious look fixed to her face.

Sicaro held the rifle up sideways to her, firm in his massive hands.

As though curious to inspect the weapon, she stepped forward. "Can I hold it? To see the other side?"

"Don't take me for a fool." He glared at her but reversed the rifle in his grip to display the other side.

Doubting that she could wrest the weapon away from the giant—at least twice her body mass—the steel chest was her only other choice. A locker held eight darkcore rifles and four pistols. With any of them, she could blast her way out of this place.

Unfortunately, *he* was in the way. She tensed to leap past.

But before she even moved, he shoved the point of the rifle muzzle into her chest.

Her body crumpled to the floor, overwhelmed with a sudden heaviness—just like the time Sarah, her tech assistant when she worked as a design engineer, had accidentally dialed the gravity in their orbital lab too high. *Damn him. Damn this gravmancy.*

"You disappoint me," Sicaro said, then moved back to the steel chest and lowered the weapon inside. As the gravitational pull normalized, his sneering henchman pinned her arms behind her. "Judging by your intention, it's clear that you could grant my request. It is saddening, however, that you would instead concoct a deception to use one against me."

"What do you expect? Kidnapping me from my bed and dragging me into the center of a barbarian horde? Into a damn harem!" Her anger boiled over, quashing the rational part of her mind that told her to shut up and keep quiet. "I will never help you, you evil bastard."

"'Never,' can be a fickle word. You'll come to your senses. Better the *Queen's Quarters* than a dungeon, don't you think? I am a generous man—I'll give you a day to change your mind," Sicaro said placatingly. "And you need not worry. I'm not like Harek. I have no need for doxies. I won't be spreading your legs anytime soon." He looked her up and down as though to do that very thing. She had never felt so naked within her flightsuit. "My daughter seems rather taken with you. Think on this. 'Tis a better option than being stretched on a rack. Karisa will need handmaids once she is queen at my side."

After a moment to unravel Sicaro's words, a surge of revulsion struck Meila—his intent too obscene for her palate. Her fists clenched involuntarily. Sneer tightened his grip on her forearms. Although Jaks had talked of Karisa's past abuse at the hands of their father—to hear him speak of its resumption was as offensive as the smell of a rancid pit. "You are sick. Karisa is your daughter, not your wife. You disgust me," she hissed through tense lips.

Sicaro smiled while shaking his head. "Such old ways of thinking are why Voros and Ascoria need a new regime. Soon, once I am formally coronated, I will declare my queen," he said, and then leaned down to her eye level. "I will give you a single day back in your warm and cushioned chambers. When I see you again, I expect your full cooperation. Anything else, and it will be to the dungeon and a torturer to help you see reason. One way or the other, you will give me these weapons."

From the palace vaults, guards escorted Meila back to the harem. With an ultimatum coming the next day, she needed to hasten the escape she had planned with Karisa and the other women.

But Sneer had orders, additional to returning Meila to the room. Karisa was unlocked from the pillar by the weaselly henchman and led past in chains. Her face turned ghostly white, and her shoulders slumped.

Meila grabbed the younger woman's arm. "Leave her alone. You can't take her to that beast."

A guard rushed up and pried Meila's hands off Karisa and shoved her to sit on a velveteen sofa while Sneer dragged the girl out of the chamber.

"Stay strong," Meila called to Karisa, in a weak effort to empower the cursed woman-child.

Without her main conspirator, the once starship captain contorted her mind for hours, computing an achievable escape plan with her cognitive implants and gray matter. There had to be some way out. If she had had access to her wrist comm and one of the zinger droids, she was certain she could've found a route. But, the last she knew, the wrist comm, along with her darkcore pistol, was hidden under her bed back at the Academy.

One critical piece of information, which they had drawn out of the chambermaid Rasish in the past two days, was a way out of the building: a sewer dump beneath the palace, in a room carved out of the rock substrate, and blocked by nothing except a rusted grill.

But getting there, past the many palace guards, was a problem that even this human-computer could not solve without more information about the guard movements, palace layout—or a bunch of armed fighters. The only real possibility was if they could remove Karisa's slave collar and slip past the guards under the cloak of her illumancy. Then they could seek out the sewers.

Finally, late that evening after the other consorts had retired to their plump sofas and cushion beds, the harem doors opened and Karisa flowed into the chamber.

With head hung low and with red, puffy eyes, she was garbed in a traditional Ascorian gown, the kind Meila had only before seen on Dunberrin noblewomen. It was crimson and stitched with golden thread, embroidered with patterns that curled and wove around her bodice. Karisa's golden hair spilled over her shoulders, freshly combed, and as majestic as the clothing she wore. A stark contrast to the silks and ponytail that she had left the room with that afternoon.

A guard followed and locked her slave chain to the central column.

Meila stepped forward to grab Karisa's arm. "Tell me this is not what it looks like."

The king's daughter ignored her demand and shrugged off the touch.

"Talk to me, Karisa. Say you haven't made a deal with that beast," Meila spluttered in her eagerness to break into the other's consciousness. "We can escape together, all of us. We'll figure a way to get that collar off you, then we can get to the sewers, to the river, just like Jaks did. We need you."

"Leave me alone," Karisa murmured. She picked up the slack in her iron chain and flowed to a wide, round divan. There, she collapsed into the piled cushions and tunneled her head beneath.

Shocked at the transformation in Karisa, Meila muttered a curse at the woman's father—what threat or tainted thought had he planted in her head, for her to agree to this madness? Surely, she could not willingly consent to becoming his queen?

She sat on the divan and placed a hand on the girl's shoulder.

Karisa turned away, dislodging the touch once again and, before Meila's eyes, illumanced into nightwraith dark, retreating even further into her hiding space.

***

Several hours later, the grim light of dawn slashed through a gap in the curtains onto Meila's face. She hadn't slept, but instead had activated a rejuvenation protocol to replenish her neurotransmitters; normally, a process she would only do while navigating a long and complex flight path. Lying beside Karisa's sleeping form through the night, she had needed to stay alert in case the girl woke clear-headed and willing to talk.

Yet, Karisa remained withdrawn, and the countdown ticked away. At any moment, the doors would be thrown open and Meila forced to decide her fate. Release the darkcore weapons and bear the shame of mass murder? Or deny him and face torture and death?

Escape was the best path, but she needed Karisa. Without her, the alternatives were futile or suicidal. Meila gritted her teeth and looked at the seam of morning light.

A rattle at the main doors, and Rasish the chambermaid entered the chamber. She smiled, with her empty chamber pot in hand, then frowned when Karisa didn't respond to her greeting. "I was going to give her these," the girl said, holding out several small hairpins.

Meila grabbed them, and once the girl had left, she bent down and pushed the tip of one pin against the floor to bend it. She sighed with relief when it held its shape.

She climbed onto the divan beside Karisa and pushed the cushions aside. She shook Karisa's shoulder and repeated her name, louder each time. "Come on, wake up. I've got new pins." Without waiting for her to wake, she grabbed the padlock.

Karisa awoke at the first pull on her neck and sat upright. She stared at her crumpled gown and then at Meila. "I thought it was a bad dream . . ."

"He's coming for me this morning. We might never

get another opportunity," Meila said, holding up the bent hair pin to show Karisa. "Let me have a go at the padlock. We can get out of here."

"I can't," Karisa interrupted. "I have to stay."

"Why? You don't owe him anything."

"It's better for everyone if I cooperate."

"Don't be stupid!" Meila leaped off the divan and glared at her. "No one benefits from this madness. No one except *him*. And it's just wrong. It's sick." She steadied her breathing and calmed her voice on seeing Karisa's face crumple under the burden of truth. "Look. If I can unlock your collar, we can start a fire to distract the guards—"

"He'll kill them." Karisa looked at the other women in the chamber, who were rousing at the sound of Meila's raised voice. "All of them, and you . . . if I disagree." She lowered her legs off the divan and rose to her feet. "It's not such a hardship, being a queen. It's normal in some countries, Father says."

"Abhorrent countries. Countries that kill their babies at birth and become so inbred that the children become malformed and feeble-minded." It was impossible to restrain her anger while trying to drain the poison that Sicaro had injected into Karisa's mind. "Your father is manipulating you, just as he did when you were a child. Blackmailing you. You're an adult now. You can't let him use you like this." But Meila could see the fatal despair behind the girl's eyes.

Desperation driven there by loyalty to save the people she loved—as it had been with her mother.

"There's no point. We can't escape. There are guards everywhere, hounds, dragons . . . we would never escape. If I try, he says he will kill all of you, one by one, in front of me. It's the only way I can stop him." Tears flowed from Karisa's eyes. Takola wrapped her arms around Karisa and pulled her to sit, then kissed the top of her head like a mother to a child. The three other courtesans hastened over and added their embraces.

With Karisa lost to her father's blackmail, Meila turned to her last resort.

She grabbed several silk shifts from a basket and began tying them into a makeshift rope. After the final knot, she pulled back the curtains to the bay window and arched her neck to examine the grassy courtyard below. The window slid up only enough to reach an arm through. She would need to go *through* the glass.

As she weighed her options again and questioned her sanity, a rattle at the chamber doors announced the too-early arrival of guests. The doors swung open, and a guard shouted, "Stand for the king." She then stood aside for Sneer and the hulking figure of the Vor monarch.

No time left.

Meila ran back several steps and turned to the window. Someone shouted at her, but she ignored them.

Bounding forward, she pumped her arms and sprinted for the window, aiming for the center pane.

She would likely injure herself, but it was her last chance for freedom. She had to reach the river.

"Stop her!"

A yard from her target, she leaped. Her head shattered the glass.

But as she hurtled forward, a weight whipped around her ankles like the tentacles of an octopus.

Her body slammed to the floor under the influence of gravmancy. A bleeding deadweight, she slid back into the room.

Her escape was denied.

Chapter 15

The Bear King

King Sicaro—The City of Irin, Ascoria

His new subjects called him the "Bear King." Not simply because he towered over them in his black plate armor and furs, but that King Sicaro's sudden appearances at the barracks of his warriors and dens of his beasts-of-war subdued both men and beast equally with fear. Vor warriors fell to their knees and hounds nuzzled the floor as he neared, compelled by his power whether they willed it or not. His first task was to make sure all bowed to his throne.

The dark rod always in hand, he strode at the head of his contingent of twenty and seized the attention of all until the room or hall or courtyard was hushed. As he inspected each man and woman, they would breathe, "Sire," and lower their eyes. Those that displeased him met the ground with force, unable to inhale or expire, their chest or throat crushed in the grip of an invisible titan. The Bear King was no trivial nickname, for all were torn down to their knees.

Gone was the gentleman lord of Sanford. Done was the comradely general of Ascoria. These Vors respected none of that. All they respected was a king of power.

Even when Karisa had been coronated at his side—not as princess, but as queen—none dared challenge this revolution in Vorosian monarchical law. Only the Ascorian Bishop of Irin—who had remained in his cathedral after his flock had fled—had said a word. He decried it a moral corruption, a violation of nature, and a sin against God. The man had died in seconds.

King Sicaro displayed her frequently—removing her collar for those occasions only. And despite any reticence his subjects might have carried about the relationship of the new queen to the king, her astonishing beauty swayed them all in his favor. Not that he cared what they felt, as long as it boosted their loyalty to his crown.

And such was his climb in popularity, aided by rumors of this glamorous new queen back on mainland Voros, that over the winter, shipfuls of colonists dared the seas to see their new king and queen, and receive an allocation of land to toil in the spring. Then, as the lands warmed, Vor farmers brought breed stock to greening meadows, and gardeners and orchardists plowed and seeded fertile soil in the conquered southern provinces.

But now that summer was coming, it was time to stir.

Hibernation was over, and the Bear King hungered for Ascorian blood.

Chapter 16

The Battle for the Border

Jaks—Border between the provinces of Irin and Dunberrin

Jaks's left eye twitched as the horizon darkened with the arrival of the Vor horde. He shivered, despite the warmth of the late-afternoon sun, unable to dismiss his growing horror at the sheer numbers of warriors and beasts of war that he and the Ascorian army would face.

He was standing atop a fortress at the center of a two-mile-long palisade wall closed in on either side by mountains. It was here that King Silas had rallied his army after the defeat at Irin and awaited reinforcements promised from the Pact Countries—but they never arrived, and so the Ascorians stood alone.

Jaks had spent the last few months under Mulgrave's instruction, cursing himself for not blocking his father from kidnapping Meila. Focused to master his lightning, one could find him on the pier or the roof of the Academy—when not assisting the grandmaster—

practicing his electromancy and reliving the fight from the day she was taken. No longer a slave to fear, he channeled the emotion into his magic, and honed his skill until he could reliably channel lightning into the ocean and the skies like a blade. And today, he would use that power to fight an army. Only then could he hope to reach Meila and Karisa.

His hand rested on Meila's velocannon where it sat on its steel frame. The barrel gleamed brightly as the square case with the darkcore gun inside weighed down the back and tipped the weapon skyward. One or two successful shots with the weapon and Jaks could change the course of the invasion.

Two scorpion bolt-throwers and their crews shared Jaks's tower top with barrels of spears waiting to be loaded and fired. And amongst them, a squad of soldiers in steel cuirasses and armed with crossbows stood ready to fend off dragons that might attack from above.

On the palisade below, along a raised walkway, more of the deadly siege weapons waited, stationed every hundred yards for the entire two miles. And alongside them, thousands of Ascorian soldiers and conscripts waited to defend this hardened line across the valley. The Jurn warriors and the Uwama, too, he was sure, were here somewhere. He'd caught glimpses of some tribesfolk but had not lingered to engage them. Jaks was sure they would be staring out now, as he was, wondering how their enemy had arrived so quickly.

As soon as summer flowers had sprinkled the

meadows, the enemy had poured out of the City of Irin. The Ascorian generals had expected the invaders to pillage the less well-defended provinces first; however, they marched directly for the border and King Silas's main army.

On top of fears of overwhelming Vor numbers, disturbing rumors had circulated for months that a *new* and even more brutal king now led the armies of Voros. But no one knew for certain.

Even Jaks's spying, using the zinger droid high over the Vor-held City of Irin, had found no certainty of a coup. And, although he had spotted his father's frigate moored in the river, he could not trace him from the clouded altitude that the droid flew to avoid another scrape with patrolling dragons. And of Meila or Karisa, he could not see them directly, but he knew in his heart they were there somewhere.

"It's those skyships that worry me," said Grandmaster Mulgrave, standing beside Jaks and holding a magnifying scope to his eye as he examined the distance.

"And the damned gargantors and their warriors do not?" King Silas replied to the mage, standing on the other side of the grandmaster.

"Of course, they do," Mulgrave said patiently. "But unless we can counter their ships, they will have a free hand to rain down missiles and explosives. There is already disquiet amongst the troops; it won't take much to shatter their resolve."

"Yes, yes, we should retreat to the capital. It is much safer there," the king said, in a sudden swing of mind that revealed the taint in his character following an immense betrayal some months before.

After his father had kidnapped Meila, Jaks had sent a message to the king to warn the monarch of his father's treachery; however, the warning had been dismissed as the rant of a disgruntled son.

So, when Lord Sicaro returned to the king, Silas had welcomed him with a hearty handshake. It was said that Jaks's father, with a poisoned knife in hand, had then attempted to stab the king. If not for the sharp eyes—and sacrifice—of a nightwraith guard, Ascoria would have lost its king. But Jaks knew in his heart that it was not his father who had wielded the tainted blade, but his father's assassin, Craeg Vesenira. A tapering blood trail was the only trace of the assassin after he escaped.

But despite the killer's failure to plunge the knife into Silas's chest, a nick of the blade had been enough to sicken his target and leave him bedridden for weeks with delirious sweats and shakes. After he'd recovered enough to walk unaided, the poison's toll became clear: the king quickly spiraled into a debilitating paranoia. For months after, he locked himself away, refusing visitors, and communicated through a slot in the door.

Subsequently, in the uncertainty of the king's mental state, morale plummeted, and soldiers deserted their posts. Whole bands of soldiers and conscripts stripped their insignia and slipped away into the mountain forests—preparation to repel the invaders began to fall apart even before the enemy arrived.

Only in the last few weeks had the king been coaxed out of his tower and returned to a semblance of leadership.

"Not what I meant, sire," Mulgrave gently countered Silas's anxiety. "If Grandmaster Hazeldine can get her experimental skyship stable in the air, it will increase our strength in the skies. If we could delay the enemy until her ship could fly here from the capital? Perhaps consider sending out nightwraiths to sabotage the building of their siege weapons, or raiders to attack their supply lines? With the skyship, we could raise our velocannon high enough for a clear shot."

Jaks nodded. Even up here, at the highest spot of the fortress, they were still not high enough to get an accurate shot and ensure they wouldn't destroy the Ascorian defenses with the back-blast of the velocannon. Meila had said the explosion could destroy anything within a half mile. If they could get the weapon onto Hazeldine's experimental ship, *that* would be the ideal vantage point to fire it from.

However, the king would take no risks and refused to do anything other than shore up the defensive walls.

There would be no delaying the Vors.

The next morning, a fur-coated figure rode out of the enemy line up to the Ascorian fortress gates.

The rest of the Vor forces, camped two miles back, stained the far hills and fields. Overnight, siege towers had started to rise, assembled from wood and materials their army had carted from Irin. Similarly, the giant frames of trebuchets under construction stood out amongst the tents of the enemy encampment.

The Vor rider stopped at the main gate of the palisade wall.

Ascorian sentries trained crossbows and scorpions on the enemy warrior as though she might attack them alone.

From his station beside the velocannon, Jaks studied the woman. Except for a blue motif tattooed on her cheek, she reminded him of Vixhana. Tall, muscular, and with eyes that glinted steel.

"A message from the king of Voros for your pathetic leader," the woman called out to the sentries on the wall above her. She held up a leather scrollcase.

A liveried herald dashed out of a side gate to retrieve the scrollcase. For a moment, Jaks thought it was Minto, but the official was far too old to be his childhood friend. He wondered where his past companion was in this chaos of war. Although he'd kept a watch out for him, Jaks had not sighted him even once since returning from Irin. He had heard rumors that Minto was on some secret mission for the king. Wherever he was, Jaks hoped for his friend's sake that he was somewhere a lot safer than here. As Jaks's thoughts wandered, the older herald returned through the same gate from which he'd approached the Vor messenger and pounded his way to the king's tower at the opposite end of the fortress.

Several minutes later, to Jaks's surprise, the herald, accompanied by two guards, puffed his way heavily up the tower stairs toward him. After a few seconds to catch his breath, the official instructed him, "Go with the guards to the king." Jaks dutifully followed the pair back, wondering whether they would have manhandled him if he had refused. His neck tingled with a sense of a foreboding.

Panic and fury echoed in the king's tower chamber as Jaks entered. "There he is. Son of the viper!" The silver-haired king pointed at him and strode up. Then, just as quickly, he backed away as though frightened. "Your father. Your father! How can this be?" the king spluttered. Although armored in embossed steel plate, he lurched in dramatic steps as though struggling with its weight.

"The lad has nothing to do with it, Silas," Mulgrave said in a controlled voice. "The son doesn't control the father any more than the cub controls the lion."

Jaks gaped in confusion. The words of the king and the grandmaster were falling like missing pieces around a puzzle.

The brunt of King Silas's erratic rage then diverted to a piece of paper he held in his hand. He waved it as though it were on fire and threw it to the ground. He then slumped onto a heavy oak chair, shaking his head and muttering nonsensically to himself.

"Look at it, lad." The grandmaster inclined his head to the letter on the ground, lying beside the discarded scrollcase.

Jaks uncurled it and read. In beautiful cursive writing, the document demanded the immediate surrender of all lands of Ascoria to the king of Voros.

However, it was the name of the king that caused Jaks to sway on his feet and grip the paper tightly—*King Sicaro Rauhalik*, Ruler of the Burned Lands, Chief of the Clans, Lord Commander of Voros.

"It can't be . . ." Jaks began, then stopped. It was starting to make sense. The invasion landing in Sanford. His father's heroic escape and return to King Silas's folds. The assassination attempt. And ultimately, his father's frigate in the center of Voros-controlled Irin. His father's hunger for power and control had never let up. It had festered into a grandiose scheme to dominate *both* realms, Voros and Ascoria. If Jaks hadn't been so distressed that his father had caused his country's collapse, he would have nodded in appreciation at the clever timing and alignment of wheels and cogs to bring the devious plan to bear.

Silas unfolded from his chair with the aid of a young squire. "Surrender? Mulgrave, is it the only way? His army is far greater than mine. We have already lost every battle. Yes, I must surrender! We cannot win."

Silas grabbed the grandmaster's arm. The king's face pleaded for the wisdom that seemed to have fled him.

"Out, out! I will speak to the king alone," Mulgrave ordered the guards and servants from the chamber. He looked at Jaks and flicked his head for him to leave as well. "Word of surrender mustn't reach the ears of the troops. Go now." The mage's words trailed behind them as they left: "Pull yourself together, Silas. Your words are poison to the ears of your soldiers . . ."

As Jaks teetered along the palisade wall back to his tower, he maneuvered past dozens of soldiers. Half were armed with spear-and-shield, whilst the other held bows and carried quivers filled with bodkin-headed arrows. Seeing him leave the king's tower, a few grasped his arm as he went by and asked anxious questions.

"Is it a request for surrender?" "Does the king hold his courage?" "How many warriors do they have?" "Is he going to retreat? If we do, I bet half will run for the mountains."

He brushed past them without replying. His mind was elsewhere.

If his father now held the Vor crown, it meant he held its prisoners. A shudder jolted Jaks's shoulders as he despaired at the thought of both Karisa and Meila within his father's vile hands. Perhaps he had dragged them in chains to the battlefield? He wouldn't put it past his father's controlling ways. They could be as close as a field away.

Another thought horrified him. If Meila and his

sister were in their midst, and he fired the velocannon at the Vor forces, the blast would kill them. The very two people he had vowed to rescue.

He shook his head. If he used the destructive weapon, he'd make sure it would be against the distant flanks, away from the center or rear, where any hostages would be held.

On his return to the velocannon, it seemed to Jaks that the Vor siege towers had grown even taller, and the ridge of warriors thickened even darker along the horizon. *Were their siege weapons finished so soon?* Vor dragons circled the ocean of enemy warriors, and behind them, several masted skyships hovered as though waiting to dive forward. The sun continued its morning ascent as the two armies waited and stared at each other across the hills and fields that now seemed as narrow as a garden path.

A quarter hour later, Grandmaster Mulgrave appeared on the palisade wall with the royal herald.

The Vor messenger standing beside her horse, with the sun to her right, scowled up at them. "Where is your cowardly king? Why does he not show himself?" she called out.

Ignoring her questions, Mulgrave glared down at her. "Go back to your kennel and tell Sicaro that he shall find nothing here but pain and death," he said. His words were addressed to the surrounding troops as much as to the Vor messenger. "Tell your compatriots that your new king cares nothing for your country and thinks nothing of destroying it for his own greed and power."

Bits of paper scattered in the wind as Mulgrave tore the letter of demand apart above the messenger. The empty scrollcase followed, thudding to the soil at the forehooves of her horse.

"To the ashes with you," said the tattooed woman. She spat, then mounted her stallion.

Jaks watched the messenger ride away, the certainty of battle sealed with her departure.

He tugged on the chest straps of his torso armor with trembling fingers and rubbed the pommel of his shortsword to calm his nerves. To replace his original armor—abandoned in a pit outside Irin—he'd acquired a new set of finely crafted fighting leathers embedded with steel plates from the Academy's armory. However, his sword was the same as he'd carried since the start; albeit its blade was now rippled and warped with black lines left by the lightning that had coursed through it several times now. Although it couldn't hold an edge like it once did, its true deadliness, in the hands of Jaks, was far greater than its maker could have ever imagined. Little comfort to Jaks, however, as he contemplated the tens of thousands of Vor warriors thirsting for blood a mere few miles away.

As the sun reached its zenith, horns blasted from the Vor line.

The siege towers rolled forward, and trebuchets slid,

the latter lifted by gravmancers and pushed by warriors from behind.

More horns blasted up and down the frontline. The wind carried their shouting and chanting to Jaks's ears as the horde advanced.

"The flanks . . . The forest!" a signaler called from his post behind Jaks. The man, holding a telescopic lens in one hand, pointed left to the central mountain range where the palisade wall curved away.

Within the woods that lined the valley, a mile from the Ascorian wall, a jet of flame blasted through the green canopy for a moment. Two pillars of smoke rose nearby, and battling figures spilled out of the woodland onto the edge of the plains.

The battle had begun.

Jaks stood behind the velocannon, gripped the left handle, and stuck his hand in the back for the darkcore gun. The metal barrel appeared dull, as clouds masked the sun above, and the fins at the far end lay limp and lifeless. He tilted the barrel up and down, then left and right. Well-oiled on its steel frame, it moved easily. Avoiding the central mass of Vors, he squinted through the targeting sight at the west flank. He shivered at the formidable, undulating mass of warriors that blacked out the tubular lens as he panned across the horizon.

As ready as he could be, palms sweating, Jaks looked around for Grandmaster Mulgrave. The veteran mage was nowhere to be seen amongst the Ascorian soldiers dashing around the towers and walls and readying the scorpions, ballistae, and mortars. Jaks frowned, needing his master's direction for when to fire the weapon—the responsibility for the first shot was too much for him to take alone.

An Ascorian signaler from the king's tower blared three notes from his warhorn.

In response, the thump of Meila's gravfire mortars sounded as they fired flaming bombs. The missiles sang as they arced through the air and landed a mile away within the Vor lines. Tiny explosions marked each as they struck a hapless warrior or exploded between their ranks.

"Too far. Aim for the center-most tower," a woman wearing the winged helm of an Ascorian general shouted from the wall further down from Jaks.

The two mortar crews within earshot redirected their weapons, and the following bombs landed closer to one of the siege towers. "Thirty yards left," the general shouted, correcting the teams again.

Much further down the line, a lucky mortar crew hit a tower to the right flank. A cheer broke out as the top burst into flames; however, their glee sank a few minutes later when a figure leaned out of an arrow portal and the flames magically extinguished.

"Damn pyromancer . . ." a conscript muttered nearby.

The tidal wave of Vors surged toward them.

They were close enough now that ladders could be seen carried and dragged. The warriors were eager to scale the walls even before their siege towers could catch up.

Ascorian scorpion bolt-throwers thudded along the wall and from the two towers as the enemy finally marched into range.

"Take that, you fuckers!" shouted a soldier from behind a bolt-thrower he'd just fired, several yards from Jaks's position. His spear and others slammed into the Vor frontline, impaling many, but doing nothing to slow their march. If anything, the leading edge sped faster.

Jaks looked around, desperate for someone to tell him what to do. Mulgrave was strangely still absent, as was the king. He leaned over the tower crenel and looked at the general, hoping she might give him direction for the velocannon. But she was preoccupied with sending reinforcements along the wall and did not even hear his shouts above the cacophony of war.

Anxiously, he wiped his hands dry on his leggings for a surer grip on Meila's lethal weapon. He'd have to decide on a target and make the call himself.

He squinted at the east and west flanks. Ascorian reinforcements had engaged with the ambushing Vors. Warlions pounced onto the tattooed axe warriors, their riders lunging with spears from their backs, preventing the Vor flankers from skirting around the far ends of the long wall. He couldn't fire near them for fear of killing fellow soldiers. The center he wouldn't risk either, not with Karisa and Meila possibly there.

Fretful, Jaks's sweaty hands slid on the velocannon's steely grips as he swiveled it back and forth.

There.

A pair of trebuchets, a mile from his tower but only a half mile from the wall to the west.

Surrounded by ranks of warriors clattering axes and swords against shields, the great throwing arms of the siege weapons bent down to receive their massive, rounded missiles as huge counterweight blocks rose at the other end. Normally, a trebuchet could only throw its projectile a hundred yards further than an arrow, but with gravmancers multiplying the power of the weapons, they could reach over twice that distance. Soon, the deadly boulders would thunder like meteors at the Ascorian defenses.

Jaks's breathing grew faster. The closest Vors were well past the trebuchet line. *Grafuk! They're so near already. I should have fired much earlier.*

"Wind your crossbows! They'll be in range in a few minutes," yelled a captain of the bow, on the wall below. The man then swiftly wound the ratchet on his own weapon.

Phooom!

An explosion rocked the tower.

A hot wave of pressure staggered Jaks into the velocannon and pivoted it wildly. Dazed and confused, his hands slipped from the weapon.

The rear edge of the tower was covered in a pool of

flame and two soldiers stumbled around within it. They slapped at themselves, yelling in pain and fear.

"Get it off me!" screamed one flailing man whose shield still clung to his arm uselessly while his other arm and his legs burned.

Several other soldiers rushed to help but could do nothing but kick at them, trying to push them out of the spreading fire.

Dozens more explosions of red and yellow flame burst around the tower and walls. Some engulfed soldiers, but elsewhere, they just ignited the wood or stone surfaces they struck and burned with black, oily flames.

Fire was falling from the sky.

Far above Jaks, a Vor skyship sailed overhead. A few seconds later, flaming balls plummeted to the ground behind the tower and splattered a line of soldiers waiting as reinforcements. Each explosion burst with the same sticky substance and created new blazes. Burning, shrieking men and women ran and collapsed amongst the flaming buildings and tents of the camptown.

And further along the Ascorian defenses, even more skyships on short sails floated over and rained down hellish fury.

The only airborne defenders they had were caught in a maelstrom of talons and fangs halfway up to the flying ships. The Ascorian war dragons swooped and screeched in mighty clouds of bronze, gold, blue, and red, fighting for the skies against their Vor cousins. Streaks of breathed flame and globs of black acid were traded back and forth. The dragons, preoccupied with their own grim battle, left the skyships free to deliver whatever devices they wished to deal.

A hand grabbed Jaks's arm. Grandmaster Mulgrave pulled him to his feet.

"The king has lost his mind. He is calling a retreat! I cannot convince him otherwise," the bald mage shouted at him above the clamor of explosions, roaring flame, and screaming men and women.

Jaks's face contorted in surprise.

Mulgrave released him and began deftly unbolting the velocannon from its frame. "We must get this back to Dunberrin. The wall here will hold long enough for us to make an escape. Damn the man, he has turned utterly spineless."

Jaks shook his head in frustration. The velocannon could have helped, or maybe not. He wouldn't ever know. They'd lost the battle for the border before it had truly begun.

"Shoot the bastards. Fire!" a voice commanded from somewhere. Ascorian crossbows twanged as the enemy charged across the last few hundred yards of the battlefield.

The Vors thrust forward oval shields whilst those behind turtled beneath shields held overhead. Iron-tipped bolts sank into and glanced off shields. However, some of the deadly missiles found gaps in the shield wall and pierced the fleshy targets behind them. But even as the victims were trampled by their comrades, shields shifted to close the gaps.

The grandmaster shouldered the velocannon. Although the weapon was as heavy as a pot-bellied merchant and as long as the cart he might drive to market, the gravmancer carried it as easily as a broom. "See you below," he said, then jogged to the rear of the tower. With a glance at Jaks, the mage leaped over the side.

A cry of surprise formed on Jaks's lips at his master's seeming suicidal act. But his frown then eased. Despite the chaos and panic all around, he laughed at his unnecessary worry—of course, a gravmancer could control his fall without danger. Jaks regretted his own powers couldn't do the same.

Forced to the stairs instead, he picked up his shield, palmed his sword pommel to keep it still, and ran past several crossbowers and a scorpion crew.

At the rear of the tower, he winced at the sight of the two burned corpses of the soldiers caught in the first explosion—the pool of fire had been extinguished but clearly too late for the men.

At the bottom of the tower, Mulgrave waited, studying the disorder around him. Jaks caught his breath beside him and followed his master's gaze. More than a quarter of the canvas tents and buildings burned fiercely.

Regiments that had been waiting to reinforce their

comrades now rushed about, whacking down flames and throwing precious water onto the fire—but their efforts were of little use and the blaze continued to spread.

"Follow me. Hold the end so it doesn't get damaged." Mulgrave tilted the finned muzzle of the velocannon to his apprentice. "Hopefully, the draft horses haven't taken loose."

The pair of Academy mages jogged through the ranks of a sword regiment battling fires and wound their way through the camp. Flaming tents and buildings reddened Jaks's face with their heat as they passed.

Halfway through the camp, a warhorn pulsed out a five-note rise from the fortress behind. The motif was repeated into the distance by other signalers.

The order to retreat.

Jaks glanced back, concerned for his fellow countryfolk. Hundreds of ladders peeked over top of the palisade. Faces filled with bloodlust topped the scaling devices but were stabbed and chopped down before they could clamber over. The top of a square siege tower neared the fortress where he had been stationed minutes before. A ramp fell forward to bridge the gap to the wall. Vors charged out of the tower, screaming defiantly even as spears and bolts knocked them off the ramp.

"We'll take this cart. Go get two of those draft horses before they bolt, lad," the grandmaster said, pushing the velocannon onto the back of a cart as they reached one of several on the far side of the camp. Fortunately, the fires hadn't reached this far yet.

Jaks coaxed two stocky, long-maned horses out of the corral. The other beasts, thirty or forty of them, stamped and snorted. An eye on the approaching fire, Jaks left the gate open for their escape.

An entourage of mounted soldiers in the Ascorian king's purple livery galloped past their cart as Jaks and Mulgrave hitched the horses to it. At their center, King Silas rode unhelmeted and without a glance sideways or back. Behind him, his army appeared to be holding back the Vor attackers at the wall. Jaks couldn't make out whether they retreated or not, despite the order to do so.

When their cart reached the hilltop, Jaks looked down on the valley. The consequences of the king's panicked withdrawal were apparent. Thousands of Ascorian soldiers darted through the flames of the burning camp—fleeing in a chaotic swarm. Clouds of smoke veiled the battle at the wall, but through breaks in the hellish swirls, brave defenders remained to stave off the attackers. Enormous boulders pummeled the fortress and palisade, some flying over to smash into the burning encampment. Vor skyships yawed, escaping the pillars of smoke, and turned languidly to the flanks. Exhausted of bombs, they descended as though to swoop on the remaining defenders directly.

"We must hurry from this disaster," Mulgrave said. He shook his head and flicked the reins at the horses from the cart they sat upon. Jaks, at the back of the cart, stared at the defeat in futility.

Fleeing the border, the Ascorian army fought as they retreated. Entire regiments that had been ordered to remain and hold back the attackers were slaughtered. But even with those sacrifices, thousands more were massacred as the Vors took up the pursuit.

Only when night fell on that terrible day and the nightwraiths were in their element did the Vors stop their chase. Even the most blood-thirsty brutes couldn't fight through the deadly shadows that ambushed them in the darkness.

Over the night and the next several days, the Ascorian survivors—half of what had first manned the border—limped back to their last refuge.

The Battle for the Border was lost. Only one Ascorian hold remained—the City of Dunberrin.

Chapter 17

Unrelenting Storm

Jaks—The City of Dunberrin, Ascoria

Six days after escaping the border, and three since arriving at the ivory-white walls of the capital, Jaks stood atop the battlements beside Ranger Cromer. The last of the Ascorian army—those that hadn't deserted—had straggled in the day before, and now the city locked down for its final defense.

"Do you believe in evil?" Jaks asked the master ranger. "Is it born into me?" He glanced at the veteran's hawkish profile and immediately regretted spilling his worries to the man who had once been his harshest trainer.

Ranger Cromer fixed his gaze on storm clouds darkening the horizon, pausing so long that Jaks was sure the man hadn't heard him.

Cromer surprised Jaks with a reply a minute later. "Evil? It's not something you believe in, it just is."

"So, it could have been passed to me." Jaks rubbed

his arms as though to expel the curse within. Since the revelation that he had caused his mother's death, and denied his own hand in it for years, he had to know what else he hid from himself. Perhaps an evil equal to his father's?

"We all do evil deeds from time to time. There's no denying. But nothing is black or white," the ranger said. "Your sister saw things that way. And it is what probably near-killed her." His jaw tensed as he spoke of Vixhana. During earlier travels, the two of them had shared an intimate attachment. "Heroes and villains, good and evil. She thought she always knew the clear path."

A moment of guilt stung Jaks at his part in injuring her.

"But is she free of evil?" Cromer said, while still glaring at the brewing storm. "You know she has killed more men and women than most soldiers would in an entire lifetime of war? Many in cold blood. Could a person do that without taking some satisfaction from extinguishing another?"

Guilt twisted Jaks again. This time at the thrill he'd felt personally after he had channeled the wave of lightning through the Vor warriors at the siege of Irin. Hundreds had died and dozens were burned into cripplement. There was no question he had reveled in killing them. Evil, then, *did* seed his core.

But, as though to counter his thought, the ranger continued, "Yet, there is no *force* of evil that compels you against your will. It is always your choice how you act when the sun rises or the blade swings." The man straightened as though finished with dispensing his wisdom.

Jaks swayed against a wind gust that blew over the battlements and eventually nodded in agreement. The ranger was right. No matter how much his father's blood indwelled him, his path was his alone to carve.

Minutes later, lightning speared the horizon and danced across the distant plains. Thunder boomed in response, as though to applaud the furious spectacle.

"It's heading away from us, toward those damned Vors. Hope it drowns them," said the ranger. "The trial flight can go ahead. Let's go back down to the others."

Reminded of their actual purpose for scaling the battlements, Jaks cleared his head and turned his attention to the mustering fields in the military district. There, below, prepared their last hope against the enemy invaders and his father: the velocannon bolted onto Ascoria's one and only flying ship.

Chapter 18

———

The Skyship

The skyship, Grandmaster Hazeldine's invention, would have been a pitiful sight stranded in the middle of the dirt field, had it not bristled with scorpion bolt-throwers, and been armored with steel plating along its sides. A decked, flat-bottomed galley, it measured forty yards long. However, with oars removed, the only feature its past crew might have recognized was its central mast. Its crossbeams and boom, though, no longer flew a sail but instead carried a squad of war dragons, the size of wolves, assigned to protect it.

Although gravmancers from the distant nation of Zura had mastered flyers over two hundred years before, the chariot-like vehicles with their small sail—like the one stored in the Academy's museum area—could only levitate the mage alone and relied on the wind for propulsion. Hazeldine's masterpiece, in comparison, held up to fifty crew, a dozen dragons, and cut through the sky on the power of runestones and mages.

Jaks needed to get to his station on board the ship. A reeking squirt of dragon excrement lay in his path. He screwed up his nose and stepped over it to catch up with the ranger. A ribbed gangplank led up to the deck of the ship nicknamed, by its crew of gravmancer engineers, "the *Kingfisher*" for its tendency, during earlier test flights over the harbor, to dive unexpectedly, bow-first into the water like its bird namesake. Although the eight gravmancers who gave the ship the ability to fly had since learned to synchronize their levitations and declinations well enough to glide the skyship wherever the captain directed, Jaks had crouched and gripped the railings with whitened knuckles during the one previous time he had flown on it.

Grandmaster Mulgrave met them at the top of the gangplank. "Good to fly?" he questioned the goateed man.

"Aye," Cromer replied. "Let's take this god-forsaken deathtrap for a ride." The grimace on his face suggested he regretted Mulgrave hand-selecting him for the skyship crew.

"How about you, lad? Will you hold your guts in this time?" The mage raised an eyebrow.

"I skipped breakfast, and I think dinner is too far past to return. I'm ready." He patted an empty leather pouch at his hip—just in case—remembering the previous day when he had skidded over his own vomit and ended up teetering over the ship's edge.

"We haven't fired the cannon since Meila was taken. I think we had best make sure it still works while we're up there this time," Mulgrave said. "Once we're clear, Master Cromer will spot a target area in the mountains . . . make sure you hit it."

Jaks nodded. A missed shot could destroy the buildings of a mountain village or a mining settlement. That was assuming the potency of the velocannon on water translated into an equally devastating effect on land.

Only Meila could have told them what to expect. His heart sank at the thought of her. He twirled the strands of hair he had recovered from her pillow and kept coiled in his pocket. Her medikit, clipped around his waist, was the only other thing of hers he had saved —it could only be useful.

An ear-splitting whistle broke the air and snapped Jaks's focus back to the deck.

Well-trained to the commanding blast, the thunder of war dragons leaped from their perches on the ship and buffeted the air with their wings. Hisses and screeches added to the momentary chaos, and Jaks flinched as a red wing brushed past his head.

Seconds later, the dragonmaster—with no weapons but her whistle and illumancy signals—blew two more bursts in a code, and a swirling conjuration resembling a hurricane appeared above her head. With further screeching, the deadly beasts split into a multi-layered patrol above and around the skyship.

With the galley lightened of its draconic load, and expecting the captain to call out the skyship's own take-off drill, Jaks jogged to his assigned position at the prow of the deck and clipped a rope dangling from the railing to his belt. Just in time.

A horn blew. High pitched, then low. *Prepare to fly.*

"Cast off the anchors, you damned slouchers," the skyship captain shouted.

Captain Gant's voice was never less than a shout. The cantankerous seadog had been Grandmaster Hazeldine's choice to command her flying ship, and a better one, she could not have found. After decades of commanding a three-masted cruiser, chasing and sinking pirate ships along the trading routes of the northern seas, his maritime prowess was the glue that bonded the skyship crew into a tight-working unit. That he was also a master gravmancer able to comprehend the complex machinations of the mages below deck— responsible for harnessing the gravity-wells and grav-floats that moved the vessel—uniquely granted him authority to command this unusual fighting platform.

The world swayed beneath Jaks's feet as the ship lifted off the ground. His stomach heaved, and he ducked below the railing and held on. Laughter boomed behind him. The veteran crew were clearly amused at the antics of this dirt-footed novice.

"Damn you, idiots, secure those shafts," Gant

shouted as several scorpion spears rolled across the deck. Two sailors fleet-footed over to grab the wooden shafts and secured them point-down into an ammunition barrel.

Thirty sailors, drawn from Gant's cruiser, bore crossbows and stationed weapons around the ship. They were unrequired for the regular duties of sailors, such as rowing oars or rigging sails, so their role was simply to repel boarders and defend the ship—as well as Jaks's skin.

Everything rested on him and the velocannon. Despite all the gravfire mortars, flamethrowers, blinding barricades, and other devices that the Academy had invented, Meila's velocity cannon was the only one that had a chance of stopping the relentless advance of the Vors. Although he had charged up the cannon twice yesterday, he had not pulled the trigger. In fact, he hadn't since the day they tested it at the Academy. But today he would.

Once the skyship cleared the highest building of the city—the flute-glass-shaped royal palace—the deck tilted and wind rushed through his hair as the ship sped forward. Jaks leaned away from the invisible force of the gravity-well, pulling him toward the prow of the ship. He had little understanding of the magic involved but knew that once they reached the captain's desired speed, the gravmancers below would cease the conjuration, and only then would he stand with ease. Compared to the Vor flying ships he had studied through the zinger droid's sensors, Jaks was confident the *Kingfisher* could out-fight any that his father commanded; however, theirs was only one, to the several or more that it might have to engage in combat.

Jaks looked to Grandmaster Mulgrave and Ranger Cromer, standing mid-ship, also tethered to the railing by braided ropes and iron clips. The mage wielded a staff capped by a red orb the size of his fist, and the ranger carried a composite bow and a quiver of arrows.

"You remember the mountains," said the ranger, who had slid his way up behind Jaks. The pull of the gravity-well relented, and Cromer wobbled on his feet as he adjusted. "Different view, but the same that we trained in."

Jaks didn't need reminding of those awkward days as a conscript, but he nodded, recognizing some of the distant contours several miles ahead of them.

"Draper's Peak, then north." The ranger's finger pointed at a barren mountain face. "Nothing around there but rocks and goats for miles. Won't be any patrols either—at least not ours—too exposed to hide anything. Let's see what this thing does."

Thankfully, not a place the dryads would visit, either. Although he didn't know how far the velocannon's effects would reach, the forest dwellers' habitat was on the opposite side of the mountain range and surely well beyond anything the cannon would damage. Jaks's heart warmed. He hadn't thought of the tiny creatures and their hidden orchard for a long time.

All eyes were on him; his back itched from the attention. The skyship was gliding a mile above pasture lands, green with springtime, but dotted with cattle and sheep—ready to be herded into the city streets at the first sign of the invaders. Grasping the handle and grip of the cannon, Jaks swung its long barrel and aimed at the pale outline of the mountain face.

"I'll line her up for you, boy." Gant manipulated steering rods at his helm. The ship yawed port-side, straightening Jaks's aim onto his target. The gruff captain then yelled at the dragonmaster, "Get your damned pets out of the way."

The handler sent a withering look back at the pirate-chaser and then signaled her dragons with a series of whistle blasts; the winged beasts of war swooped into the wake of the *Kingfisher*—safe from the danger at its prow.

The air pulsated around Jaks. "Stand back!" he yelled over his shoulder, fearing that the ranger or one of the crew might stray close enough to attract the electrical current to themselves.

He checked again that the orange dot overlay the target. The pale mountain. He willed lightning through his hands. The familiar smell of metal filled his nostrils. The steel fins hanging at the end of the barrel flipped erect, as though standing at attention, and the velocannon whined a high-pitched buzz. His finger hovered over the trigger.

Shouting erupted behind him, so loud and

desperate that it broke his concentration. The fins of the barrel flopped as the electromancy dissipated, and he twitched his finger away from the trigger.

Several sailors, leaning against the ship's railing, yelled and gesticulated back at the city.

Smoke clouds billowed up from the capital, too thick and wide for workshop furnaces, too many for an accident.

"The city's under attack," yelled Gant. "Bring her about, you apes." The captain came into his own at that point, as though preparing to chase down a pirate ship. His bellowed orders commandeered the flight-plan from a mere exercise to battle stations. "Recon for attacking force."

The *Kingfisher*, its gravmancer engineers over-eager to turn the ship about, spun on its mid-point, pivoting from bow to stern in less than half a minute. At the abrupt movement, Jaks grabbed at the railing with one hand while desperately holding onto the velocannon with the other.

Shouted curses and swearing erupted around the deck as sailors fell and bashed against hard points around the ship. Tethers snapped on some of the heaviest sailors, but fortunately, tall steel plates balustraded the sides and kept any from being tossed overboard.

Reeling from the maneuver but now facing the city, Jaks had a clearer view of the devastation ahead.

A dozen huge fires, each the size of a city block,

spewed smoke and flames from locations all over the peninsula. As the ship reversed its rearward travel and accelerated toward the city wall, an explosion blew a cloud of debris and smoke up from the market district, starting a new fire amongst the stalls and shops. But there was no horde of invaders, nor enemy ships, in sight —only tens of thousands of people panicking in the streets.

Captain Gant steered the *Kingfisher* in a loop around the city, and every eye aboard searched for attackers. However, no one, not even the master ranger, could spot a source of assault.

But Jaks knew. Months ago, he had observed through the zinger droid a hooded agent on his father's frigate reporting on sinister deliveries. The information had been far too vague to identify the locations or the corruption that would hatch at each. But now he knew. Now, they all knew, and could see it for themselves.

The barracks of the Hog Legion and the Royal Pikes spewed smoke and flames over the military district. A half-dozen residential blocks were smothered in choking clouds. And outside the city walls in the industrial sector, a cotton mill and two oil distilleries layered black fumes and exploded to spread fire to surrounding buildings. Scores of pump-carts with firemen spraying water at the flames looked pathetic against the fiery monsters they fought.

"At least the Academy and the Royal Palace are undamaged," Jaks said to himself. But he shivered at the thought of how the Ascorian king might react to this new threat. Already a brittle shard, the monarch, he feared, could easily shatter and throw the remains of himself and Ascoria at the feet of the Vors, pleading for mercy against insurmountable odds.

As Captain Gant sought a landing site amongst the smoke and flames, Ranger Cromer called out another unexpected sighting. "Ships to the west," the hunter said. "Tracking the coast. Can't be our fleet. We don't have that many left. Vor, I think."

Indeed, an armada of ships filled the sea off the distant coast, visible at this distance to Jaks only by the sheer number of them. Unable to distinguish their affiliation, he trusted the master ranger's sharper, more experienced eyes. But Captain Gant, wanting to confirm the identity of the ships for himself, barked orders to reconnoiter the approaching fleet.

"Bastards. It's too much of a coincidence they turn up at the same time as these fires," the captain of the ship spat.

"A signal? Or a distraction?" Mulgrave shouted above the rushing wind. "Get closer, Gant."

"That's what I'm doing, old man," the captain shouted back and scowled at him, clearly not liking being ordered around on his own vessel.

An idea flashed into Jaks's mind. He slid his clip along the railing, detaching and reattaching it to bypass those of other crew members, and approached the trio of Gant, Cromer, and Grandmaster Mulgrave.

"Captain, I can scout out those ships before we get too close—if they have dragons, they might attack us." He dug into his belt pouch and drew out the zinger droid, Slasher. "My droid can stay well above them and show us what we need."

With the dented and scratched droid as the last of its kind—the other destroyed by his father—he kept the device close and reserved it for essential tasks. The last time, yesterday, for the king's generals, it had darted over the Vor land forces closing on Dunberrin—confirming their location, three days' march away. Similarly, scouting out this flotilla of likely enemy ships equally warranted sending the droid into danger.

"Go to it, lad," Mulgrave replied. "Hold off, Captain. Our best weapon could be surprise."

Gant scowled again at Mulgrave but nodded to Jaks and pulled on the ship's controls to return it to circling the smoking pillars of the troubled city.

Jaks sat cross-legged and propped himself against the ship's side. Closing his eyes, he merged his mind to the droid through the wrist comm, commanding the flow of circuits with pulses of electromancy. It sprang out of his hand and sped toward the gathered ships.

The droid returned images as it flew over the ocean. As the first ships came into view, Jaks watched in dismay as Ascorian flags heaved at full sail ahead of the main mass of vessels. Fleeing, pursued, remnants of the royal Ascorian fleet cut through the waves to escape the wooden sharks at their sterns. Two hundred ships streamed the Vor naval flag—a tiger and an elephant fighting each another on hind legs. They tossed and rolled on the high seas behind the ten Ascorian ships. Dragons circled the pitiful survivors: blues and bronzes, bodies the size of dogs and talons the length of daggers. The winged beasts dived at the Ascorian sailors. Exposed heads and shoulders were slashed, and an occasional sailor lifted bodily off the deck and dumped screaming into the churning sea.

The ships of the pursuers teemed with sailors and warriors and appeared so overloaded that their decks were dark with jostling bodies. Jaks wondered whether the invaders intended to land these thousands of screaming fighters directly onto the docks and pebbled beaches of Dunberrin. The only downside, for the overburdened Vor ships, was that they could not catch up to their prey, despite the dragons harassing the Ascorian crews.

Jaks sent Slasher spiraling above the clouds, gave instructions to circle and evade, then broke his connection to it. Opening his eyes, he hurriedly reported his findings to the expectant captain. "Couple of hundred Vor ships chasing a few of ours. Scores and scores of dragons." He stood, rocking on his feet for a second. "Their ships are heavy with troops."

"Damnation." The grandmaster shook his head. "No warning. They must have taken out the signaling tower at the Point," he said, referring to the northwestern tip of Ascoria where the fleet had been holding off the invader's ships.

"How many left?" Gant questioned while pulling at his beard.

"Ten? But they're slowly getting away."

The captain's proud shoulders slumped, and a pained look overtook his face. "Not good, not good. Even added to the score of ships in port and patrolling the rest of the coast, we haven't near enough to fight off that many of the bastards."

"Unless we reduce the odds," Mulgrave said, slapping a hand on the captain's shoulder. He pointed at the velocannon. "There could be some danger to our fleeing ships from a wave surge, but if we target the ships at the rear, they might be far enough ahead to escape undamaged."

Ranger Cromer stepped between the two men and pointed to the master signaler at the aft of the ship. "We should signal Dunberrin and ask what the king wants us to do."

Gant shook his head. "No time. Even if the Dunberrin tower is still in action and monitoring us, it'll take hours for them to get Silas to respond . . . if they can even get through to him at all. When we chase down pirates, we don't ask permission first." He pointed to Jaks and ordered, "Get to your station, mage. I'll take us close enough to sight your target . . . the rear-most ship. Smash 'em up good, you hear."

Jaks unclipped from the railing, staggered to the

prow of the ship, and re-secured himself next to the velocannon. Then, shaking with both excitement and fear, he took hold of the weapon, then angled the barrel down at the enemy armada. Still a splotch on the ocean at this distance, dots against an immense green-blue expanse, he waited until the *Kingfisher* flew close enough for him to single out his target—a galley boat lagging the fleet by three hundred yards.

Every few seconds, the skyship sliced through tufts of cloud, blanking out Jaks's view through the aiming scope. He turned to the captain, pointed to the deck, and shouted, "Down." He hoped the man would comprehend his request to drop below the cloud line.

To his relief, the *Kingfisher* descended, and the air cleared of the pockets of moisture. But even with a clear line of sight, the aiming scope at this distance—a dozen miles—swung wildly back and forth over the galley. A dilemma. Wait until the skyship nears enough for a steady aim and risk becoming the target of enemy dragons, or shoot now and risk missing the galley, wasting a precious shot?

Captain Gant yelled at him across the ship to shoot; sailors shouted, relaying their captain's order.

Jaks waved off their demands—and waited.

A few minutes later, as the *Kingfisher* overflew the first of the fleeing Ascorian ships, Jaks's aiming dot was finally steady on the laggard galley.

"Do your fucking magic now, mage, or else I'll come up there and squeeze it out of you," Gant yelled, so loud that he must have been invoking sonomancy to project his voice. The old seadog clearly had many gifts.

The dragonmaster, leaning over the railing, also looked at Jaks and shouted to reinforce the captain's message, "Now, boy. Their wings have spotted us. They're flying up toward us." The woman then blasted her whistle and pointed below. A cacophony of screeches and shrieks responded, and their own multi-colored cloud of winged beasts dived to meet the enemy dragons.

It was time. Aware that it would be the first time he would fire the velocannon in combat and unsure whether it would even work, Jaks rested his finger on the trigger and gritted his teeth. Electricity sparked around him, and he channeled it into the cannon. The weapon sang a high-pitched whine and its metal fins sprouted outward, trembling as if with the same anticipation coursing through Jaks's shoulders.

The bustle of the ship, the shouts of the captain and crew, all faded to nothing as Jaks's senses needled down to the two things that mattered: channeling the lightning and keeping a steady aim.

He squeezed the trigger.

The velocannon shuddered, and a scream tore from its alien throat.

An enormous white mountain erupted from the sea like a fist of God punching an uppercut from the salty depths. Seconds later, the *Kingfisher* bucked and a mighty rush of air roared past. Jaks's feet lifted from the deck and thumped back down. Holding onto the velocannon kept him from a heavier fall, unlike several of the sailors, who soared and then plummeted to the deck. Screams and anguished shouts cried out.

Focus disrupted, Jaks's magical channeling cut out, and the velocannon's power died away as quickly as it came.

As the skyship leveled, the shouts of Captain Gant drowned out the curses and swearing of the crew as they recouped. He bellowed orders for reports of ship damage—none.

Jaks stared down at the tsunami caused by the velocannon blast. Having reached its apex, the mountain of water crashed back down and radiated out immense waves, further adding to the waves already pushing ahead from the initial explosion. Ships at the rear of the armada, like tiny pieces of driftwood, were swamped; some, the lucky ones, rose back up, but scores vanished forever.

As the leviathan of water rolled beneath the closest of the Vor armada, ships rode the surge. Several more vessels overturned with the watery assault, but many— still more than a hundred—survived. Pushed and pulled by deranged tidal currents, they swirled in disarray.

Only two of the Ascorian ships faltered. Hostages of the hostile sea, they toiled within the chaotic currents. The remaining Ascorians, however, hastily recovered and continued their escape.

"Damn good work. That's given our ships time to

gain some distance, mage," Gant roared. "The opportunity is ours to take."

Grandmaster Mulgrave nodded agreement from where he stood surveying the carnage.

A few hundred yards below the *Kingfisher*, the air was filled with swooping and thrashing wings. The Ascorian reds and greens, with the advantage of height, slashed down upon the Vor dragons with razor-sharp talons, ripping the wings and bodies of their enemy brethren. A dozen blues and bronzes fell to the onslaught, spiraling or plummeting to the ocean surface below.

But, despite the Ascorian dragons' initial advantage, the aerial fight was far from over. Pairs grappled in midair, falling as they fought, slicing and biting at one another. Others broke off and pumped their leathery wings for height, only to swirl and dive again at an enemy below.

The battle was too fast to follow and figure out which side was winning. Jaks hoped that if Vor dragons endangered the *Kingfisher*, his mastery of electromancy would be nimble enough to catch the darting beasts.

Even now, the velocannon's aftermath left the sea churning and swirling unnaturally. Jaks stared at the weapon in awe, barely believing that this hunk of metal could cause such devastation and destruction—a quarter of the Vor ships sunk and many more limping and crippled.

"Now, son," the captain shouted at Jaks several

minutes later, the Ascorian ships now well ahead of the pack. "Fire it again. Get the rest of the buggers."

If Jaks had been close enough to see the faces of the enemy sailors and warriors reeling from the mammoth assault, he might have felt pity for them. If he had been close enough to hear their terrified screams, he might have felt guilt for his second attack on them. But he felt neither.

The armada, having lost interest in their prey, had slowed, with many ships at a quarter-mast. *Regrouping,* Jaks thought. And perhaps puzzling together what had caused this oceanic eruption.

The second velocannon blast engulfed the center of the Vor fleet. A three-masted frigate disintegrated, and a watery monument towered in its place, filling the air with vapor.

The sea surged once again and pulverized the surrounding ships. Jaks laughed with glee even as the *Kingfisher* was buffeted by the blasting wind again. Heady power pumped through him. *Damn them, they deserve that. Destroying our peace.* Once the skyship stabilized, he grinned as hoots and cheers sounded behind him—the sailors of the *Kingfisher* celebrating a win.

Once the vapor cloud cleared, he finally relaxed his grip on the velocannon and gazed down on the angry ocean and the few Vor ships that were left afloat. He thumped the side of the weapon in awe.

Only then did his euphoria dwindle, replaced by

worry, on seeing that the metal fins had melted to gray lumps and tiny lines marred the surface of the barrel. It was destroying itself with each shot. He had fired it only three times in all. How many more could it handle? Could it even do one more? And then, would it just fall apart—or explode, destroying him and everybody aboard? He looked around and, seeing no one else had noticed the damage to the weapon, kept the secret to himself. No need to cause alarm.

Mulgrave appeared and pounded Jaks on the back. "Well put to the squids, lad!" Only a handful of ships remained below, drifting directionless amongst the fragments of their smashed allies. "Shan't worry about the remnants. We'll turn the tide of this damned war with this. Bless the lass—she would have been happy with the results." He beamed a smile.

Jaks had never seen him so excited. He'd tell the grandmaster about the lines later.

"We've done well today," said Mulgrave. "Today it was their navy, soon their armies." The rest of the crew were similarly joyous. Untethered but locked together with crooked elbows, they jigged around and hollered with pride—their little skyship was far deadlier than anything they had sailed before.

The Vors' dragons had suffered a similarly brutal defeat. The aerial battle had thinned their numbers and savaged the remaining few so severely that they dove with fearful screeches for the mainland. In a stretch of mercy, the Ascorian dragonmaster sounded orders for her beasts to break off and return to the skyship. She clucked proudly and threw chunks of meat to the monsters for them to snatch out of the air.

Despite the chain of defeats and losses across the country since the Vors invaded, this one struggle, at least, had been won, Jaks thought. Perhaps a small win, but surely enough to dent his father's gathering forces. And certainly enough to foil whatever plan they had destined this armada for.

In the distance, smoke still plumed over Dunberrin. Jaks shuddered at the thought of the carnage that would have resulted had the naval invaders ambushed the city in the midst of that chaos. For now, though, he could only pray that they would bring the fire under control before the main force of the Vors arrived at the walls. And hope that the *Kingfisher* and the velocannon would hold together long enough to challenge his father's armies in battle—the ultimate battle that would decide the fate of Ascoria.

Chapter 19

A Horde at the Gates

King Sicaro—Province of Dunberrin, Ascoria

The Bear King gestured impatiently for a signaler to attend him as he stared at the thin white line that was the city wall of Dunberrin. A seemingly impenetrable peninsular city to a casual observer, but not to him. For, standing on a grassy hill with his retinue and personal guard, the fields he saw below were not the green of the cultivated meadows and farms that had surrounded the road leading to this rally point, but the black and brown stain of his Vor army. So vast it was that, even from this elevated point, his eye could not distinguish the furthest flanks; thus, he depended on a chain of signalers to organize this seething sea of foot and mounted warriors, hounds, dragons, a few captured warlions, and gargantors.

Sicaro's greatest wish was that he could have crushed Silas once and for all at the border battle. But the coward had made a habit of slithering away at the

290

last moment. And, as he should have guessed, the Ascorian and most of his army had bolted at the first engagement, with the loss of several thousand who stood courageously and died as their craven compatriots fled. Like a dog with its tail between its legs, Silas had run until he could run no more and was now holed up in the city before him.

The signaler arrived and saluted to him, then quietly awaited his orders.

"Send a message for the supply wagons to stop here," he said to the signaler, who fidgeted nervously with her polished-steel signaling cone. "Except for the siege wagons and arrow carts. Each torgue and regiment should carry enough food and water for the last few miles."

The woman nodded, then retreated to message her counterpart at the supply battalion a mile to the west.

"Craeg," he addressed his personal assassin, standing at his side. The scar that split Vesenira's ear and reddened the right of his face had paled over the few months since his failed attempt to kill the Ascorian king. Disguised by illumancy to look like Sicaro, he had got close enough to stab his victim but was foiled by one of Silas's personal guards. Shamed, Vesenira had snuck back to Irin and materialized at the gates to have himself presented to the newly crowned Vor king. Sicaro, despite his disappointment, had ushered the shadowdancer back into his fold—but not before extracting a death-promise from the man.

"Sire? Shall I seek out the Ascorian now?" Vesenira replied, his hands palming the pommels of his swords, as was his habit.

"That faux king is still holed up in his palace, my eyes report. Although the fires didn't come near his hideout, the damage to the city was extensive and as much as could be desired." Indeed, two days of fires had destroyed much of the market district and dozens of residential areas. But best of all, a few of the incendiary bombs had burned down several barracks and storehouses of the Army District, leaving only charred stones and the skeletons of hundreds. "But without the armada follow-up, the opportunity has been lost to end this battle tidily." Sicaro's face flickered with anger for a brief moment. "Much of the city could have been ours by now, and we would be preparing for the final blow, but for the betrayal."

"Uncertain, my king," Vesenira reminded him. "They say it was a giant wave—"

"Impossible. Two hundred ships. By a wave! They were not rafts and barges. No mere wave could sink such deep-hulled ships." Sicaro spat out a bitter taste in his mouth. "Mutiny is what it was. That traitorous bastard."

He should not have trusted that pot-bellied pillager who was always with a flask in his hand. Captain Narler had been Harek's best and most reliable raider, or so he had been told. "Who knows where he's led them . . . or defected to? Damn him to his pirate hell."

Rumors of the fate of the missing fleet had been sent by his spies in Dunberrin. The most ridiculous reported destruction by a freshly erupted underwater volcano and the most believable stated that the fleet admiral had mutineered the armada to foreign waters. If those traitors ever neared these shores again, a volcano would be an apt description for his retribution on them, Sicaro thought.

The Vor king returned to his original reason for summoning his assassin. "A change of mind, Craeg. Rather than have you slink into the city to finish off Silas, I will save that pleasure for myself. Over the wall and through the city, I will climb his fluted palace and crush his head in my hands."

Vesenira nodded assent. "Sire, as you command. I shall remain at your side, your shadow where there is none."

<hr>

The Vor army trampled farmland and orchards as it approached the enemy's capital city. Mounted scouts ranged ahead, while legions of axe-wielding warriors and crossbowmen marched in columns of thousands. Teams of horses followed, dragging great wagons of timber and parts that would be used to reassemble their dismantled trebuchets, ballistae, and siege towers. Gargantors trailed even further behind; their handlers kept them distant from the main army to prevent the beasts from becoming overstimulated and attacking their own side. Overhead, a dozen skyships with billowed sails glided with their loads of bomblets and bolt-throwers. And all around them, dragons spiraled and looped.

Ceaseless, the sea of invaders marched to within a mile of the outer district of the city. There, standing empty and abandoned before them, lay the smoking ruins of factories, warehouses, and residential slums that had, over the decades, outgrown the limits of the city wall and spilled out into the plains.

As he stood surveying Ascoria's last refuge, the acrid smell of smoke wafted over Sicaro. The firebombs that his agents had planted months before had incinerated three-quarters of the mile-wide industrial area, leaving rubble and ash—many still smoldered and trailed strings of smoke. He shrugged. No great concern. The slave camps were crammed with plenty of hands to rebuild it once this business was resolved.

A nearby white-washed farmhouse, the last before the city, collapsed as a gargantor leaped onto its roof.

Sicaro's horse, a seasoned destrier that stood several hands above common mounts, flicked its head and flared its nostrils at the menace—a whirlwind of claws—a hundred yards ahead of them. Nearby warriors varyingly responded with laughter or fearful cries.

He shook his head at the mindless destruction; the monsters had a predilection for smashing human constructions, as though buildings and other man-made structures offended their senses. Another reason the destructive beasts were usually kept distant from cities and towns. That they could be tamed enough to fight was a miracle—and he had a dozen of them at his command. A leathery head reared amongst the ruins and, as though swatting a child's block tower, a massive paw smashed through a wall and sent splinters of wood flying into the field outside.

"Why isn't that thing with the others?" Sicaro yelled at the cluster of generals and commanders behind him. They were debating over a table of maps that had been brought up and placed beneath a tattered pavilion. Several of the gray-bearded generals jerked upright at the king's voice and looked at each other.

"They should all be on the coast flank, readying for the water. The damned thing needs to be kept away from the siege towers," he finished. He raised a finger toward a distant paddock where workers hastened to build one of many fifty-foot-tall wheeled constructions.

Arlo, the man who had infiltrated the Vor council, and risked his life to poison King Harek—paving Sicaro's path to the Vor crown—responded to the command. Recently promoted to a full general, in reward for his loyalty, the square-faced Vor gestured at a junior officer and sent him jogging off to the beast's agitated handler.

The king swung down from his horse and approached the open-sided war tent.

"Sire, all looks in order for attack, come morning,"

Sneer reported as Sicaro strode in. "Regiments from west to east are all in place, sealing off the peninsula—ready to take their final positions at dawn. Trebuchets and tower-bridges are on time to be completed this evening for the gravmages to advance them under the cover of dark to their final staging points. Two torgues will stay with each to guard against any sabotage attempts by nightwraiths."

Sicaro nodded and leaned over the map table. "The outer district still provides good cover, despite the fire damage. Silas should have let it all burn down," he said. "Our center attack will have plenty of cover in the streets."

"You will remain at the rear during the attack, sire?" A general with a tattooed bald head raised an eyebrow.

"Indeed not. I will be where needed," Sicaro replied. Vor tradition required a leader to lead from the front; hence, the importance of a king who was the fiercest of warriors. "Where the threat is most high."

"As to that, sire. A private word, if you wish. You won't like this . . ." interrupted Sneer, touching the king's elbow.

"What is worse than the loss of a fleet of ships?"

"Your son, the younger Rauhalik, breathes. Sighted this week within the city, traveling to and from the Academy of the Arcane." Sneer's eyes narrowed as they often did when he delivered ill news to the king, unsure whether it would trigger an outburst of anger or days of furious activity to attack the issue; however, laughter was not what he expected.

"Ha. Tough little shit. Harder to kill than I would have thought. The boy has more of my blood to him than I would have guessed." The king rested a hand on Vinton's Rod resting at his hip, and the glimmer in his eyes faded to dark coals. "Although his lightning is a dangerous weapon, he has little experience on a battlefield. With my mentoring, we could have routed entire battalions with strikes to strategic points. But as it is, I doubt he can do more than kill a few dozen here and there. No great loss to our superior numbers."

"That's not all. The Ascorian flying ship. It is to *that* he has been traveling, along with his master."

"Yes . . . their ship." The Bear King stared at one of the Vor equivalents landing on a trampled cabbage field nearby. "And what has he to do with it? Is it he who makes it move so quickly?"

"I can't say what the boy does for the ship. Highly guarded. Even to Helena. She cannot get close enough to study the secrets of it." Sneer steepled his fingers as he mentioned the city-guard sergeant they had paid with a kingly coin and promise of lands of her own.

Sicaro stroked his beard. "Nevertheless, there is no need to delay our plans due to one ship. It's time to grind Silas into the gravel. The boy, I'll deal with, if he shows up. He will present no problem." Vinton's Rod sparked as he ran a massive hand over its caged runestones.

Chapter 20

The Battle of Dunberrin

The next morning, a skyship flew below the cloud line, so small in the distance it looked nothing more than a bird. If it hadn't been pointed out by a marksman, gesturing at it with the end of his crossbow, Sicaro would not have noticed it.

"Can only be the Ascorian skyship, Sire," the man—one of his personal guards—said to him. "Ours are but rising just now." He tilted his head to the fields where the Vor flying ships had rested overnight and where the first had just parted the knee-deep fog.

The dawn sun blinded Sicaro momentarily as he looked out over his army to the east.

Columns of his best warriors assembled. The swirling white of fog around their legs steamed off, while the glint of steel from their weapons and armor reflected their menace. Trebuchets were already throwing boulders against the city wall, and siege towers were rumbling toward the edge of the canal. Although Ascorian mortars—their only weapon with enough range to respond—lobbed explosives back, they were few and did nothing to dampen the Vor army's final preparations. Dunberrin was sure to succumb quickly.

In the first assault, the gargantors would swim across the bay and gain the granite walls under the assistance of their skyships and dragons. Once underway, the distraction would open the way for his siege towers to extend their gravmancy-aided bridges across the waterway and for thousands upon thousands of his warriors to stream onto the walls. He knew the defenses better than any man. Strength of numbers, guile, and surprise would take the day. Nothing could stop him.

He gestured at a signaler as he looked up at the Ascorian skyship roving above the city walls—its captain likely too scared and out-numbered to venture any closer. "Send a signal to Commander Fritchar and his skyships to deal with that. Five should be adequate to corner the thing, or at least chase it away from the battlefield." Though only seen from afar, Sicaro's skyship captains had reported the Ascorians had succeeded at building a faster, fleeter ship that was twice the size of theirs and undoubtedly more heavily armed. However, even the largest of gargantors could be brought down—as could the largest of ships. Feints, maneuvering, and superior tactics would overwhelm any enemy, no matter how quick or strong.

Continuing his orders, he spoke: "Five more of the

skyships are to go defend the gargantors during their crossing." He expected little resistance from the Ascorian navy—the few ships they still had remained moored along the opposite edge of the city, leaving just ballistae and bowmen to protect the commercial docks where the monsters would set ashore. "The last two ships are to stay in reserve at my command." The limp-faced Sneer, nearby, nodded, then gestured to the signaler to begin his task.

Black steel plate, the same he had worn in the campaigns to unify Ascoria over a decade ago, covered Sicaro from neck to toe. Said to have been crafted in an ancient volcanic furnace from a metal rock found in a lost subterranean city, the articulated armor was invulnerable to physical weapons swung by anyone other than another powerful gravmancer. Many times, he had carved his way through a melee, blades and points glancing off him unnoticed, leading the charge to victory.

Sicaro grasped the warhammer Sorrow in his right hand and Vinton's Rod in his left. With his weapons and his gravmancy, he feared nothing.

It was with some surprise, then, that a brilliant flash drew his eye to the west flank of his army.

In less than a blink, the meadows that had lay under the smear of Vor warriors disappeared in a blinding explosion.

BOOM!

Sneer grabbed at his king's arm and screamed in his

ear, but his voice was drowned out by a groan from the earth itself.

Sicaro staggered, then fell as a blast struck him like a cart of rocks.

All around, warriors were thrown to the ground. Horses toppled like toys, and war dragons tumbled through the sky.

For several seconds, he lay stunned by the blow. Blood streamed from his unhelmeted head where something had struck him hard. Gray cloth lay across his legs—a tent torn from its pegs. He pushed it aside and rose to his feet, pushing on the shaft of his hammer for support; even under such duress, he never released his grip on either hammer or rod.

A stone thudded to the ground next to him, followed by a shower of pebbles and dirt. The air clouded for as far as he could see—thicker toward the source of the explosion. He invoked a gravmantic shield, warding aside the falling debris. An uprooted tree smashed to the ground nearby. Rocks the size of melons slammed about while stones and pebbles rained down in a freakish hailstorm.

Eventually, the downpour of detritus ceased, and the dust began to settle.

To the west, where the explosion had originated, it was devastation. Nothing stood, not even the ancient oaks and ironwoods that had dotted the landscape only minutes before. Of thousands of warriors, there was nothing left but crawling figures and corpses on a pitted wasteland.

He found his voice and shouted at one of his generals nearby, struggling to his feet. "What caused it? Did you see?" The man, however, still confused, tripped and fell away.

Another man, a thin man holding a dented round shield over his head, edged his way closer. Sneer peered out from under the dome. "My lord, you are injured," he said, staring at the king's face.

"It is nothing," Sicaro replied, wiping the blood on his brow into a smear. "What is the source of this chaos? I've never seen anything like this."

"The last thing I saw before the explosion was the briefest of flashes on the Ascorian skyship. I was looking up at the craft and saw a bright light at the exact time of the explosion. Perhaps this was the purpose of your son on the ship?"

"It cannot be. He doesn't have enough power to do this . . . no one does."

"No one of this world," Sneer offered.

Sicaro froze as realization struck. "That bitch. She has made a fool of me."

"Who?" Sneer dropped the shield to the ground. "The woman?"

"The weapon at the Academy. I shouldn't have believed her. She deceived me to destroy something lesser. I should have destroyed the entire building." Sicaro spat a curse, then lifted his gaze to search the skies. He must get to the Ascorian ship and destroy the weapon. If it fired again, it could end his assault, end his army and his hold on Ascoria.

Several men and women, finding their king, scrambled to attend him and begged for orders, unable to make sense of the devastation surrounding them. Desperate fear swirled in their eyes, reflecting the screams of the wounded in the fields.

Sicaro gazed around. The west flank was decimated. Fifteen thousand fighters gone. Almost half his army destroyed in one earth-splitting attack from the Ascorian skyship.

He had grossly underestimated the outworlder woman and her creation. He gripped his weapons tightly as anger threatened to cloud his mind—he quickly stifled the emotion and assessed what he had left to work with.

The east flank remained—albeit disarrayed for the moment, fear obvious in the disordered lines of assembled troops, but mass panic had not yet taken hold. A quick assessment and he gauged there were still enough warriors to take the city once the gargantors assaulted the flank and the siege towers were uprighted.

"Deal with this," Sicaro ordered Sneer and several commanders stumbling toward him. "Rally the troops. We continue the attack."

"Sire, perhaps we should retreat and regather," said a torgue captain with a trembling voice.

A tiny voice at the back of his mind cried out in

agreement to the captain's plea. Perhaps the best course was to retreat his army? Gather more warriors—form a slave army to command from the thousands that had been captured—and attack another time? He grimaced at the thought. No, he couldn't show the slightest weakness, even after such a sudden turnaround of fortune. He would see Silas crushed before him today.

Sorrow smashed into the side of the captain's head, pulverizing it to mush. The decapitated body tumbled several feet into the dust.

"We continue the attack," Sicaro repeated with his bloodied warhammer held at the ready for another dispute. No one challenged his command. "See it done," he directed Sneer.

He lowered his weapon and stalked toward a mired Vor skyship in the distance as his shadowdancer appeared behind him. "I have a bigger problem to deal with."

Chapter 21

Skyward

Jaks—Onboard the Kingfisher above the City of Dunberrin

J aks stared in disbelief at the savaged earth below. From a second after he had fired the velocannon, he had lost sight of the ground as the *Kingfisher* bucked ferally and sent him flying until his tether snapped tight and he fell to all fours. Dust had then obscured everything as it billowed up around the skyship, quickly followed by a pounding of flying rocks and stones to the underside of the vessel.

But now, several minutes later, as Captain Gant and his gravmancers finally leveled out the ship, and the air cleared, the destruction was vicious and raw. But was it enough to turn back the invaders?

Visible through the tainted haze, a massive crater had hollowed out a segment of the cultivated farmland. What had been a patchwork lined by hedgerows and thin cart roads was now a black gouge surrounded by a brown stain for miles around. And where, minutes before, Vor columns had inked the countryside, multitudes of dust-covered bodies and body parts lay scattered and unmoving amongst the churned earth.

He blinked his watering eyes and coughed dust out of his throat. His stomach churned, and he expelled its contents—whether a result of the rolling deck, the elation of conquest, or the excise of guilt for many thousands of murders, he felt it all.

"Get yourself together, lad," said Grandmaster Mulgrave, pulling on the railing up to Jaks's position. "A better result than I could have imagined . . . but we need another. Many of their legions on the other side of the field still stand and are regrouping."

Jaks wiped his mouth and followed the mage to the velocannon. He pushed the guilt aside. It was either the Vors or his countryfolk.

"The barrel looks damaged. I'll cool the metal and examine it closer." Mulgrave laid hands on the metal shaft and a frigid breeze spiraled around him. "Not too quickly or it might worsen those cracks," he said.

A minute later, he spun the weapon on its holding bracket and gazed into the dark barrel. Wide enough to reach inside, he thrust his arm into the round opening and felt around. He frowned and pulled his arm out, then ran his hand over the exterior as though to smooth the cracks on its surface.

"How does it fare?" Jaks asked. It had only been fired four times. Surely, it could do more. Then he remembered it was just an improvised contraption made of wreckage. They were lucky it even worked.

"The cracks threaten to strike all the way through the barrel." The grandmaster shook his head.

"Just one more time and it'll all be over!"

"Another time might destroy it." The grandmaster grimaced. "It would kill all of us with it. No, we need to return to the runic forge. I can weld steel bands around it for reinforcement."

Distracted by a movement below, Jaks staggered a step. His voice pitched high. "We don't have time, Grandmaster." He pointed at several flying Vor ships and a cumulus of draconic forms.

The bald mage squinted over the prow. "The fiends just don't give up."

"Their ships soar our way. Coming for us. Coming to stop us," said Jaks. The hairs on the back of his neck rose. He sensed an angered grief rising toward him, seeking revenge for the tragedy of thousands killed.

A whistle pierced the air. The dragonmaster sounded her device twice more and illumanced a commanding rune into the air. Red and green beasts leaped and dove from their perches on the masts and railings of the *Kingfisher* with a flurry of wings and bursts of breathed fire. Having overcome his initial fear of them and becoming accustomed to their contained ferocity on the ship, Jaks found pride at seeing the powerful creatures once again leaping to the ship's defense.

Captain Gant bellowed for his sailors to prepare for battle. Ballistae clanked as they were ratcheted tight and loaded with quick, light spears. Heavier spears and grape-shot canisters waited nearby in case the Vors neared for ship-to-ship combat.

"Five of the devils!" Gant shouted for all to hear. "Outnumbered, but we're more than their match. Their tubs are nothing compared to our lady. Let's show them how we fight in the Ascorian navy!" Bold words, but ones that the veteran seadog doubtlessly believed.

The crew, emboldened by his words, cheered and shouted as one, "*Kingfisher!*"

Jaks's reports of the zinger's recordings over the past weeks supported that confidence—as long as his observations of the enemy ships were accurate. Although half the size of the *Kingfisher*, his father's ships took twice as long to change direction and generally flew half the speed; however, with raised sail and wind to fill it, the longboats could speed like an eagle on the wing.

Yet, both the strength and the weakness of the Ascorian skyship was in its human engine. Designed by Meila and Grandmaster Hazeldine to allow eight gravmancers to coordinate their magic, it relied on the skills and control of those eight gravmancers who sweated in the gloom below deck.

Captain Gant relied on a set of four levers to signal his course adjustments to the gravmancers. Each lever manipulated ropes and springs to adjust dials in front of each of the eight mages seated with knees around a large runestone. According to the dial instructions, they would alter their gravmantic "well," and the combined gravity fluxes then resulted in changes of speed, direction, and/or elevation of the skyship. Sometimes all at the same time. It was a delicate dance of gravmancy that had taken many hundreds of hours for the captain and crew to master. Mastery now tested to the extreme.

"Hold on!" Jaks shouted to Mulgrave as the ship jolted and pressed him against the side rail.

"We take the fight to the enemy. Target the rightmost ship. Toss firebombs when we pass over," the captain cried out from the helm. With a height advantage going into this fight, his sailors could rain down oil flasks like flaming meteors with impunity.

The air ahead and below exploded into a hurricane of red, black, blue, and green. Dragons dived and swooped, screeching and slashing with razor-sharp talons, biting and snapping at all within reach. How they distinguished friend from foe, or whether they even knew, Jaks wondered at the terrible spectacle.

The *Kingfisher*'s ballistae thunked and clattered as the crews reloaded and fired spears into the fray. Either the sailors had a clearer idea of which dragons were theirs or did not care which of them they hit.

"Protect the ship," Mulgrave said to Jaks. "Do what you can. I'm going back for my runestaff." He waved a thick finger toward the ship's stern, where the ironwood staff was gripped in a weapons stand, its fire gem glimmering a life of its own.

As the mage retreated, a flicker at the edge of Jaks's vision and a deafening screech caused Jaks to flinch. If he had been the target, the slight movement would not have saved him, but the black dragon's prey instead stood at middeck, lifting an armful of spears. The dragon hurtled toward the sailor, first spitting a glob of dark liquid at him and then raking claws over his astonished face. Thrown back and screaming, the man's blood misted the air as his jaw parted from his skull. He thrashed on the ground, clutching his mangled face. Black acid bubbled where it splattered his exposed skin and armor. Spear shafts clattered to the deck and rolled chaotically around the dying man.

More screeches. Several draconic figures swooped in from all directions.

Abandoning their ranged weapons, the sailors picked up fighting spears and sabers, and poked and slashed back at the dragons in defense.

Another sailor was lifted and dragged until his rope tether tightened and tore him out of the dragon's clutches, only for the man to collapse with blood spraying from his ragged neck.

The captain's second mate, a haughty Fauconian, speared a blue dragon as it dived. But even with a shaft through its chest, the winged monster fell onto the hairy-chested man, slashing and biting at him as it died. Wings and arms entwined, the duo convulsed in a death match until a red-faced sailor stabbed the dragon several more times, but not in time to save his shipmate from disembowelment.

Bolts of fire spat from the rear deck. Grandmaster Mulgrave, with a dome of fire over his head and shoulders and runestaff in his hands, invoked fiery projectiles left and right at dragon shapes harassing the captain's helm. Backed up to the mage, Captain Gant held up a round shield and a stabbing spear at the swooping figures. The pair danced a defense to clear the ship up to the central mast.

Jaks fell into his battle training. He diverted the terror of the situation into an invocation and created a web of electromancy, thick and deadly with lightning. He drew his sword.

Several yards away, a red dragon and another midshipman fought. The beast flapped in midair with talons grasping the edge of the man's shield. It hissed and then breathed fire at the sailor. The man screamed as the jet of flame blinded him and burned his face.

"Let go of the shield!" Jaks shouted.

Whether in response to Jaks's command or the agony of his blistered face, the sailor released the shield and fell to the deck. And, as Jaks anticipated, the dragon gained height with the shield in its grip—high up enough for the electromancy to spare the man below.

He swung his sword. Lightning flashed through the gap from steel to dragon, snapped like a whip, and filled the air with brilliant white. Where it struck, it exploded and blasted the beast into a starboard arc over the ship's side.

But no sooner had he lowered his sword than another of the hell-born creatures plunged toward him. His reflexes too slow to react, he could barely twitch his sword to the new threat when his mage shield reacted and burst with a blinding light.

Outstretched talons exploded, and the dragon's electrified body thudded to the deck. A wing knocked Jaks's feet out from under him. Head striking the deck hard, his surroundings blurred into darkness.

Jaks roused to a woman's face close to his and her hands gripping his shoulders as she shook him. "Get on your feet, mage. No time to nap. The battle isn't done," she yelled and flopped his arm over her shoulder and pulled him up.

He groaned and stood, thanking the sailor before she stepped back to reach for her spear and shield. His waist feeling unusually free, his gaze trailed down to his rope tether—blackened and smoking, it dangled, burned to a wick by his electromancy.

A distant shout followed by several thudding noises about the ship raised Jaks's dazed attention. Through gaps in armor plates at the prow of the ship, he saw only clear skies ahead: no dragons or skyships.

"Below," Ranger Cromer shouted from the middeck. "Ships below. Prepare to repel boarders!"

Leaning through the gap, wind stinging his eyes, Jaks's gaze fell on four flying longboats below. The fifth Vor ship spiraled wildly in the distance, clouded with Ascorian war dragons. On the nearer skyships, he could see battle-enraged faces sneering from the deck and their bearers flourishing axes and knives, their blades begging for blood.

A manic web of ropes spanned the air between the Vor ships and the *Kingfisher*. A second later, yet another of the strands hummed through the air on the tail of a whaling harpoon, disappeared beneath the skyship, and thunked. Several bearded Vors pulled on the rope and reeled in their catch with beefy arms. Spiders entrapping a wasp.

"Cut the ropes." Gant gestured with a falchion in his hand. "Climb down if you have to."

Jaks watched incredulously as five sailors unquestioningly obeyed the captain's order and clambered over the sides, sure-handedly clinging to mooring ropes and hawsers. He shook his head, admiring their bravado and loyalty.

But soon after, the first of them screamed as he plummeted into the vast gap below. Missiles pelting the underside of the skyship sent one after another of the sailors to their deaths. Their lives sacrificed for only three of the many harpoons to be cut free.

With crossbow bolts pinging off shielding along the

rails, no other sailors dared follow their mates over the edge. Instead, they turned to hurling oil flasks topped with flaming rags at the Vor ships.

Most missed their targets, but a few scored hits on two ships below. Glass smashed and splattered over warriors and wooden decks. Oil ignited and burned black as it consumed screaming men and women—several became so confused, they jumped from their burning ship into the abyss.

Ruthless flames engulfed a canvas sail on the Vor ship closest to them and the captain's helm on the furthest.

At the other end of the *Kingfisher*, Grandmaster Mulgrave pointed his runestaff and projected an immense blade of fire. Scorched by the intensity of his magic, ropes binding the ship fell away, braids burned to charred ends within seconds.

Chaos. Burning deck, panicking crew, and flapping ropes sent the first enemy skyship wildly adrift.

The second damaged ship, too, tiller ablaze with its captain unable to approach the burning controller, lurched and then rolled upside down. Its crew and warriors, untethered, tipped out of the ship and fell screaming with arms flailing uselessly.

"Enjoy the view down!" a red-headed sailor shouted at the rolling ship and laughed.

Jaks's eyes dropped to the farmlands and city below. The skyships, bound in a tangled web, drifted above the main battlefield.

The battle for the walls of Dunberrin raged, with tiny dots of infantry and beasts of various shapes marring the landscape. Plumes of smoke and roaring fires smeared the already demolished outer city; siege towers and bridges forded the canal moat. From this height, Jaks couldn't discern the sway of the battle. Disappointed, he realized that if he fired the velocannon at the Vors now, the blast would most likely demolish the city wall and its defenders as well.

Shouted warnings from the crew behind him renewed Jaks's focus on their battle for the skies.

The last three skyships pulled level with the *Kingfisher*, pulling in their harpoon strands. The two ships to Jaks's left were lined with terrifying, bearded demons, gesticulating with wicked axes and swords. They balanced on the edge of their longboat, vying to be the first to leap the quickly narrowing divide. And to his right, the third ship rose. Warriors hurled grappling hooks. All fell short, but it wouldn't be long until they could secure their prize.

Teeth gritted, arms trembling, and fighting an impulse to run away and hide, Jaks turned to the dual ships on the port-side.

Warriors, from the land of his father and his ancestors, but as different from him as Zurans, Ranilians, or any other barbarians from a far-off land, jeered and yelled across the gap of only forty yards. "Rip off yer arms," "Tear off yer head," and "Fuck yer skull," they screamed. No doubt they would if they boarded. But they wouldn't get that far if he could help it.

"Take cover, mage, you'll get shot!" shouted a sailor, himself winding back the cord of a crossbow to fire back at the enemy.

At Jaks's command, filaments of electricity warped around him. Seconds later, a Vor crossbow bolt seeking to lodge in his chest struck the elemental shield and exploded, its fragments repulsed and impotent.

With their snarling faces and burning hatred still piercing his shield, he gathered the pool of fear brimming in his head, feeling oddly confident yet utterly terrified, and visualized a scenario for the Vors' destruction. Another minute and the ship would be within range of the invader's grappling hooks.

Clouds swirled and brewed above the pair of skyships, darkening and pulsing brightly several times. A sound like whips cracked the air.

The skin on Jaks's arms prickled, and the smell of metal invaded his nostrils.

With palms stretched toward the clouds pent up with crackling energy, he drew them down.

Forks of lightning barraged the Vor skyships in a storm of electromancy.

Wooden masts detonated, timber decks erupted, and bodies exploded.

White flashes, faster than the eye could follow, danced across the ships, lightning bolts seeking anything they could lash at.

"Get the fuckers," yelled the Ascorian crossbowman, who a minute before had been fearing for Jaks's safety. "Take that, fucking squidbait!" The sailor twanged off his weapon, but it was a needless effort.

Under the blasts of the lightning storm, the pair of skyships splintered apart. The prow of the nearest broke loose and tumbled as though falling off a cliff—men and women aboard uselessly grabbed for anything that could stay their descent; several seconds later, the flaming remains of the fractured skyship followed, leaving a trail of smoke and tumbling crisped bodies. Storm clouds lathered the second skyship with sheets of lightning, each bolt smashing parts off even as it plunged out of control.

The debris of the two ships falling smaller, Jaks clapped his hands together and broke off his invocation. The arcs of white energy disappeared in an instant and the clouds receded and dissolved.

He slumped forward, gripped the rail, and gasped for air—unaware he had starved himself of breath throughout the storm.

"Mage." The crossbowman clapped a hand onto Jaks's shoulder. "Master, their last ship is upon us. You must help." Though still light-headed, he turned to the sailor's gesture as the last of the Vor skyships, grappling hooks grasping, crunched into the side of the *Kingfisher*.

Dozens of warriors aped over the sides of the Vor skyship. Sailors stabbed and slashed to repel the boarders, but those who fell were ruthlessly trampled by their eager comrades pushing up from behind. Jaks prepared his sword, the melee too close for broad strokes of lightning.

"Boy," a familiar voice cut to Jaks's soul.

All else fell away as King Sicaro, black steel from neck to toe, descended like a dark angel from some hellish aerie. With arms outstretched, left hand gripping a triple-stoned rod and the other a giant warhammer, he alighted the deck.

"There is a reckoning to be had for what you have done."

Jaks fell, compelled by his father, to his knees.

Chapter 22

The Duel

Jaks—Deck of the Kingfisher

"Demon child," said Sicaro to Jaks. "I always thought it would be the older one who would be the thorn in my side . . . but it turned out to be you."

Jaks stared at his father, his cheek pressed, paralyzed, against the deck, gravmanced with invisible slabs like everyone else he could see from the corners of his eyes. Warriors and sailors, Ascorian and Vor alike, lay sprawled and unmoving under the warrior king's magic, groans and gasps for mercy barely heard above the howling wind.

The dark clouds above grew smaller as the *Kingfisher* hurtled uncontrolled toward the ground, dragging the Vor skyship down with it.

One of the three runestones on the spiral rod that his father bore pulsated gray and midnight black—no doubt fueling or magnifying his gravmancy—the red and green glow of the other two stones simmered, waiting.

"First mother, then sister, and no doubt craving to murder your father and king as well," he continued. "And how about the other sister? Slit her pale throat and make it complete?"

The words burned in Jaks's mind. The truth being, more than anything, he did desire to kill him. No one had brought greater pain or suffering to him than his father. No one more shame or guilt. But unable to even breathe, his chest crushed by the gravmantic giant, he could not shout his rage nor focus his power to invoke a stroke of lightning—he could do nothing but strain his lungs for air.

"Enough!" Grandmaster Mulgrave shouted.

On the edge of Jaks's dimming vision, the stocky mage pushed to his feet on the middeck with the timber of the central mast at his back. Leaning on his staff, he pointed the orb atop its shaft at the Vor king. "Enough, Sicaro. Destroying us all will make no difference. The battle is lost. The invasion is lost. You have lost."

Fire burst from the grandmaster's orb and enveloped the steel-encased bear. Heat so intense, ironwood decking warped and blackened beneath the roaring flames. Bodies beneath the path of flame caught fire; if they still lived, they made no sound as they burned.

Abruptly, the weight lifted from Jaks. Chest heaving, he sucked in the sweetest-tasting air. Released.

He rolled flat on his back, with his vision sharpening and strength replenishing.

The upward rush of air around the *Kingfisher* slowed and the sounds of humanity returned with gasps and then groans of pain.

"Ancient fool," Sicaro bellowed from within the raging cone of fire.

Forging to his feet and backing up to the skyship railing, Jaks groaned as the flames retreated, revealing his father unharmed by Mulgrave's pyromancy except for his beard and hair scorched to stubble and his face an angry red.

"Your fire is pathetic, old man." The Vor king held Vinton's Rod before him—the red runestone within its spirals glowed brilliantly, having absorbed the grandmaster's pyromancy. "Once I destroy this ship along with the two of you, Ascoria will be mine." He made a peculiar gesture with the rod, pointing at Jaks momentarily, although his eyes remained latched on his veteran adversary.

Mulgrave called out to Sicaro, "Look . . . your army is breaking. The few legions you have left will soon dissolve into a rout." Jaks followed his father's gaze to the battle on the land below. The *Kingfisher* had leveled out from its plunge over the Vors' rear line. Low enough that the cries of both humans and beasts rose to his ears. "Your towers are destroyed. With no passage across the canal to aid your monsters, they fall one by one." As though cued by the mage's words, a gargantor, prickled by pikes and engulfed by unnatural fire, toppled from the wall and splashed into the canal below.

A clamor of bells then rang from the city walls.

The canal frothed, but it was not the great, gray monster returning; instead, several of the city bridges broke the surface, returning to their peacetime positions. Was the grandmaster mistaken? Had the Vors taken control of the vital bridges and city gates?

The truth manifested when the gates crashed open and armored warlions bounded out of the giant portals— the beasts roared as they sprang into the midst of the Vor legions. Bodies were torn and tossed aside. Catapults and trebuchets were abandoned as the invader's panicked and fled.

Warriors and sailors aboard the skyship, many limping or pained from Sicaro's paralyzing assault, had retreated to opposite sides of the deck to recover. But at the sight of the turning tide of battle below, the Vors dismissed their injuries, began chanting, and raised their weapons in defiance.

The Vor king lifted his hammer and howled a war cry, signaling his warriors to attack.

A coiled snake, Sicaro lunged across the deck, the spike of his warhammer swinging at Mulgrave's skull. The mage's magical staff lashed out to counter the blow. A ball of raging flames erupted around the pair and obscured them from view.

And all down the skyship, the melee renewed as both sides roared and met with a clash of steel on steel.

At the stern, Captain Gant hefted a saber, leading five of his sailors as they defended the steps into the belly of the ship. Middeck, the fight degenerated into a brutal bloodbath of axes, knives, and fists; the combatants wrestling and stabbing at whatever enemy they could.

Movement flickered on the edge of Jaks's vision. He twitched toward it. There it was—a pool of shadow with no source—a memory from the night.

Confused, he scrambled back from the darkness slithering across the deck. Were his eyes failing? Was he hallucinating fragments of Vixhana?

Then it lunged.

Pain stabbed through Jaks's belly.

He stared incredulously at a steel blade sprouting from the front of his leather doublet.

A hand materialized around the dagger's handle and continued to sink the blade up to the hilt.

"That'll do you, whelp." The rest of Craeg Vesenira materialized in front of Jaks, cords of muscles protruding on his tattooed neck and down into his arm. His father's assassin did not smile or grimace at his deed; instead, bitter sorrow shadowed his face.

Jaks fell to the deck, dagger embedded in his front and blood seeping from the wound.

The bare-chested Elliptan stood over him with a second dagger in his hands, readying a deathblow.

Jaks raised a hand against the blade. Electromancy responded to his fear.

Serrated lightning and a deafening clap tore between Jaks and Vesenira.

The assassin was hurtled backward, lifted into the air by tendrils of white. His body crumpled against the far railing, smoldering and spasming for a few seconds until finally going limp, a grotesque mask twisting his face.

Jaks gasped, sickened at the sight of the dagger protruding obscenely from his body. No one around to help—the clashing sailors and boarders showed no sign of abatement and the fiery ball surrounding Mulgrave and Sicaro flared even greater than before. He spilled Meila's medikit around himself, groaning with every movement . . . weakening with each second.

He had studied the contents earlier that day and racked his memory for what Meila had instructed each was for. It was the medigel bandage that he needed right now. The miraculous healing particulates that would stop the bleeding.

He gritted his teeth and yanked the leather-handled dagger from his gut. He screamed, almost passing out in pain. Breathing heavily, a minute later, he lifted the edge of his doublet and slapped the bandage to the seeping wound. The doublet fell in place, and he pressed the pad to his skin. Despite the agony, he didn't seem to be bleeding much. Hopefully, there wasn't much internal bleeding either. Perhaps, off-center, Vesenira had missed his vital organs and vessels.

Pain—there was something for it. Meila had shown him before.

The green bottle. Tiny pills to numb the body. He threw several in his mouth and slumped flat on his back. A dozen breaths later and the pain had receded to a dull ache, and his energy slowly returned.

He pushed himself up onto his hands and knees.

His father stood with chest heaving on the middeck, staring at the grandmaster, his warhammer and Vinton's Rod held to either side.

Mulgrave, his back to Jaks, panted heavily with his mage's staff raised to his opponent.

Their fiery shield had extinguished, but its aftereffects smoked and burned around them. Several human forms twitched on the deck, charred and disfigured. Flames ran up the central mast and out along its beams.

On the far side of the burning ship, the remaining warriors and sailors continued in a whirl of stabbing and swinging blades.

Where the Vors had boarded, their skyship now drifted free from the *Kingfisher*, its tethers and grappling hooks hanging loose.

"Apprentice . . . how bad is it?" the grandmaster shouted to Jaks but without turning his head. The veteran battlemages appeared at an impasse, fatigued and swaying heavily. Mulgrave stumbled, almost falling, but caught himself by leaning on his staff. His right leg was awkward at the knee; his arm, on the same side, fell limply; and blood poured down his brow.

The Vor king grimaced, also showing wounds— chest plate cratered inward and the left side of his face blistered, red and raw.

"Fine, Master. I'll be fine," said Jaks, wincing as he rose to his feet, never taking his eyes off his father. Injured, the man looked even more dangerous and terrifying.

The Vor king tossed down his fisted hammer and tore off the dented chest piece. He cast it aside, and his breathing eased. Vinton's Rod thumped into his palm and he met Jaks's eyes.

"Your master is nigh dead." Sicaro flared a disdainful look at the bald mage leaning on his staff. His eye blazed through the ravaged side of his face. "And you will soon join him, frightened little boy."

Jaks placed a trembling hand on the grandmaster's shoulder and pressed him to retreat.

It was time to face the source of his greatest fears.

He paced to within three arm-lengths of the man he had once called "father." His lips thinned to a line, thinking "torturer" would have been more apt. The quivering fear of a minute past pivoted toward a shaking anger.

"You don't intimidate me. My powers are far greater than yours." He raised his crippled hand. Sprites of lightning jumped between the remaining fingers. "You cut me, you beat me, you deceived me . . .

but you have not conquered me." His other hand lifted, and sparks danced back between his palms. "I have made mistakes, but the blame is on you. You are right, there is a reckoning to pay . . . but it is *you* who will pay it."

"Enough," snapped Sicaro. "Time to finish this—" Two strides and the giant vaulted toward Jaks with Vinton's Rod swinging in an overhead arc at his head.

Energy surged through Jaks's hands. Bitterness tainted his mouth.

A brilliance of lightning caught his father in midair, focused on the artifact swinging in his hands.

The blast reversed the weapon's descent, sending both attacker and weapon flying in separate directions.

Sicaro hurtled backward. He struck the charred center-mast and slid to its base. Vinton's Rod, torn from his grip, spun through the air and disappeared over the side of the skyship.

The Vor king slumped, wheezing through blistered lips, his chest visibly labored through the gap in his armor.

Jaks searched for a weapon. He reached down for a long-bladed rapier in the cindered hand of a dead sailor. Still weakened from his belly wound, possibly bleeding internally, he hefted the weapon with both hands and walked toward his father.

Sicaro groped for the closest weapon—a spear with a blackened haft and tip. Leaning against the mast, he stood to meet his son.

"No magic . . . sword against spear," the giant declared.

Jaks shook his head and electrified the blade of the rapier. He would not trust his father to honor any arrangement. Jagged lightning rippled along the steel. Wisps of blue flickered off the tip.

Sicaro lunged. Jaks's arms sank, encumbered with an unnatural force, dragging the rapier blade to the deck. With speed belying his injured state, Sicaro drove the spear at his son's undefended chest.

But Jaks needed no shield to defend, nor blade to attack.

A column of white and blue surged from Jaks's arms. Lightning enveloped Sicaro mid-stride and paralyzed him statue-like as forks of electricity raged over his body.

The gravmantic weight vanished and Jaks raised the rapier in front of him. He double-stepped, knocked aside the spear, and plunged the electrified sword into his father's chest.

The blade pierced the gambeson and slid between the ribs. Realizing he had been screaming as he did so, Jaks took in another breath and then pushed again until it went no further.

Sicaro groaned, spitted on the end of a sword and broiling at the hand of his son.

Shuddering uncontrollably, a glob of blood ejected from his mouth. His eye bulged in its socket and gray vapor fled his skin.

Dead weight then pushed against Jaks's hands. He released the rapier and stepped aside for the body to fall to the deck.

Tendrils of lightning fizzled out, and he collapsed beside his father's corpse.

As consciousness slipped away from Jaks, a sense of great evil disappeared with it. He had overcome and destroyed that which he feared the most. Sicaro was killed and Ascoria was saved from his tyranny and deviant visions.

Jaks fought to uphold his failing strength. There was one thing left to do, an oath to fulfill, but the darkness couldn't be denied—it enfolded him in its grasp.

Chapter 23

Sisterhood

Karisa—The Palace of Irin, Ascoria

Muffled voices from outside the chamber doors woke Karisa from a troubled sleep. Her head rose from her pillow to listen closer.

The voices grew louder. A moment later, the rasp of steel escaping its scabbard cut through the dark. A shout, right outside the doors, was followed by the unmistakable clash of sword on sword. A hound growled but then went silent. Grunts, thumps, and more yelling grew louder.

Karisa pushed aside the silk veil surrounding her canopied bed and slid out barefooted, ignoring the chaffing slave collar around her neck. She gestured and a hovering globe flicked into being to light the room. She had to find out what was happening.

"My queen, what is it?" said Takola, the eldest of the handmaids—not so long ago a courtesan. She rose from the other side of the grand bed, grabbed a long, elegant robe, and held it out for the wife of King Sicaro with trembling hands.

Karisa donned the garment in a swift motion. "I don't know. Quickly, gather the others and hide in the steam room." She gestured at the four other handmaids, also staring terrified at the guard-room doors.

No sooner had the women retreated than the chamber doors burst open; a couple of them screamed as light from the guardroom sliced through their quarters.

Karisa stood in front of the door to the steam room, her arms spread wide as though to protect her servants. The chain to her neck was stretched to its extreme. The hovering globe vanished to be replaced by a curtain of darkness that enfolded her, the chain, and a yard in every direction.

"My queen. Queen Karisa. Are you safe? Where are you?" The silhouette of a warrior holding a broadsword stood in the doorway from the guardroom. "Deserters attacked us," the figure said.

Recognizing the captain of the guard, Rachella, but uncertain of the danger still about, Karisa spoke through the veil of her illusion. "What do you mean, deserters? What are they doing here?"

Sheathing her sword, the captain scanned the room but seemed unable to pinpoint Karisa's location. "They're saying the king is dead. The garrison has turned to looting. I am afraid the situation has become dire."

"Dead . . .?" Karissa's voice trailed off. She lost focus

and the veil of illumancy fell away. She stumbled against the wall.

Captain Rachella saluted her bewildered queen but then glanced back to the chamber doors as though wary of more intruders. On the other side, four bodies lay dead: one female guard, the hound, and two heavily bearded men. The fight had been quick but deadly. "A signal message from the front says the king was killed. At least half of the assault force was destroyed, and the rest are in full retreat."

"Gods be thanked!" Takola strode out of the steam room and began a tiny dance. She raised her hands and jabbed at the air.

"No time for rejoicing, handmaid," admonished the captain. "The queen is in great danger." She placed a hand on the pommel of her sword.

"What was the fight about?" Karisa walked to the door and stared at the blood-filled room. Far away, shouts sounded from the central staircase of the palace.

"You." Captain Rachella followed her and kicked the largest man's body. "Forgive me, my queen, but you are nothing but chattel to them now. You and your handmaids are treasures for the rapists. We must flee before more appear."

"Thank you for your loyalty, Captain." Karisa touched the female guard on the arm. "Will you release me from this collar?" Much relied on the guard's goodwill toward her. To her relief, the sturdy woman extracted a key without hesitation and freed Karisa from her binding. There were still some good people, even amongst the Vors.

A small figure dashed into the guardroom from the outer hall and skidded to a stop. Captain Rachella swept out her sword and pointed it at the intruder. "No further!"

"It is only the chambermaid, Captain. She is no threat." Karisa touched the small girl's arm. "Rasish, are you harmed?"

The girl stared in horror at the blood and dead bodies but shook her head and stammered a reply. "My lady, you must hide. There is chaos outside. They say the king is dead."

"Yes, so I have heard. It is hard to believe."

Deep inside, a tone of pure joy sang in Karisa's soul. Her father was dead. The spider that entrapped her, the leech that drained her, the monster that used her, was dead. She could not prevent the smile that slowly creased her face. She knew she must look like a madwoman with the danger lurking the hallways around them, but she could not shed the release she felt. Even if she died tonight, she would die satisfied knowing that the devil had died before her.

"Listen to me," said Karisa, taking command of the group, enacting a plan that she and the chambermaid had prepared for such a day. "Rasish will lead us down through the servant's stairs to the dungeons. There, she will give us torn and dirtied rags to disguise ourselves." She looked at the young girl.

The twelve-year-old girl nodded, pulling her servant's tunic tightly around her shoulders.

"Captain Rachella, if you are loyal to me, you will come and help us escape. If not, please leave me now. Take what you want from my chambers and know my thanks for protecting us from these two." Karisa shifted her gaze to the would-be rapists and bent to pluck a sword from the hand of the closest. She had never seen the man before, but then again, they all looked the same behind their matted beards.

The guard captain, without a pause, bent to help and replied, "My lady, I would follow you to the ends of the world."

With the help of the captain, Karisa removed and then donned the dead guard's leather jerkin, holding back her nausea as the cold, congealed blood on the inside of the armor pressed against her skin.

With a glance in both directions down the hallway, they slipped out into the darkened palace. Six ex-courtesans, a chambermaid, and a guard.

At the grand staircase, voices rose from the lower floors, accompanied by the sounds of stamping boots, scraping furniture, and doors being slammed open and closed. Episodically, muffled screams would break through the sounds of looting—palace servants caught and exploited for sport.

Following the chambermaid—zipping through palace shortcuts like mice in a barn—they bypassed a trio of Vors carrying sacks over their shoulders by sneaking through side corridors as the warriors brazenly trashed room after room. "Queeny, oh queeny, which room are you in?" one of them called. Not guards who knew the palace layout, but simple axemen on the prowl.

They similarly evaded two more groups of looters until Rasish opened a small door leading to a narrow spiral staircase.

The escapees inched down the cramped and creaking stairs, lit only by globes of light that Karisa illumanced in front and behind her. Joslyn, the timid ex-courtesan, only a year older than the chambermaid, wept quietly as they descended.

A tomb-like chamber hewn into the rock foundations of the palace claimed them at the bottom. Then, after a few more twists and turns through a labyrinth of storerooms and tunnels, they arrived at Rasish's stash.

"Change into the most ripped and torn clothes," said Karisa, poking about a pile of stinking clothes in a corner of the room and pulling on a ragged robe and a tatty brown scarf over her pilfered armor. A box of unburnt incense and censers resting beside the garments scented the air with a heady spice.

"But they stink," complained Takola, holding out an ambiguous garment.

"The worse you stink, the better the ruse. You are no longer a queen's handmaids. You are Plague Sisters." Ascorians and Vors all avoided the Sisterhood, who on every continent had nuns traveling through towns and cities to take in anyone ostracized for their deformities or chronic illnesses. Associated with sickness and disease, they were paid to then move along as quickly as possible. A perfect disguise for a group navigating through dangerous lands.

Karisa continued, "You, too, Captain. Cover yourself. But hurry, I need you and Rasish for one last task before we leave. I need to access the dungeon."

The prisoner lay curled in a corner of the cell, facing the wall. A woolen blanket covered the childlike form, and a single finger clutched its edge.

They had burst into the prison guardroom minutes before, Captain Rachella and Karisa, with bared swords ready to incapacitate or kill the guard, but the man was nowhere to be found. Now, they and the others stood at the end of a corridor of iron-barred cells.

"Is this her?" Karisa asked of Rasish, her voice rising in horror as she clutched the bars and stared inside. "What an awful place."

Inside, the figure stirred.

"Meila, it's me. It's Karisa." She cast a globe of light through the bars and into the stone cubicle.

After King Sicaro and his armies had forged north, leaving just a small garrison to guard the city and his queen, Rasish—on Karisa's instruction—had bribed the prison guard with one of the queen's ruby rings to allow the young girl to attend the tortured and abandoned outworlder.

The Ascorian king had banished torture many years before—bringing an end to the barbaric practice in the realm—but the new Vor king had no qualms about reintroducing it; as such, a cell had been modified into a dungeon to extract cooperation from the resisting foreigner.

Meila had been welcomed by iron chains dangling from rings hammered deep into the stone walls, and by a wooden bench with a tidy row of instruments and tools. Shackling her in irons, her torturer—a silent, thin man with long fingers—had wasted no time in taking to her with his emotionless eyes and steady hands.

His pliers crushed her fingers, toes, and any fleshy part he could find; his hammer shattered the bones of her hands and feet; and his scalpels carved lines into her back and torso. Her grunts and groans had echoed the depths of the prison for days. But she did not relent.

Each morning, Sicaro and Sneer visited and offered her release from the attentions of the gaunt man in exchange for unlocking the darkcore weapons. But each morning, she would reply with the same—a shake of the head.

What they did not know—Meila had told Rasish in the days after—was that she could dampen the pain and fear with secret devices inside her head. So, although fractured and mutilated, she persevered and never released the weapons.

Only when the thin man began amputating fingers and toes did her resolve erode. The sight of her bloodied stumps and her digits lying on the dungeon floor agonized her. Even special implants could not prevent the mental anguish of their loss.

But the memory of two people fueled her tenacity, she had told the chambermaid. A brother and sister. A girl who sacrificed her freedom for the lives of first her mother and then her sisterhood of slaves; and her brother who sacrificed his freedom and safety for the lives of little boys, honest tribesfolk, and her. Heroes who made no claim to heroics.

Then one day, the silent man entered her cell, but instead of taking up his instruments, he hunched in front of her and stared. After an hour, he stood and said, "God, take you now." He scooped up the ten withered digits he had removed from her hands and feet, dropped them into a pouch, wrapped his instruments, and left the cell.

Sicaro had then returned one last time. "No matter, I have power enough. The rats can have you," he said and departed.

For days after, Meila drifted in a morass of grief and despair. Hunger and thirst tormented her. Darkness smothered. Even the prison guard stopped visiting.

So, the chambermaid had been met with a cry of relief when she had first appeared. Rasish had unbolted the irons, wept with her, and then fed her, beginning her restoration.

But even knowing the horrors of the torture submitted on Meila, through the chambermaid's reports, Karisa was not prepared for the pitiful vestige of her friend.

Meila pushed herself up. Twisted, deformed hands, with torn cloth threading the stumps, dropped the blanket from a wasted body. Bandaged feet appeared at the ends of thin legs as they unfolded before her. Red and purple lines etched her chest and arms in a lattice of scars. Only her face was untouched, one of the few graces her torturer had granted her.

"It's not that bad," said Meila. She grasped the top of her gray cotton shift to conceal her chest. A weak smile forced its way to her lips.

Tears rolled down Karisa's face. She addressed Captain Rachella. "Does your key open this?"

The cell opened and Karisa swept to Meila's side. They embraced, and the younger woman's tears flowed into the other's hair and down the scars on her back.

"He's dead. The Vors are routed and are retreating," said Karisa. "We must escape before they return."

The "Plague Sisters" bore Meila through the city. Karisa and the loyal captain carried her on a stretcher while the others swung incense burners and chanted as they shuffled along the avenues in the mists of early morning. As they passed, Vor warriors reeled away with their sacks of loot, covering their faces and scowling, eager to avoid these harbingers of disease.

The city gates were abandoned. They passed through a side gate swaying open in the wind and began their journey to Dunberrin.

Chapter 24

New Beginnings

Jaks—The Academy of the Arcane, Ascoria

Jaks and Mulgrave gazed over the rooftops of Dunberrin. A late afternoon breeze swept in from the ocean, cooling the scorch of the day.

In the three weeks since the Vor horde had been rebuffed at the city walls and routed through the fields and farmland to the south, the city had lost no time in rebuilding.

Although sections of the city still lay in rubble, much of the ruins had been sorted and cleared by a worker army of citizens and refugees. Construction crews had re-dug foundations, and now, block after block, buildermages steadily regenerated the city. Buildings rose, and excited chatter spread amongst the homeless crowded into the parks and squares.

A pain spasmed Jaks's belly and distracted him from his survey of the city. Leaning against a merlon, he winced and cupped a hand over the spot.

"A wound like that, you'll carry for the rest of your life," said Mulgrave, standing at his left.

The bald mage's own injuries—smashed bones and black-purple bruises from his confrontation with Sicaro—however, were healing far slower than Jaks's. One arm in a sling and one over a crutch were markers of how close the grandmaster had been to death.

"You're lucky to even be alive," said Mulgrave. "We both are."

"Thanks to the Uwama," Jaks replied, recalling the blurry days in the Royal Infirmary under the care of the Jurn chieftess. "She and the medigel. Without both, I'm sure I would be ashes in one of those giant pyres."

Even now, two weeks since the last of the enormous mounds of dead had been cremated, whiffs of smoke and scorched flesh lingered in his memory. Their ash now covered miles of farms and pastures, and their charred remains lay buried in pits that would fertilize the soil for decades to come.

And the land to the west, where the velocannon had split the earth and killed tens of thousands of Vors, was a giant crater—a half-mile wide, and deep enough that the sea seeped through cracks in the bedrock and was reclaiming it as a lagoon.

"You would have had your own pyre—" the grandmaster said.

"Such a privilege," said Jaks, half-heartedly. He straightened as his abdominal pain receded.

"I would have cremated you myself," said Mulgrave with a glint in his eye.

No such honor had been given to his father, though. The head of the Vor king had been removed for presentation to the Ascorian king and the body thrown onto the first of the funeral pyres. It should have been joy that Jaks had felt when he watched Ranger Cromer decapitate his father's corpse and drop the head into a sack; instead, it had been intense sadness.

"So, what of your research, Master Jaks?" the grandmaster said, addressing him by his new title.

"You shouldn't call me that. It makes me sound old." Jaks shook his head but was secretly delighted at the sound of it. With the surety of position, the permanence of a role, and a purpose to fulfill, he had found his security as a Master of the Arcane. The council of grandmasters had decided that the title of apprentice, or even journeyman, did not befit Jaks's manifested power. A conjurer of lightning and a manipulator of storms, his mastery of electricity had turned the tide of war. So, they had said, he would be Master Jaks, electromancer.

"You'll get used to it." Mulgrave laughed. "Being *named* master is just the beginning."

Jaks frowned and wrung his hands together. "As for that . . . re-examining Grandmaster Vinton's writings has been little help," he said. Searching for a focus for his research at the Academy, Jaks had pored over the work of the last known electromancer. "It's clear he was obsessed with destructive power; hence, the rod he created." He thought of the artifact, blasted from Sicaro's hand during their confrontation, that had been found and now rested in an Academy vault.

"You think there is a better use of your magic?" said Mulgrave.

"I know there is." The electromancer reached into a pocket and brought out the egg-sized zinger droid. It hovered in the air, circled his head, and then returned to his palm. "Devices such as these. You used to say that knowledge is a power greater than sourcestone. You were right. It is knowledge that created this droid and the velocannon."

"You think you can make these things?"

"Not yet, maybe never anything as extraordinary. But I can study Meila's devices, dissect them, and see what I can learn from them. Maybe technology we can use in other things—new signaling devices, skyships, or those engines to replace waterwheels that she talked about." Jaks brought the zinger up to his face and squinted at the familiar dent it had received from the dragon's talon. "I'd not damage this one anymore, though. Perhaps I will start with the salvage at her workbench."

Mulgrave nodded. "Aye. You might as well take her things. Take over her workstation . . ." The silence that followed left unsaid what they both suspected—Meila was dead.

For days, as he had lain infirmed, he had sped the zinger back and forth over the governor's palace in Irin and the rest of the city for signs of Meila or his sister. His gut told him they were there, but the eyes of the droid denied success. Instead, he found looting, savagery, and chaos as the Vors took what they could and fled—some to the south, but many sailing back to their motherland. If either of them was still alive, he could find no trace.

The grandmaster yawned and rubbed his face. "I've been up on this crutch for too long. I need to straighten out for a while." He bade his leave and hobbled away.

Alone on the rooftop, Jaks walked to the far side near the family of blue dragons that made it their home, coiled up around one of the turrets. They hissed at him when he approached but quieted as recognition set in. They were no threat. The beef chunks he threw them when he visited had placated them to his presence. Beautiful creatures. He toyed with the idea of adopting one of the baby dragons for a pet but doubted the adults would simply allow him to snatch one of their young.

He stood for a long while, staring at the sea and the yellow globe dipping on the horizon. His mind drifted, ruminating over the past year and a half, from when he went from being a conscript tormented by bullies to a master who crafted lightning and storms. He commanded power that none other had possessed for almost a hundred years. He could kill and disfigure. He could demand fear. But he could not abandon the oath he had made to his mother. In a few days, now that his wound was healed enough to travel, he would take to horseback and take his search in person southward for signs of Karisa, and Meila too.

"Hey there, Sir Hero," a man's voice called across the rooftop. One of the dragons screeched at the newcomer. It leaped off the tower and beat its wings until it soared around the towering runic furnace.

Minto's familiar face rounded the brass dome, and Jaks dashed forward to greet his childhood friend. Time had worn his face thin; however, the amiable grin and impish sparkle in his eyes were unchanged.

"Who let this rabble in?" said Jaks, smiling. They clasped arms, and Minto punched him lightly on the chin, raising a laugh from both.

Along with a yellow cap sporting a rakish red feather, the herald's attire presented him as someone of importance. Jaks looked him up and down. "God, it's good to see you, Minto. I thought I would've seen you at the King's Triumph. I asked around, but no one seemed to know what had happened to you."

Minto tapped the side of his nose. "Secret stuff. I wasn't dressed in this foppery for the entire war, you know. Tell you later. But I am disappointed that I missed seeing you paraded around like a trophy. Rather spectacular, I heard. Mister 'Defender of the Realm and Hero of Ascoria.' I heard the king has even commissioned a statue of 'The Stormcrafter' for his halls. I'm surprised they didn't make you a grandmaster straight away."

As his friend was enjoying the ridiculous-sounding

titles the king had awarded him, Jaks reddened and waved them off.

A wry smile then curved the side of Minto's mouth. "But you'll have to spill the details later . . . I'm actually here on official business."

"Official?" said Jaks. Minto held no document bag or scroll that a herald might present on royal business. It was then he noticed two guards, bedecked in the king's purple, at the turret door. A cloaked figure appeared at the stairwell and limped toward him, supported by a third guard.

"His majesty commanded a royal escort," replied Minto. He stepped aside and made an elaborate flourish to introduce the important personage. "Master Jaks, may I present—"

"Jaks, you wretch," interrupted the figure as she turned down her hood.

His jaw dropped, and his knees threatened to fold.

Meila.

Incredible, clever, *alive* Meila. Sunken eyes and hollow cheeks distorted her face, but despite those features, Jaks would recognize her anywhere. His heart pounded at the sight of her. She reached out for him, and he swept her up in his arms and laughed.

Alive but not *whole*. Scars crisscrossed and puckered the exposed skin of her arms and chest below her neck. Fingers were missing on each hand, the stumps at odd angles to the remainders, and the hands themselves contorted and twisted as though they had been mangled by the wheel of a wagon.

"Meila," he said. "I'm sorry. I thought you were dead. There was no trace of you—" He spluttered an excuse about the futility of his search and the limitations on him imposed by his belly wound. Tears of joy welled in his eyes as he realized his mistake.

"Shut up. Come here. I've missed you." She wrapped her arms around his waist and pressed her face against his chest.

Dropping his arms around her shoulders, he pulled her tight. He closed his eyes and kissed the top of her head. "I'm glad you're back." She looked up at him, and his tears dropped onto her face.

A look of resolve crossed her face. She crooked a hand behind his neck and pulled him down until their lips met. Passionate and needy, they pressed together with urgency. Murmuring to each other between kisses, they continued until an embarrassed cough interrupted them.

"Our duty is done here. Please excuse us, my lady." Minto bowed to Meila. Then to Jaks, he addressed, "Master," and tipped his cap. Turning, the herald nudged the grinning soldier back along the walkway.

Then alone, with the horizon a lingering glow, Meila pulled him by the hand to sit together on the battlement between a pair of merlons.

Even in the dim of twilight, the deformed hands and

scars on her arms were stark. Jaks frowned in concern at her wounds.

"Who did this to you—was it my father?" asked Jaks. He touched her cheek and placed a hand gently on her thigh. "What happened?"

"His man," she replied. She told him of her imprisonment and Sicaro's intent to torture her into submission. "I couldn't give up the weapons. They weren't as powerful as the velocannon, but used well, they could have countered it. Don't worry—after a couple of years, the scars will fade. You know how fast I heal. Once you have medigel particles in you, everything heals fast." She placed her right hand over Jaks's maimed left. Two cripples holding hands. "My fingers, though . . . what is done, is done."

"I'm glad I killed him. Had I known he had done this to you as well—"

"What would you have done? Killed him again?" said Meila.

He shook his head at the confused emotions his father's death had left him with and changed the subject back to her story. "How did you escape?"

She told him how Karisa and Rasish had freed her and how their commune of "Plague Sisters" had escaped the city. "They carried me north while I could not walk. Your sister is a fine leader, Jaks. Resilient and smart, as seen in few. You should be proud of her."

"I am." Jaks smiled. Few people talked of Karisa

well, except for her appearance and grace. It pleased him to hear someone acknowledge her other attributes.

"I bet you *didn't* know that she wields a swift blade as well?" She quirked an eyebrow. "We crossed paths with hundreds of Vor warriors fleeing south. Most chose to leave us alone. Incense burners and her illusions of boils and pox were sufficient to warn most of them away, but she could not cover all nine of us. Several of the predators needed a sharp sword. Reflexes of a snake, Jaks. One blackbeard, she pierced through the throat as soon as his eyes glazed over with lust, staring at our little Joslyn. Another, a tattooed monstrosity, she dodged as he went to grab her, and her dagger was in his kidney three times before he could even turn."

Jaks gawped, wide-eyed at the description of Karisa's martial feats. If it had been Vixhana, he would not have been surprised, but his little sister? "Hells, it sounds like I've been short-changed some fighting skills," he said, and then chuckled.

Meila responded with a laugh, then continued. "Then, two weeks ago, we spotted riders flying the Ascorian flag. Your sister signaled them, and they took us in," said Meila. "We arrived today. I wanted to come straight here, but the city guards took us to the king instead."

"How did he receive you?" asked Jaks. Rumors held that King Silas was temperamental even following the defeat of the Vors. Although the paranoia that had afflicted him during the latter days of the war was less, the Ascorian king was a shadow of what he had been.

"Must have felt sorry for me. Discharged me from duress of the court."

"He freed you?" Jaks laughed. "It wasn't as though we were holding you, anyway."

"Didn't want me wandering off, however." She winked. "Say hello to your new Royal Science Advisor." She bowed her head with faux humility as Jaks congratulated her. "Nothing much changes, though. I'll live and work here like before, except I'll be paid for it." The evening enveloped them, and Meila twirled a finger in a flourish and conjured a yellow globe to bob in the air beside them.

Jaks clapped his hands. "We can work together. Make things. Like these wrist devices. I was thinking that if we could make more, they could be helpful for fleets at sea, or merchants making trades, or people lost in the mountains. That sort of thing." Although the ideas came out of his mouth, his imagination dwelt on Meila and him being together like the magesmiths Doeg and Shazair—working and living together. Jaks looked hopefully at Meila.

"On this planet, without the infrastructure, we couldn't produce anything as advanced as the wrist comms, but there are alternatives," she replied, appearing bothered by a concern. "There is still this problem of the United Worlds Federation returning. They would make the Vor invasion seem like a mere distraction in comparison. Eventually, a starship, or an entire terraform fleet, might appear. Maybe years or decades. But we'll have to be ready. I'll have to convince them that this world is worth preserving . . ."

"Still?" asked Jaks. Meila's previous life was puzzling and mysterious to him. The threat presented by what she called the UWF was almost incomprehensible.

"Of course." She looked at him as though annoyed. "It's why I was sent here in the first place. To assess the planet for repopulating."

"I mean, you still think it's worth saving? After you've seen how we live compared to your world? Wouldn't it be better if your people came and we could have the flyers, giant buildings, and all of those amazing things you showed us?"

She shook her head. "They cleanse the planet of whatever is leftover of the old colony. Indigenous populations cause problems, claim rights, start riots and wars."

He frowned. "We could fight them, then."

Meila laughed. Then, seeing he was serious, stroked his hand. "No, we couldn't. It would be like trying to dig a hole in the ocean. Every scoop would be refilled with water and would drown anyone that tried."

She leaned forward and kissed him lightly on the lips. "Don't worry, we'll think of something. But let's not worry anymore of it today."

Jaks nodded and would have been content to fold

her in his arms for the rest of the night, but one last question burned in his mind.

"Karisa. Where is she?"

Meila looked at the darkened rooftops. "She had some business to take care of. Had a message for you, though—meet her tomorrow at noon at the usual place. I assume you know where she's talking about."

He did. There was only one place.

The next morning, Jaks tiptoed out of the room, leaving Meila asleep in his bed where they had lain together. She had not refused the offer to share his bed this time. Although the pains of their wounded bodies kept them from anything other than taking comfort in each other's company, they had slept curled together.

At a brisk walk past the Academy gates, he roamed the city streets, restless in the time before he would see his sister again.

It had been several days since he had last witnessed the rapid pace of the city being rebuilt. At a couple of building sites, he stopped briefly to marvel at gravmancer builders floating massive stone blocks and huge timbers into place. Construction crews then hammered and screwed each into place before the gravmancers returned with the next. Dunberrin healed from its wounds as quickly as Jaks and Meila did.

He paced the walls outside of the Army district.

Although the guards would have welcomed and saluted the "Hero of Ascoria" into the military zone, he had no formal business there that morning. However, he could not completely escape his newfound fame.

A trio of off-duty conscripts recognized the famous "Stormcrafter" and ran toward him with awed faces. One waved a drawing of Jaks that had been recently printed by a local news press. After zealous salutes, the recruits assailed him with questions about the fight with the Vor king: "Was he really your father?"; "Is it true you fried him to a husk?" Jaks's annoyance grew, as did the size of his audience, when they begged him to summon a lightning storm for their entertainment. At the limit of his patience, the storm in his eyes, however, subdued their excitement. Muttering excuses to leave, he pulled the cowl of his cloak to shadow his face and parted the circle of adulators as he strode off.

The bells of the Cathedral of Dunberrin tolled midday, and Jaks walked onto its sacred grounds.

The ornate building had survived the war unscratched and had served as an infirmary for the wounded during the final battle. Today, the grand monument continued to house hundreds of refugees still fearful of returning to the southern provinces from where they had fled from the path of the invaders. Eventually, they would go back, but only after their farmlands had been secured and rid of the deserters from the Vor army who still lingered.

Children ran and played around the gray

headstones and trees of the cathedral's green spaces. A groundskeeper admonished and waved them off, but it was apparent to Jaks that the man fought a losing battle —quicker than he, they treated him as much a part of the game as the hideouts and treehouses they had built.

He arrived at their mother's gravestone and discovered a single white rose resting there. He looked about for his sister, but only an old man with a tattered bag and a scruffy, gray dog wandered the rows.

Alone, Jaks bowed his head and whispered, "Oh, Mother, it could have been so different. If only it had been *him* who went down those stairs that time. If I had never been such a coward. If I had stood up to him. You would still be alive. And this war might never have been. They think I'm some sort of hero, but if only they knew."

"We can't change the past, Jaks . . ." For a second, he thought it was his mother answering. But the voice came from behind. He turned, and it was the old man.

"Who are—" Jaks began.

The man continued, ". . . but we can change where we are going." The illumancer mask then fell away and revealed a familiar face. "And you did," said Karisa, in her pure form.

Jaks smiled, and so full of joy, he hugged her, lifting her off the ground. She squealed and laughed, squeezing him back. He had practiced what he was going to say when he first saw her, but all that came out was, "You haven't changed!"

She shared the same timeless beauty of their mother, and seeing her face caused his heart to ache for the past. The same haunted eyes stared at him, scarred with unspoken pain, but even deeper now. But, in contrast, her blazing smile and golden hair, as always, lifted his spirits with delight.

"Still picking up strays, I see," said Jaks, as the scruffy dog sniffed at his leg. Unimpressed, it wandered off.

Brother and sister then jabbered at each other for a minute until they broke off laughing. Their joy of reunion shared, they sat at the foot of their mother's grave to talk less hurriedly. Jaks had worried that Karisa would be cold and accusing—blaming him for her capture and enslavement, and then failing to help her even when he had come so close. However, his fears were dispelled. He should have known that his sister's resilience would take her through those dark times, attributing blame directly to those who captured her. In the end, she did not want details of Jaks's last fight with their father, only assurance that her abuser was truly slain.

"I made an oath to look after you—" Jaks began, his lingering guilt forcing its way to his consciousness.

"You and Vixhana are obsessed with oaths."

Jaks shook his head, reminded again of his broken oath, and continued, "I failed in my promise to you, Karisa. You ended up kidnapped and enslaved. I couldn't rescue you—"

"As I see it, you killed the one who has enslaved me all my life. That is the promise fulfilled." She parted her cloak and revealed a longsword and dagger at her hip. The dagger slid out, and she pricked the end of her thumb. A red drop formed.

"What are you doing?" said Jaks.

Karisa pressed her thumb against Jaks's cheek and smeared the blood down his face. "No more oath. I am marking you free of the promise you made to Mother. I can look after myself and don't need you worrying about me anymore."

He nodded as she sheathed her dagger. She was the weaver of her own fate. "But what will you do? Where will you go now? Will you return to the stage and live in the manse? You and I are its only heirs."

"I burned it down last night," replied a stony-faced Karisa. "I couldn't bear to know that the place stood with everything that had gone on in it."

He nodded a second time.

"I saved this for you, though." She swung her bag around and reached inside. She revealed a rolled canvas. Holding the top edge, she let it drop open.

He gazed at the family portrait she had cut out of the frame—four of them but not Father—when they had last visited the estate with Vixhana.

He smiled tensely at the last visual remnant of their mother, knowing that it meant as much to Karisa as to him. "You keep it," he said.

"No. I won't be in one place for long enough to hang

it up." She cast him a side-long glance. "I am back with the troupe. We've booked a ship leaving tomorrow. We're going to Zura."

"Zura! It's so far away," he said. A journey of several months, sailing from port to port. He might not see her again for years—if ever.

"I can't stay in Ascoria. It's different now. People were talking about me even before I arrived." Karisa's face flickered with worry. "People will learn that I was 'the Vor Queen.' There are rumors already. I can't stay here. I need to restart my life, somewhere far away." Her eyes then flickered with excitement. "I hear there are provinces where they only allow illumancers to live. Imagine the mystique!"

Jaks knew he could not stop her, that he should not, now that his oath to her was retracted. She was a survivor and just as capable—*no, more capable*—than he. If she had been the one gifted with electromancy, their father would never have been able to propel the invasion to the last walls of the kingdom.

Karisa rolled the portrait in her hands and tied it with string. Her eyes took on a mischievous twinkle and a wry smile edged her mouth. Curiously, as she proffered the canvas to Jaks, it *floated* from her hand.

The rolled painting levitated in the air between them.

Jaks grabbed for the canvas, fearing it would fall to the grass, but as he wrapped his hand around it, the familiar lift of gravmancy met his fingers: gravmantic lift he had known aboard the *Kingfisher* when it ascended into the sky. "You, too? You could become a nightwraith, with Vixhana," he said as the weightless painting regained its slight heft.

She laughed. "I'll leave that to her. Where is she, anyway?"

A breeze swept over them, and a voice spoke from a shadow in the row of gravestones behind them. "Here . . . barely. After my little brother almost killed me." A tall figure materialized from the puddle of darkness.

"Vixhana!" Karisa cried out with joyous surprise tinged with horror, for the once imposing battlefield assassin was a skeletal, pale remnant of her former self. Her black armor hung loosely on her body. Where muscles once undulated and bulged beneath leather and hidden steel plates, her limbs were thin; where her face was once handsome, it was gaunt. However, although her eyes were sunk deep into their sockets, they still glinted with steel. She resembled what Jaks imagined a mythical wraith might look like.

But despite her muscle loss, Vixhana stood tall and straight with her longsword at her hip, just as she had a year and a half ago at this very spot.

"I'm so sorry, Vix. I don't know if you ever heard my apologies back in the Jurn village. I sat by your bed—" Jaks began.

The eldest sister laughed and strode over to her younger siblings. Her voice was thinner but still held its commanding tone. "All forgiven, Jaks. I have no memory of the incident, but Cromer explained it all as we traveled back from Jurn." She looked to the avenue running alongside the cathedral's grounds and nodded to the ranger, who was waiting there with two horses. "What happened, happened. I'm just glad that the three of us survived." Opening her arms wide, Vixhana gathered Jaks and Karisa into an embrace. They leaned in and affectionately pressed their foreheads together for a celebratory minute.

"I'll recover," Vixhana then said. "I have to. I still have a duty to uphold and a country to protect . . . thanks to this one." She winked at Jaks, who gave her a small, humble nod.

"You're tough. We're all tough," Karisa said as she looked at the last surviving members of their family. "We're lucky to be alive after what all we've been through." Jaks and Vixhana nodded in solemn agreement.

At the foot of their mother's grave, hours passed by as they shared their ordeals of the past months and spoke of old times.

Even after his father's death, Jaks had still felt laden with a sense of unfulfilled duty. But seeing his sisters both here, the disturbance finally lifted. They were all safe and free to make their own choices. The kingdom needed to be restored, and there was still the threat of Meila's people returning to claim their world. But for now, he had a sense of arrival. A job completed.

Vixhana departed first. She would return to the nightwraith barracks and rebuild her strength until she could return to her military duties. Dependable and loyal, Jaks knew she would most likely serve the kingdom with the elite soldiers for the rest of her working life. In the distance, Ranger Cromer rested a supportive hand on Vixhana's arm and handed her the reins of her horse.

"I need to go gather some clothes and provisions for the voyage tomorrow. It'll be a long trip. Take care, Jaks," Karisa said and threw her arms around him one last time.

Sadness engulfed him, knowing he might never see her again.

Their farewell was interrupted by laughter as a little boy ran down the cemetery row next to them, chased by an equally small girl waving a ragdoll in front of her.

"Good luck, sister," Jaks said as they parted.

"Farewell, brother." Karisa turned away, her face transforming back into her old-man's mask.

Her canine companion sprang to its paws, stretched on front legs, and shuffled to her side.

Jaks watched Karisa and her dog exit the gates of the cathedral grounds.

This chapter of his life was sealed.

An evil king, a cruel father, was torn from power, and a brutal invasion repelled.

He would only look forward, for he had clearly chosen his path. No longer submissive to fear, he was its conductor: controlling and manipulating the very emotions that once chained him.

He had chosen the path of courage—a warrior in the face of fear.

He was the Stormcrafter.

The End

Don't miss out on future books by J.T. Moy
Signup to J.T. Moy's mailing list to receive special offers
and updates about upcoming releases.
Mailing list: https://linktr.ee/jtmoy

About the Author

J.T. Moy is from Auckland, New Zealand. A medical doctor and careers consultant, he retired in his mid-40s to write scifi/fantasy novels. He is married and has two children.

www.jtmoy.com

04022022